MARGARET'S

MARGARET'S
Dove
A Novel

GARY J. GEMME

MILL CITY PRESS

Mill City Press, Inc.
2301 Lucien Way #415
Maitland, FL 32751
407.339.4217
www.millcitypress.net

To Donna

The love of my life

As always and

Forever . . .

Table of Contents

PART THREE

PART FOUR

PART FIVE

Acknowledgments

I would like to thank my wife, Donna, for all of the time she spent reading and critiquing my manuscript. Her encouragement kept me on a steady course toward completing the novel. My eldest son Michael's edits, suggestions, and literary background helped me greatly. He has his dad's thanks, appreciation, and gratitude.

A thank you to my daughter, Jessica, for borrowing some of her childhood stories and my son Matthew for introducing me to Radnor Lake State Park. My thanks to my sister Mary for her artistic help with the front cover.

The Mill City Press manuscript evaluation provided me with a summary that helped me put the finishing touches on chapter size and formatting. My thanks to the entire Mill City team involved in the editing and production of Margaret's Dove.

My further thanks to Elizabeth Earl Phillips for reviewing the initial draft of my story. Her critique and advice are much appreciated.

To the extent that the reader finds value and enjoyment in the novel, the credit is widely spread. Otherwise, I take full responsibility.

Part One

Psalm of David
Psalm 23

The Lord is my
Shepherd; there
is nothing I lack.

1

25 December 1971

*S*omething did not seem quite right.

He could not see. *Is it night?* he wondered. He wasn't sure.

Focus on your senses, he told himself. *Smell,* there was a smell he couldn't recognize; the taste of the air was somewhat familiar. His perception of time and distance, the present and the past, were distorted. He couldn't recognize what taste or smell he was experiencing.

He felt he was still breathing.

Pain, he thought. *I should be feeling pain.* But there was no pain. He tried to move his arms and feel his body. He had no feeling; he wasn't sure he moved his arms.

Sound. Is there sound?

Is there sound? Did I just think that, or did someone just say the word sound? The sound he thought he heard he didn't recognize, but it gave him a sense of quiet and made him feel a calmness not of this world. *How would I know that? What world would it be?*

How much time had passed? Am I conscious or unconscious? Am I dreaming? He heard no answer. He thought he spoke but wasn't sure.

His mind said to focus. *Focus on what?*

Sound, that was it. Sound, sound, sound.

He felt a sense of quiet. Yet there were sounds that fatigued and drained him. *Was it a humming or buzzing? No, it's more of a swooshing sound. Buzzing, humming, swooshing, humming, swooshing,* a constant softening sound creating a sense of calm, of quiet. It was soothing. Sedating.

The sound was fading. He was fading.

He'd lost his soul. The fire consumed him. His death was overdue.

2

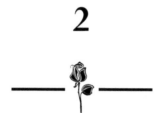

24 December 1971

Dressed in his weatherworn, olive-drab combat fatigues, Nicholas sat in the makeshift chapel thinking about his Catholic upbringing and how alienated he was from his childhood beliefs.

He knew he should go to confession and ask for forgiveness. That, however, was not possible. Penance and reconciliation in the eyes of the Catholic Church required he have sincere remorse for the sins he had committed.

He had no remorse. He only had an aching sorrow driven by his guilt, and that was inadequate for absolution by his faith. No amount of penance, without remorse, would absolve him from his sins.

Nicholas continued to sit quietly, and with his own soundless words recited in his thoughts, he began his confession. He wished all the angels and saints on display in a real church, who would be looking down at him, could hear his tale. He hoped they would take pity on his soul before he died and was condemned to hell for all eternity.

Bless me Father, for I have sinned. I can't remember my last confession. I am guilty of violating several of the Ten Commandments.

My Lord, who is all good, I do not ask your forgiveness.

I unknowingly violated the Sixth Commandment: Thou shalt not commit adultery. I knowingly violated the Ninth Commandment: Thou shalt not covet thy neighbor's wife. And without remorse and with vengeance, I killed a man and broke the Fifth Commandment: Thou shall not kill.

While he said a few Our Fathers and a couple of Hail Marys reminiscent of the childhood penance he typically received, he was only reciting them from rote memory. He knew his prayers were inadequate. He owned his sins.

As a Catholic, there was no denying that one day he would stand before his Creator in final judgment. His only thought was *The sooner that happened, the better.*

3

Boston, MA — May 1971

*N*icholas had slept late, and as he woke, he sensed Meg's absence from the warm bed. He smiled at the thought. In their short time together, he'd learned she was an early riser. She would quickly escape the confines of whatever place they were staying and explore the outdoors.

Meg loved the early morning coolness. She wanted to be outside to experience the day's first light. When she returned, she was always smiling and excited. She couldn't wait to show Nicholas her newest discovery. She called them her keepsakes.

They were simple — unusual shapes or colors. There was a shell from the bay, a pinecone from one of the many varieties of trees that make the Cape Cod landscape unique, and a wildflower growing naturally wherever they visited. Meg would hold her treasure long enough to share it with Nicholas. She would then store what she'd found in her memory scrapbook to recall whenever she needed.

Meg, with her slim figure, short black hair, brown eyes, and cream-colored skin, radiated the innocence of a child on Christmas morning. It was her desire to share her joy in the little bits of happiness she'd found in the things most often overlooked that moved Nicholas the most.

Seeing her excitement, his eyes would always well with tears. At these times Nicholas would think of his mom. Her absence in his life had created a vacuum that Meg was quickly filling. Years alone with just him and his dad, Nicholas had no experience with the comforting presence of a woman. He liked it; it felt good. He wanted more from Meg than the friendship vows they'd exchanged and the inexpensive rings they'd purchased from the talkative street vendor in Provincetown.

Nicholas longed to marry Meg in a Catholic Church and spend their lives together as husband and wife. Reflecting on this, he drifted back to sleep.

When he awoke for the second time that morning, he immediately knew Meg had not returned. He quickly got out of bed and began to dress. He would go out and look for her. After spending five days on Cape Cod, they'd only arrived in Boston the previous afternoon. Neither was familiar with the city, and he was concerned she'd somehow gotten lost.

As he was about to leave, he reached for the room key and noticed a note in Meg's handwriting addressed to him. He felt a temporary relief, believing Meg was just letting him know she'd be out longer than usual.

Smiling, he picked up the note and started to read.

My Dear Nicholas, I love you so much, and I know you love me. Our love is not enough. I have another life . . . You will not understand this, but because I know how much you love me, you will protect me, and that means you must never find me. Please take comfort in the time we've spent together. That will comfort me, and help me endure. I love you so very much, and know that not a second will pass when I'm not thinking of you.

Nicholas couldn't recall how many times he read Meg's note or how long he sat on the bed replaying the events of the past week. His solitude was interrupted by a knock on the door and a voice calling out, "Housekeeping."

He was emotionally drained. He couldn't get a grip on his feelings. The tears had stopped, but his eyes remained moist. He knew he had to leave the room; his time there was over. He took a deep breath, trying to capture the last floral fragrance of Meg's presence. He wanted to hold onto it and always remember the sweetness of her scent.

Nicholas threw his few belongings into his vinyl bag and prepared to leave the room when he noticed Meg had left her favorite book behind. She cherished the novel *Love Story*, Erich Segal's best seller. Meg idolized Jenny, the main character. She loved everything about her, particularly her strength. She admired her for going to college, being brave, and for marrying a man who loved her.

Nicholas couldn't quite remember something else Meg had said about Jenny or the book; it had to do with great love stories, and it was always the woman who died. He would continue to search his memory trying to recall Meg's exact words, words that would haunt him forever.

Nicholas folded and placed Meg's note into her book and then zipped them into his gym bag. He would read *Love Story* and trace the words on her note with the tip of his finger many times. It was a way to feel connected to Meg and feel her love. He would hold onto the book and the note, and pray she would come back to him.

As Nicholas walked out of the hotel, he was chilled by the cold, wind, and rain. He couldn't control his emotions.

He knew his eyes were tearing, and he didn't care. Nicholas couldn't quite make sense of Meg's note. When he'd felt the ridges on her back last evening, she'd said, "Shh, tomorrow." He now thought, *there's no tomorrow. Meg's gone.*

Nicholas wondered about the other life. He couldn't believe Meg had a secret life. *What did that mean?* he asked himself. In his mind he reasoned, *she couldn't be married.* It didn't seem possible to him. He felt Meg was good, caring, loving, and innocent; she was so very special. She'd given him her love and helped him shed the sadness he'd carried in his heart since he was a young boy.

Nicholas knew he'd violated the teaching of his religion when he and Meg made love the night before. Adultery was a word so removed from his upbringing; he never would have considered violating the Commandment. Having experienced Meg's love, he no longer cared if she was married. He knew their love was real. He ached to be with her now and forever. He told himself, *Married, divorced, single—it doesn't matter. I love her.* Then he realized he would never hurt Meg. He could never look for her. He could never find her. He vowed to always protect her. They would never be together.

4

*M*eg sat in a coffee shop and watched the cold dreary rain fall from the sky. She had a view of the hotel where she and Nicholas had stayed the previous night. She was determined to remain there long enough to see him leave. She wasn't sure how long the wait would be, but it didn't matter. Seeing Nicholas one more time was something she needed to do.

In her heart, Meg was hoping he would see her in the window of the coffee shop and come rushing toward her. But she could never allow that to happen. She could only think of her love for her parents and how her recent behavior had affected them. She would never intentionally hurt or abandon her parents. They loved her and cared for her, and now they desperately needed her.

Meg had truly fallen in love with Nicholas. When she fled her home in Tennessee the second Saturday of May, she hadn't even thought about falling in love. Her trip north to visit the College of the Holy Trinity was meant to create memories she could later draw on for strength. She wanted to walk the campus hills, sit on the green grass in the oval courtyard, see the red brick academic buildings, and sit in a classroom as if she were actually a student. Most of all she wanted to visit the chapel with its stained-glass windows and white marble statue of the Virgin Mother. Meg had dreamed all her childhood of graduating from Holy Trinity just like her dad and one day getting married in the same campus chapel as her mother and father had.

While Meg continued to wait at the coffee shop window outside the hotel, she thought of her first day at Holy Trinity, just six days earlier. She had been strolling along the tree-lined walkways, admiring the colorful flower beds when she found herself at the highest point. She'd been pleasantly surprised by the panoramic view and the ocean of green trees painted against the clear blue sky that lay before her.

Meg had no real interest in sports, but the athletic fields were also located at the highest point. She noticed a buzz of activity at one of the fields, which she ignored. As she sat on the grass, she became lost in her thoughts. Meg was imprinting an image of the rolling hills of green, the soft blue sky, and the bright sun magnifying the beauty. All that she viewed, she placed into her memory scrapbook. She had been sitting for a while when her peace was suddenly disturbed by a chorus of yelling and cheering.

Meg looked in the direction of the sound, saw the players, and realized football practice was ending. She really hadn't paid attention to them before. Meg was star-tled when she saw the players moving in her direction. She knew she wanted to remain anonymous in order to con-ceal the misery of her other life while visiting the campus.

She stood up and quickly turned away from the herd of purple jerseys.

Meg walked in a path that would allow her to avoid the approaching stampede. As she moved away from the team, she saw about ten or so young boys and girls yelling and waving. It appeared to her they were trying to draw the attention of the players. She was naturally drawn to the children and their excitement.

Meg began to walk toward them but then stopped abruptly when she saw one of the football players run over to the children. He immediately started talking with them. As he spoke, he removed his helmet. He handed it to the kids and let them each try it on. Meg saw how much the children enjoyed this. She could not avoid noticing the player. He had chestnut brown hair, tanned skin, and a big smile. It was a healthy, youthful look, the kind you get spending time outdoors in the fresh air and sunshine. His enthusiasm was genuine as he talked with the children.

Meg could hear some of his teammates yelling for him, calling him Nick, but he waved them off, and they left the field.

Once his teammates were gone, Nick really started playing with the kids. He gave each one a chance to run with the football and threw them passes as they dashed to catch the spiraling pigskin. They were all jumping up and down, cheering, and enjoying themselves. It was fun for Meg to watch their excitement. She saw them hand Nick the ball, and he dropped to his knees. The next thing she witnessed was the children piling on top and tackling him.

Watching Nick play with the kids greatly affected Meg. It brought tears to her eyes. It made her think about her own life, her circumstances, and all she was missing.

When Meg introduced herself to Nick later that day, she told him, "Nicholas is much too grand a name for me to call you Nick." Meg would always think of him as Nicholas, a name that would have special meaning for her.

As she replayed that first day in her mind from her stool in the coffee shop, she suddenly saw Nicholas leaving the hotel. He had just wiped a tear from his eye, and Meg could see he was struggling to control his emotions. Meg began to cry as she watched Nicholas walk off in the opposite direction.

Meg had never intended to fall in love on her visit to Holy Trinity. She'd risked a lot to make the trip. It was a risk she'd taken because she needed the memory of being there on that beloved campus to help her endure everything that was violent and evil in her home life.

However, Meg had fallen in love with Nicholas and was sorry for having hurt him. She hoped she would find strength and courage in the love they had for each other. Meg thought these were the types of memories she needed if she was going to survive the life in Nashville that had chosen her.

Meg knew she needed to prepare herself emotionally before returning home. She was going back to a family that would never tolerate the spirit and energy of the girl named Meg. When Margaret had fled to Holy Trinity, she'd wanted to be like the character Jenny from *Love Story*. Jenny was strong, brave, and confident.

Margaret had reasoned that if she became Meg, she could be like Jenny and create the type of memories she needed to bring back home. The Meg who visited Holy Trinity and later traveled throughout Cape Cod was the girl Margaret had always wanted to be but was not allowed to be. Meg had a burning desire to love and be loved. The place where Margaret was compelled to live would not welcome or tolerate the spirit and heart of someone like Meg. While Margaret desperately wanted to remain Meg, she would return home to her previous life.

At eighteen years of age, Margaret had been forced to forget about her hopes and dreams. She would not have the love and life she wanted with Nicholas. She loved her parents. It was the responsibility, the duty, and the guilt she felt that forced her home. Her father and mother needed her; she accepted her fate and would return to Lewis. Margaret would play her role and be the young woman everyone wanted her to be. Her only hope was that she would survive her husband's violence.

5

$\mathcal{D}$ isheartened and puzzled, Nicholas left Boston and took the bus back to his hometown. It was the middle of May and he had been gone from Holy Trinity for six days. Nicholas was back on the grassy campus he'd gazed at since childhood from the pavement of his yard. He loved the old brick buildings, the perfectly maintained lawns, and the open spaces where he could freely roam the campus. He never felt confined when he was at school like he had when he was in his old neighborhood of asphalt and concrete where his dad still lived.

Nicholas had grown up in a rough, working-class neighborhood made up mostly of multi-family dwellings. The majority were two and three deckers with a scattering of small single-family houses. Nicholas's home was a five hundred square foot cottage-style house wedged between two multi-family homes. There was no grass to cut because there was only cement. The only open spaces were the concrete walkways separating the three wood-framed structures that shared the crowded lot.

The local Catholic Church was the anchor, as it was in many other neighborhoods in his hometown. Nicholas's church had also provided schooling up to the twelfth grade. All the teachers in his parish school were nuns. The nuns who taught Nicholas were referred to as sisters, except the school principal, who was called Mother Superior.

The sisters who taught Nicholas had provided him with a good education, as well as discipline for bad behavior. Nicholas had been a little slow to understand the meaning of good behavior in the eyes of the sisters. In fact, he had excelled at earning a reason to be punished. His mischievous behavior and an occasional fisticuff had cost him many Saturdays of sports with his friends because he'd earned the honor of washing and waxing the convent's hardwood floors on his hands and knees.

Nicholas never revealed to anyone how much he enjoyed being with the nuns on Saturdays. It had been his chance to see the sisters more relaxed and surprisingly friendly, even funny. When he was at the convent, many of the nuns called him Nick rather than his given name, Nicholas. He often had long conversations with his favorite nun, Sister Mary Mark Damon. She would tell him stories of the time she had spent in Chile working in a medical clinic. She'd worked side by side with doctors treating the sick and poor. She would describe the harsh conditions and the lack of medicine and supplies. Sister Mary Mark said, "Despite all the hardship and challenges we endured, it was the most satisfying and spiritually gratifying time of my life." These talks motivated Nicholas to study hard, so he could become a doctor who would make Sister Mary Mark Damon proud.

As Nicholas's behavior improved, he continued to show up at the convent on Saturdays to clean the floors. Sitting alone in his freshman dorm room, he could still remember the conversation Sister Mary Mark had with him one Saturday morning as he was about to leave the convent. She called out to him, and he turned around to face the tall sister with the bright smile that made her glow. He responded, "Yes, Sister?"

"Your grades have much improved, and Mother Superior confirmed you will make the honor roll for the first time. I am very proud of you for working hard."

"Thank you, Sister. I'm beginning to appreciate learning in the same way I did with football. I want to do my best to be as good as I can be. I like the challenge."

"Nicholas, do I sense education has surpassed football?" responded Sister Mary Mark with a questioning smile.

"Football is just a way for me to go to college, Sister," responded Nicholas. He didn't feel ready to share his declining interest in the sport. Football was too important for his future.

Sister Mary Mark knew Nicholas well enough to let the football discussion drop. She had talked with him every Saturday he washed floors at the convent for nearly six months. When he had something on his mind, he would eventually confide in her. She knew Nicholas's mother had passed away when he was five and that he had sadness he tried to conceal. Sister Mary Mark was confident he would share more with her when he felt the time was right.

Changing the subject, she said, "Your behavior at school is also much improved. All the sisters commented on it, and Sister Mary Anne Donovan said your punishment is over. I'm sad to say you will no longer be our floor washer. I will miss the superb job you do, especially the shine."

Nicholas could feel his emotions rising, and he didn't want his eyes to tear up. He loved Sister Mary Mark and going to the convent. Nicholas turned around, opened the solid oak door, and as he walked away he politely said, "Sister, please tell Mother Superior I will be here every Saturday morning until I graduate."

Nicholas had learned about sports playing in the lightly traveled street in front of his house. It was one-pitch stick-ball in the spring and summer and a rough version of touch football in the fall and winter. Some of the best games were played when the snow lined the street where tackling into a snow bank was considered fair play. Nicholas had learned to be street tough when someone didn't play fair, and bare knuckles were exchanged. Over the years, Nicholas had gone home with a few black eyes, but so had his opponents.

For Nicholas, the best thing about the college campus was the hills. The campus was built on one of the seven hills his hometown was noted for. Many a day as a young boy Nicholas had looked up at the college and dreamed he would one day visit the school. In his youth, he hadn't given much thought to attending college. Neighborhood kids didn't attend college. They mostly followed the same paths as their parents, working in local shops and factories.

Many of the students Nicholas knew at Holy Trinity complained about the hills. Nicholas had never responded to these comments. He loved the uphill walk, and when he was alone or late for class, he would run the hills. He felt a special enjoyment pushing himself physically, an enjoyment not many on campus shared.

Nicholas was one of the few local kids who earned the grades and developed the athletic ability to gain admission to the College of the Holy Trinity. He could only attend the prestigious school because of his football scholarship.

But he no longer wanted to play the sport. It was a decision he'd made before he met Meg. He knew when he stopped playing football, his attendance there would be over. He would miss the school, yet he was sure he would find a way back without football.

Nicholas had just missed the last week of spring practice. He hadn't told any of his coaches or teammates he was leaving campus or when he would return. In fact, when Nicholas had gone to help Meg with her car six days earlier, he had no idea he was leaving or that his life would be altered forever.

Nicholas had found love with Meg. She made him feel joy and happiness. He knew he couldn't share his feelings about her with his friends. He felt they would never understand. Nicholas knew he needed to work out his emotions by himself before he could continue his education.

Meg had so much love in her heart; she would sing to him every morning in that off-key voice he loved. It was always some variation of Carole King's lyrics from her song "Beautiful" about waking up every morning with a smile. Meg had her own rendition of the song. She kept a smiley face button in her car that she called her happy face. She felt smiles were contagious, and she wanted everyone to smile. Her version of the song encouraged Nicholas by saying, "You got to wake up every day . . . With a happy face on . . . To show how much you love me." She would hold the "me," sound until Nicholas smiled and they both burst with laughter. Nicholas tried to resist smiling to see how long Meg could hold the sound. He never lasted long. He couldn't wait to smile, embrace her, and kiss.

Just thinking of Meg singing to him, his eyes began to tear. He'd spent five incredible days with Meg, traveling across Cape Cod and responding to her every impulse.

She had wanted to see and experience all that she could with Nicholas. Her desire was to see the ocean, stroll the beaches, collect keepsakes, wade in the freshwater ponds, view the sand dunes, and visit the lighthouses. Meg had wanted to meet the people who lived there, talk with them, and spend time with them. She'd loved it all.

There had been numerous stops on their drive. Meg wanted to explore the hidden paths, walk in some of the open fields to pick wildflowers, and stop at every road-side area that offered a scenic view. All the while, Nicholas would listen to Meg's constant talking or her spontaneous singing when her favorite songs played on the radio.

Thinking about it now while sitting in the quiet of his dorm room, Nicholas told himself, *It's as if Meg had been trying to pack a lifetime of memories into the shortest time possible.*

Nicholas had spent most of his life containing his feelings, his emotions. Meg changed this in him. He no longer wanted or tried to hold back his feelings. He wanted to express them; mostly he wanted to express them to Meg.

She had made Nicholas feel better about himself than he ever had, and while he was conflicted about making love with her, he wasn't naïve. He knew other kids his age were exploring sexual relations even though he'd always believed his first time would be with his new bride on their wedding night. Nicholas's love for Meg seemed pure and sacred to him. He couldn't accept that they had committed a sin.

This was where he'd felt most apart from many of his teammates and friends. The values Nicholas was still committed to had become an inconvenience to some of them.

Nicholas had a loneliness about him that was nearly impossible for anyone to detect. His loneliness was hidden behind his popularity and constant smile. It was subtle; only Meg had been able to open his heart and see its presence. She'd seen in Nicholas the loneliness he felt in himself.

Thinking about all that had happened during his time with Meg, Nicholas suddenly felt the same chill of loneliness he had when his mom died.

Nicholas knew he needed to come to grips with his desire for Meg and the pain he felt when she'd left him. He still couldn't understand how not finding her would protect her. Nicholas wasn't convinced not looking for her was the right thing to do. Yet he would honor her request and protect her. He loved Meg too much to try to find her.

Nicholas needed a way to return to college without playing football if he was going to become a doctor. He also knew it was time to leave Worcester. With his freshman year now complete, he left the campus, took a bus down to the Federal Building, and walked into the military recruitment office. He had decided to join the Navy like his dad and train as a corpsman. He would learn medicine and care for the wounded and dying. The GI Bill would fund his college expenses when he was honorably discharged, and he would never have to play football again. Enlisting would give him a way out of town and help him come to terms with the loss of Meg.

Nicholas needed to speak with his father before he left home. He had no real memory of what his dad was like when his mom was still alive. He only knew of his sad silence after she was gone. Nicholas had learned about his mother and father during those five days on Cape Cod with Meg. He'd been told about their love for each other and their spirit for life. He'd listened to stories from his parents' friends about their goodness. Nicholas had so much to say to his dad now, but he wasn't sure how to start.

Nicholas did speak to his father a few days later, just before he left for boot camp. It was a conversation he would always remember, not for how much was said, but for how little. Most of all he would remember the kiss.

His dad was sitting at the kitchen table, his powerful forearms resting on its wood surface. A bottle of beer, the saltshaker, and a glass lay resting between his calloused hands. Nicholas spoke first. "Dad, I just enlisted in the Navy. I'm going to be a corpsman, and I won't be playing football anymore."

His dad looked up at his son and took a moment before he responded, saying, "It's your decision, son."

"You're not disappointed?" asked Nicholas.

"I'm proud of you, Nicholas. Not for playing football or for going to college. I'm proud that you played football in order to go to college. You knew I could never afford to send you and you didn't ask me to. It speaks to who you are as a person. You're a good boy, son."

Nicholas walked over to his dad, leaned down, wrapped his arms around his steel worker's shoulders, and hugged him. It was the first time he'd hugged his dad since he was a little kid. To his dad's surprise, Nicholas kissed him on the forehead and said, "I love you, Dad."

His dad looked up, tears in his eyes, and said, "I love you too, son."

Part Two

In green pastures
You let me graze;
To safe waters you lead me.

6

Franklin, TN—September 1971

*W*ith pen in hand, Margaret was determined to say her final good-bye to Nicholas. Finding the right words would not come easy for her. She was emotionally drained, battered, and exhausted. She knew her life was rapidly slipping away. It was the middle of September 1971, nearly four months since she'd abandoned Nicholas's love and security. Margaret had found strength in his goodness, his kindness, and it was a time now lost in her despair. She was inconsolable, but she knew tomorrow would be better. There would be no more suffering and no more tomorrows.

Margaret became lost in her thoughts as she began to recall the summer of 1970. She was making only random notations on the paper in front of her. Tears welled in her eyes and slowly flowed down her cheeks. She was shivering as she sat at her writing table in the loneliness of her house. The house was an attractive brick-front, Tudor-style surrounded by the rich trees of Tennessee. There were

American beech, sycamores, magnolias, and many more. All the nature Margaret loved right outside her door.

Margaret had thought when she first saw the house that it would quickly become a warm and loving home, and a perfect place for her and her future husband, Lewis Isaak Barren, to raise their children. She had wanted to live in the Green Hills section of Nashville close to her mother and father, but the Barrens and her parents bought them a house, thirty miles away in the town of Franklin. Their new home was near the estate of Lewis's mother and father.

It hadn't taken Margaret long to realize her husband was not the person he appeared to be and that her new place of residence would always be frigid and vacant of love.

Margaret had always dreamed of attending the College of the Holy Trinity in Massachusetts like her father. She loved the location of the school. She would have had the opportunity to visit the beaches of Cape Cod, as well as explore the small towns of New England. Margaret had never seen the ocean but loved the thought of walking the beach, looking for seashells and driftwood. She wanted to listen to the sound of rolling waves as she sat on the sand watching the sunsets. She wanted to experience the rich history, the culture, and all New England had to offer.

As an excellent student, Margaret knew she could be selective in the school she attended. She knew that admission into Holy Trinity would be competitive. The academics were top tier, and for the first time in the school's history, her freshman class of 1970 would include women. Margaret had also been determined to attend Holy Trinity because it was a Catholic college. She'd attended parochial school since the first grade and very much wanted a learning environment that would also provide spiritual guidance in the Catholic tradition.

Margaret had been somewhat apprehensive about moving a thousand miles to attend college, but she welcomed the challenge and opportunity offered at Holy Trinity.

Margaret had been nearing her eighteenth birthday when she received her acceptance letter, admitting her into the freshman class that would begin in September 1970. It was only a short summer away. She would never have imagined that over those few months, her life would change dramatically, and she would be denied the fulfillment of her dream.

Shortly before high school graduation, Margaret accepted a blind date with Lewis Barren, the son of an acquaintance of her mother. He was tall, muscular, very good looking, and twenty-three years old. He had attended the state university his freshman year, studied abroad, and graduated from a West Coast college. Lewis came from an affluent family who owned several local radio and television stations spread out across the Midwest. He had not spent much time locally while away at school. Every summer during college Lewis had traveled and worked in the family-owned media company learning sales and marketing.

Margaret casually dated Lewis for about six weeks. Their time together was limited because Lewis worked long hours. They occasionally saw a movie when they went out, and he would telephone Margaret once or twice a week. Their conversations were generally short. Lewis was pleasant and usually arranged for the weekly date.

Lewis's interests were mostly restricted to the family business. He was outgoing but often reserved. He did not reveal much about himself, even though he could be talkative at times. He would listen to Margaret when she spoke but did not try to learn much about her. After every date

Lewis walked Margaret to her front door, where he would give her a light kiss on her cheek.

Margaret viewed her time with Lewis as more of a friendship and nothing she considered steady. She had not been ready to commit to a serious relationship. She would be attending Holy Trinity in the fall and was counting the days until she would leave for school.

It was her father's heart attack in early May that changed Margaret's life and placed her future in the hands of her mother.

As her father struggled to recover from a severe heart attack, his ability to work and provide for his family was suddenly in doubt. Margaret's future was now uncertain. She couldn't think of leaving to attend college while her father was ill. She prayed daily for his recovery and spent as much time visiting with him in the hospital as she could.

It had come as a shock when Margaret's mother sat her down on a Tuesday afternoon to tell her that Lewis had visited her. Her mother said, "Lewis came to see me last evening while you were at the hospital visiting with your father. I find him to be a very pleasant and serious young man."

Margaret hadn't responded immediately. She was much too disturbed over her father's health to be concerned about Lewis or anything else for that matter. She hadn't thought about college or dating. All her energy was devoted to helping her father recover and return to be the same loving man he'd always been for her.

Margaret's mother continued speaking, and as she did, she paused often to watch intently at how her daughter reacted to her words. "Lewis finds you to be a serious young woman and has strong feelings for you. He told me about his position in his family business, and I believe he has a very promising future. Lewis said he has tremendous respect for your father and wishes him a speedy recovery. He also told me he knows it's a difficult time for you. Lewis just wanted me to know he felt it was time for him to settle down and begin to raise a family."

Margaret continued to sit quietly as she listened to her mother's words. She began to feel anxious and a little queasy. She sensed where this conversation was going, and she wasn't prepared for it. Her father had not yet fully recovered. His prognosis continued to improve but remained guarded. She didn't know why her mother was discussing this matter with her now.

Margaret wasn't sure she heard her mother correctly when she said, "Lewis was very clear that he could provide for you financially and would like to have permission to marry you."

Margaret stared at her mother with a quizzical look on her face. Her mother recognized the blankness and with a stern voice said, "Margaret."

Regaining her attention, Margaret understood clearly when her mother repeated her words. "Lewis asked permission to marry you, and I think you should consider accepting his proposal. I'm concerned about your father's health, and I want you to be well cared for in the event he doesn't fully recover."

Margaret found it difficult to concentrate on what her mother had just said. It took several minutes to gather her thoughts. She needed to choose her words carefully. She did not want to offend her mother. Her father was hospitalized, and she couldn't believe what she was hearing. Margaret didn't know Lewis very well, and she didn't feel they had much in common. She couldn't think about his proposal, or college, or anything else. She wanted her father back. She wanted him healthy. He meant everything to her.

Margaret had idolized her father since she could remember. He taught her how to ride a bike and to swim. They both loved the outdoors, and they would often hike the local trails together. He introduced her to her two favorite places—Radnor Lake Park and Cheekwood Botanical Garden.

Margaret loved her mother, too, but there was a subtle distance between them. She knew her mother suffered from anxiety and was moody. Margaret was never sure how her mother would react to things; she had learned to rely on her father. When she was troubled, she would always confide in him. When Margaret was a child, he would read to her and tell her stories. As she grew up, they would often talk, and he would listen to whatever was on her mind.

Margaret always referred to her mother as "Mother." In this situation, she knew she needed to express herself clearly. She began carefully by saying, "Mother, you know how much your advice has guided me since I was a young girl, and like you, I think very highly of Lewis; but I hardly know him."

Margaret's mother remained quiet and expressionless as she continued speaking, "Daddy is still not well, and I can't concentrate on anything other than helping him get better. Lewis and I have occasionally dated, and I've only known him for a little over a month. We haven't had any long or serious conversations to help us learn if we're suitable for each other. I think, given Daddy's health, I don't have much time for dating."

Margaret's mother was patient and let her daughter finish speaking before responding in somewhat of a dismissive tone. She said, "Margaret, Lewis is a serious young man from a well-respected family. He has a good position working in the family business. His parents have been acquaintances of ours for many years. Lewis has come to the house once a week for well over a month, and when he speaks to us, he is very courteous and polite. He showed great respect when he requested a meeting with me to discuss his affection for you. I don't believe it's a question of not knowing Lewis; we're very familiar with him. His parents have always spoken highly of him. I think you should consider your father's health. He had a very serious heart attack, and his ability to work may be limited. I hope you know what that would mean to our family."

Margaret did not want to argue with her mother. She was very distraught over her father's illness and physically exhausted. She was spending all her time at the hospital visiting with him and praying for his recovery. Margaret responded by saying, "Mother, I'm only seventeen years old. Lewis is nearly five years older than I am. I don't think we have much in common, even if I were interested in marriage."

"Margaret, you'll be eighteen on the twenty-second, that's only a couple of weeks away. I don't expect you to marry Lewis immediately. He's a mature young man; his age is a benefit. Lewis has established himself financially and has the means to support you for the rest of your life. He has asked that he continue dating you through the summer and proposed that we all consider a September wedding. I only want you to spend more time with him. I'm very concerned for your father's health, and if something were to happen to him, well, I just think you need to prepare yourself for the future."

Margaret felt her face begin to flush, and her body started to tremble. She said, "Daddy will get well. He needs to. I need him to get better. I love him so much."

"Margaret, you need to be patient and understanding. I, too, want your father to get well, but we have to be realistic. He may get better and not be able to work. Lewis is a good, stable man. He has the ability to take care of us if your father can't. You need to spend time with him over the summer getting to appreciate all he has to offer. Don't just think of yourself; you need to think of your father and me."

With her voice quivering she replied, "Daddy will get well, I'm sure of it." She then paused, and asked, "Now, may I be excused?"

"Margaret, please think of your father. We shall not burden him with this matter. In the meantime, you need to keep seeing Lewis. His companionship will help you deal with your father's health. I invited Lewis to dinner this evening, and he asked that we have lunch with his parents after Mass on Sunday. You need a break from going to the hospital every day and night. Your father noticed how tired you look. Darling, you're a young girl, you need to think about your future. Honey, I'm only being practical."

Margaret could not believe what she was hearing. Her father was still hospitalized, and her mother was inviting the man she was casually dating to dinner. She wanted her to think seriously about a future with Lewis when she could think only of her father. Her face was now completely red, and the trembling was worse. She couldn't even respond to her mother emotionally. Margaret stood up from the chair and walked out of the kitchen. Tears were streaming down her face, and it wasn't until she reached her bedroom that she really began to cry.

7

*A*t dinner that evening, there was no talk of marriage. Lewis was gracious and behaved no differently from their previous dates. Toward the end of the evening Margaret had relaxed somewhat, but as soon as Lewis left, her concern shifted to the Sunday luncheon. As she thought about it, she felt the unpleasant, anxious feeling return.

However, the same enjoyable atmosphere was repeated on Sunday and, *More importantly*, she thought, *there was no talk of marriage*.

Margaret had been introduced to Isaak and Doris Barren for the first time at the luncheon, and she'd found them to be very gracious hosts. She thought if Lewis had intentions to marry, his parents would have brought up the topic. Since they hadn't, Margaret started to believe her recent conversation with her mother had not been as serious as she'd thought. Her father's health was stable, and he was hoping it wouldn't be too long before he'd be released from the hospital. Margaret's mother told her not to mention any of their discussion about Lewis to her father until he was out of the hospital and fully recovered.

On Monday morning when Margaret awoke, she felt the happiest she'd been since before the Tuesday conversation with her mother. Her father's health continued to improve, and if he was able to return to work, she thought she could resume her plan of attending Holy Trinity.

Margaret still wanted to speak with her mother about the conversation she'd had with her about Lewis. She needed to clarify and be sure that she'd understood her mother's intentions when she brought up his proposal.

When Margaret went down to the kitchen, her mother was sitting at the breakfast table. Margaret wanted to ease into a serious conversation with her and began by simply saying, "Good morning, Mother."

Responding, her mother said, "Good morning, Margaret. You look happy this morning."

"I do feel happy today."

"I'm sure you must be relieved that you made a good impression on Lewis's mother and father."

"I had a pleasant time, Mother. Lewis's parents are very nice."

"Well, I know they felt like they've known you for years."

"Mother, I don't know how you could say that. I hardly spoke."

"Well, of course Doris called me last evening, and she was very complimentary of you. Lewis's parents are supportive of his intentions."

Hearing her mother speak instantly brought back the anxiety Margaret had first felt last Tuesday, a feeling that now left her slightly nauseous. Despite how she was physically reacting to her mother's words, Margaret responded without revealing how she was truly feeling and said, "I don't recall any conversation about marriage yesterday."

"Margaret, of course Lewis discussed his marriage intentions with his parents before he spoke with me. I think you should appreciate Lewis's interest in you. He's a fine young man and very respectful."

Tensing, Margaret said, "Mother, frankly, I don't love Lewis; I hardly know him. I'm not saying I don't want to get to know him better, and maybe if I did, I'd fall in love with him. I don't want to marry someone I don't love. When Daddy is released from the hospital and returns to work, I still want to attend college. If I do, we'll have plenty of opportunity to date and see each other when I return home from school. It's possible that I may fall in love with Lewis. We can surely continue to see each other during the summers and at Christmastime when I'm home from Holy Trinity."

Responding, her mother said, "Your father is certain that Lewis would make a fine husband for you and will take care of you."

Before her mother could continue speaking, Margaret's face flushed. She quickly interrupted with a curt tone and said, "What do you mean Daddy is certain? When did you speak with him? I thought we weren't going to discuss Lewis with Daddy until he was released from the hospital?"

Defensively her mother responded and said, "When I visited with your father yesterday afternoon he asked me about Lewis and the lunch. Your father is doing better and, well, I just felt he should know about the proposal."

"Mother, I don't want to make Daddy upset, but you need to know that I don't love Lewis!"

"We understand you don't love him now. I didn't love your father when we first married. However, like Lewis, your father was a serious young man who would take care of me and provide for his family," said her mother patiently.

"Mother, I'm willing to continue seeing Lewis over the summer and every time I return home from college," responded Margaret.

"I, or rather, we decided, me and your father, that it's best you not attend college in the fall."

"What? What did you say?" interrupted Margaret.

"Darling, we've determined it's best you not attend college in the fall. Your father is not yet fully recovered from his heart attack, and we don't want you to be so far away. I notified the college first thing this morning and informed them that you wouldn't be attending. You know we both love you very much and only want the best for you. We need you to stay home while your father is still not well."

Margaret was stunned. She couldn't believe what was happening. Her dream of attending college was being shattered without her parents first speaking with her. She was prepared to postpone school if her father's health didn't improve, but he was getting better and would soon be released from the hospital. Tears began to drain from her eyes. Margaret's mind felt locked. She couldn't think clearly. She knew she needed to leave the room quickly if she was going to regain her composure and deal with this crisis. As Margaret rose from her chair, she could feel the trembling of her body. With frustration ringing in her words, she said, "Mother, I don't love Lewis."

As she turned away from her mother, she heard her say in a dispassionate tone, "I'm not sure I ever loved your father. You can be content in a marriage with a man who cares about you and provides for you."

Margaret stopped and turned to look back at her mother. With tears streaming, she said, "How could you say that? You've been married twenty-five years!"

Her mother responded in a tone that left Margaret chilled by how sad and resigned it sounded. "We didn't need love. Your father did his job supporting me, and I did mine, I gave him a daughter."

Standing motionless, her eyes fixed on her mother and her mouth slightly open, she was about to respond when her mother added, "We had companionship; that's all we needed."

Margaret understood the inference in her mother's words, but she couldn't accept what her mother was saying. *Marriage without love was enough as long as you were cared for.* Margaret remained silent and simply turned and walked away. Her mother's last words followed her, "You will not upset your father with this matter. Do you understand?"

8

*T*he two weeks following Margaret's Monday morning talk with her mother were the most difficult of her life. She couldn't understand why her parents hadn't discussed their decision to withdraw her from college with her. If her father's health remained an issue, she would have readily postponed college. She couldn't understand why her mother hadn't waited to speak with her father until he was released from the hospital. Margaret would now have to delay talking with him about college and the marriage proposal until he was fully recovered.

She was devastated by her parents' decision to withdraw her from college. She had wanted desperately to be part of the College of Holy Trinity community and their competitive environment. Margaret had seen it as her opportunity to mature into a well-educated and confident woman. It was her dream to attend her father's alma mater. The realization that she had so little control over her own life shocked her in a way that left her hopelessly sad about her future.

As a girl attending Catholic school in Nashville, she'd embraced her faith. She loved to attend Sunday Mass with her parents, and she passionately wanted to sing in the church choir. The choirmaster told her, "Your vocal quality precludes you from participating in the choir." Margaret knew she had a terrible singing voice, but she didn't care. She simply loved to sing. To make up for being excluded from the choir, she vigorously sang all the selected hymns from her pew in church. She loved music and the joy it provided.

Margaret had been an adolescent during the 1960s when many of the established mores and values of American society had been challenged. She was too young to relate to or identify with the new attitudes. Like many young people her age, she had very little firsthand exposure to the Vietnam War or student protests, the rising drug culture, the sexual revolution, or the so-called generation gap.

Margaret had led a sheltered life during her first eighteen years. Her parochial school education had offered a traditional curriculum with an overview of national and world events. It also provided her with a solid foundation in Catholic teachings. The study of the Holy Bible was incorporated into her religious studies.

As a student, Margaret had been schooled in the Ten Commandments. She had been able to recite them from memory since she was a little girl in elementary school. These were the same precepts Margaret's mother and father had instilled in her from childhood. She was raised to respect the wisdom and decisions of her parents and to seek guidance through her Catholic faith.

When Mrs. Gabriel notified the college that Margaret would not be attending after all, Margaret was not conditioned to challenge her parents' authority. Her reference in this situation was the Fourth Commandment: Honor your father and your mother. Margaret had just turned eighteen and was living in the home of her parents and being supported by them. She believed her obligation was to obey.

While she'd been devastated by their actions, Margaret was disposed to accept her parents' decision out of love, respect, and her understanding of divine law. True to her faith, she would continue to pray every day, seeking guidance and direction from the Lord. She still planned to speak with her father about college and Lewis when he fully recovered. She knew his heart attack had nearly cost him his life, and he would want to protect her. But he'd never before made a decision that affected her without the two of them first discussing the matter. Margaret believed it had been her father's concern for his health that caused him to make this decision without consulting her. She just wanted the opportunity to talk with her father like they always had.

Margaret felt further isolated by the absence of her two best friends. Terese, her childhood friend, had volunteered to work for the Catholic Relief Services in Haiti for the summer. Mary, her friend since the ninth grade, was planning to major in French while attending college. She was also away for the summer. She was living with her aunt and uncle in France until the start of the fall semester. Ever since her father's heart attack, Margaret had to deal with all her sorrow and anxiety by herself.

9

*O*ver a month had passed since Margaret's mother first mentioned Lewis's marriage intentions to her. When Margaret awoke on a warm June morning, she was feeling less sad than she had since that day. Her father was recently home from the hospital and improving. He was hoping to return to work in a few weeks. He would then work on a limited basis until he felt strong enough to resume a normal schedule. Margaret was hopeful she would soon be able to speak with him about college and Lewis.

While she lay in bed, Margaret said her morning prayers and began to reflect on her current circumstances. She thought about Lewis and the status of their relationship.

She had continued to see Lewis once a week and received one or two telephone calls from him between dates. He'd been very concerned about her father's health. His attitude toward her had not changed much. He was always polite, respectful, and, it seemed, more sensitive toward her. There appeared to be nothing romantic about their relationship except the soft good-night kiss on the cheek.

Margaret could not believe that a wedding could possibly take place in September. She had started to wonder if Lewis had rethought his proposal. Margaret said to herself, *Certainly a man would propose to the woman he hoped to marry. There would be talk of the wedding, too, but Lewis hasn't said anything.* Margaret began to convince herself that the whole situation was a misunderstanding.

In Margaret's view, the idea of a marriage between two people who barely knew each other was impulsive. She hoped that somehow Lewis was beginning to see it the same way she did. *After all,* she told herself, *it's not the foundation for a loving marriage.*

As Margaret arose from her bed, she decided that she would speak with Lewis about her feelings. She knew she would need to be subtle. She did not want to appear to be defying her parents. Margaret reasoned, *If Lewis was looking for a way to postpone or call off the wedding, and I told him my true feelings, that may be enough to persuade him. If that would happen, I could then think about finding a way to attend the College of the Holy Trinity.* As she thought about this, she made the sign of the cross.

Margaret then resolved to enjoy her day. Saturday was the one day of the week that she was nearly free of responsibilities. Before her father's heart attack, he normally worked Saturdays. Her mother would spend the day shopping and visiting with friends or relatives. The family had developed a sort of routine that gave each of them the freedom to make plans without creating a conflict.

Margaret always attended confession on Saturday at four thirty in the afternoon. She would then return home to have dinner with her parents. Since she'd begun dating Lewis, she would spend the evening with him, usually at the movie theater.

Margaret packed herself a light lunch to take with her and went into the garage to get her car. On her seventeenth birthday, her parents bought her a yellow Volkswagen Beetle. She loved her compact car, and she loved the color yellow. Everything yellow reminded Margaret of a yellow rose. It was her favorite flower. Seeing the soft yellow petals always made Margaret feel happy and free. She thought it was the most joyous flower God had created.

Margaret drove to a local bookstore to purchase a new novel that had been released in February called *Love Story,* written by Erich Segal. It was quickly becoming a best seller, and she couldn't wait to read it. With her new book in hand, Margaret decided to spend the day reading at the Cheekwood Botanical Gardens.

Margaret's two favorite places in her hometown to spend the day with a good book were Radnor Lake Park and Cheekwood Botanical Gardens. When she visited Radnor Lake, she always found a place to lay her blanket to appreciate the wildflowers. She particularly enjoyed the fragrance of the yellow and white honeysuckles and the deep purple dwarf larkspurs. Her other favorites were the low-growing, white spring beauties and the mountain blue-bells with their soft pastel colors. Margaret loved the old shellbark and shagbark hickory trees, the scarlet oaks with the bright red leaves, and the American sycamore, all of which seemed to enhance the beauty of the lake.

She loved the wildlife that inhabited the open wooded area around the banks of the water. She would often spot a deer with her fawns grazing peacefully among the green fern near the water's edge. She also admired the turtle families sunning themselves on the limb of a fallen river birch that straddled the shallow water and the muddy bank. Most of all she waited with anticipation of seeing a barred owl.

Every time she saw one perched on a tree branch, she would watch quietly. She'd wait for the owl to open its wings, begin its flight, and then soar. Margaret thought they were proud, beautiful birds with their vertical and horizontal streaks of brown.

Visiting the lake oftentimes made her sad; she felt it could be a much grander place if more people saw the same beauty and potential that she did. She was thrilled when a new group had formed called the Friends of Radnor Lake.

Margaret chose to visit the botanical gardens because since waking that morning, she had felt cheerful and wanted to spend the day surrounded by her favorite flowers. She loved the yellow tulips, pink azaleas, mums, and the yellow-and-purple violets.

On her way to the garden, she negotiated her VW over several side streets to get to Harding Pike. She then turned left onto Page Road, driving past the Belle Meade Country Club, and arrived shortly at Cheekwood Botanical Garden on Forest Park Drive.

She spent a couple of hours walking the gardens and then spread her blanket near the small pond to eat her lunch and read her book. She could hear the water trickling down from the little brook that nourished the pond. The sun was shining, and it was seasonally warm with a light breeze. Her light-colored skin felt the soothing softness of nature's comfort.

Sitting on her blanket she felt the warmth of the sun on her face, and slowly her eyes began to close. She began to lose her concentration, rereading the words on the page. She lay down with her head resting on her flower-spotted rucksack and fell asleep. Margaret's dream brought her back to the happier times before her mother's depression and her father's heart attack. She could feel the love her parents had for each other and for her. When she awoke, her subconscious thoughts made her energized and happy. She looked at her watch; it was four o'clock. She had only thirty minutes to drive to confession. She had barely read her book.

Margaret drove to church and hurried to confession. After confessing her sins, she knelt at the altar and recited her penance as assigned by the priest. She left the church feeling excited about her future. She drove home to prepare herself for her date with Lewis.

10

$\mathcal{L}$ewis arrived at Margaret's home promptly at seven o'clock to take her to the movies. They were going to see the newly released film starring Clint Eastwood and Shirley MacLaine called *Two Mules for Sister Sara*. Margaret loved going to the movies and was looking forward to seeing the film. She couldn't wait to see Shirley MacLaine portray a nun in the movie.

While driving to the theater, Margaret sat quietly on the front passenger side closest to the window. It wasn't unusual for her and Lewis to be lost in their own thoughts. They both often seemed to search for the right words to begin talking. The silence gave her time to think through the conversation she needed to have with him about his marital intentions.

When Margaret was ready to speak she said, "Lewis," in a soft tone loud enough to get his attention.

"Yes, Margaret?" Lewis responded enthusiastically.

"My mother spoke to me about your marriage proposal," she said cautiously.

"Yes," was all he said.

Margaret had hoped the mention of the marriage proposal would spark Lewis to elaborate on his intentions or to use it as an opportunity to gauge her feelings about it. He didn't though; this was not how she had planned he would react. She sat for a while thinking, then asked herself, *How serious can he be about marriage?* Her response was, *Not very. If he was serious,* she reasoned, *he would have asked me to marry him by now.*

They were nearing the movie theater, and Margaret did not want to arrive without learning more from Lewis. She even hoped they would become engrossed in conversation and agree the wedding was premature. Margaret felt he would be relieved the wedding would not take place, since they hardly knew each other.

"September is two months away, and we've only been dating a short while. It would be nice for us to learn more about each other," said Margaret. She paused for a second, then added, "Don't you think?"

Lewis did not respond immediately to her question. Margaret looked closely at his face, hoping his expression would reveal his feelings.

When Lewis responded a few moments later, he exposed his wide smile and calmly said, "There's no rush."

As Lewis spoke, Margaret tried to look into his eyes. Hearing his response frustrated her, and she wasn't sure if her face revealed just how much. She didn't get a good feeling as Lewis gazed back at her without speaking. Margaret couldn't tell for certain, but she thought she'd detected an odd smirk on his face as he turned away. She immediately discounted it and attributed it to the guilt she felt when revealing her frustration. *Besides,* she said to herself, *Lewis is much too respectful for that type of behavior.*

There was no further discussion about the proposal as they approached the cinema. When they arrived, Lewis parked the car, and then walked with Margaret to the ticket counter. Lewis paid the three-dollar admission fee, and they went in to watch the nearly two-hour movie. After the motion picture ended, Lewis brought Margaret home.

On the drive back to Margaret's house, there was no more talk of the wedding. The two shared some superficial thoughts about the movie. Thinking about just how little they said to each other, it struck Margaret that, *It isn't that Lewis and I don't know each other well enough to get married; it's more like we're strangers who don't know each other at all.*

Lying in bed that night, Margaret replayed her conversation with Lewis over in her head. She wasn't sure what he meant when he said, *There's no rush.* She didn't know if he meant no rush to get married or no rush to get to know each other. She wished she knew. These were her final thoughts as she drifted off to sleep.

When Margaret woke the next morning, she didn't have time to reflect on the limited conversation she'd had with Lewis the night before. She needed to get ready to attend Mass with her parents. Her father liked to be punctual; he left the house at nine thirty every Sunday morning. Margaret was excited because this was the first Mass they would be attending as a family since his heart attack. As usual, her father wanted to get to church early, so he could sit in the front row to better hear the priest. Margaret quickly prepared herself, dressed, ate breakfast, and was right on time just as her parents had come to expect.

As they drove to church, her mother asked, "Did you have a good time on your date with Lewis?"

Margaret didn't answer directly. She didn't want to tell her mother it was a frustrating date, so she simply said, "Lewis was very polite, and the movie was good."

Her parents smiled and appeared satisfied with her response. Margaret's father then said, "You looked happy yesterday. I'm glad you had a nice day."

"Thank you, Daddy, it was pleasant and relaxing. You know how much I love the botanical gardens." Margaret deliberately avoided mentioning her date.

Margaret's mother interjected and said, "I see you bought a new book. Are you enjoying it?"

"I brought it with me and found a peaceful spot to read, but I dozed off instead."

Her father then asked, "What are you reading, sweetheart?"

"The book is called *Love Story,* Daddy."

Neither parent responded, but each smiled.

Margaret, thinking her parents were smiling because of Lewis's marriage proposal, quickly said, "I haven't started it yet, but I'm told it's really a very tragic story."

Margaret's mother stopped smiling, but her father had a quizzical look on his face. He knew his daughter, and her short, quick response seemed odd to him. Margaret loved books and loved talking about them. She would share all the details until you'd felt as if you had read the book yourself.

Her father thought for a moment and asked, "How so, Margaret?"

As Margaret was about to respond, her mother quickly interrupted and said, "Not now, dear, we'll be at the church in a few minutes. We don't have the time." She then turned around in her seat to face Margaret and said, "After Mass this morning, your father needs to rest and have a peaceful day." She paused and, with a stern tone, said, "Do you understand?"

Margaret nodded her head and said, "Yes, Mother. I can tell Daddy all about the book after I finish reading it and when he's feeling better." Her mother held her glare until Margaret lowered her eyes and then looked out the window of the car. Her mother turned to face forward and with a firm voice said to her husband, "Joseph, I don't want you exerting yourself today. You just had a heart attack and you're not yet fully recovered."

11

*M*argaret had a busy week running errands for her parents and assisting her mother with many of her social and church projects. She had planned to work during the summer to earn some money for college. However, when her mother had withdrawn her from Holy Trinity, she'd also called her employer to let him know that Margaret was not going to attend college and no longer needed the job. She had suggested they hire someone who would be going to school and could use the summer earnings for college expenses.

This had been another blow to Margaret; it would have been her first job. She hadn't been allowed to work during high school. Her parents had wanted her to concentrate on getting good grades and also remain active in both religious and school programs. They were generous with the amount of allowance they'd given her, and she'd saved as much money as she could. At the time Margaret had felt especially blessed that she didn't need to work. All her energy could be devoted to the things she most enjoyed and were important to her future.

Only days after Margaret's mother had withdrawn her from Holy Trinity, she had informed her she didn't need to work that summer. Margaret was about to respond to this news when her mother had quickly added, "Your father will need your assistance while he recovers his health at home. I will also need your help with all my activities. Your time will be better spent assisting me and helping your father. These are the responsibilities you'll need to learn now that you're a young woman."

Margaret had turned pale. She felt overwhelmed with all that was happening. She was determined to keep her feelings to herself and responded in a submissive tone, "If you think that's best, Mother."

"I do and remember, I don't want you upsetting your father by mentioning college, work, or Lewis. Do you understand?"

Margaret looked at her mother and gave a slight nod of her head while responding in a barely audible voice, "Yes, Mother."

In some ways losing the opportunity to earn her own money had been as painful as the loss of attending college. Margaret had been looking forward to saving money and gaining some financial independence from her parents.

The loss of the summer job had further contributed to her despondency. Her father's heart attack had started a series of events that knocked Margaret off her trajectory. First it was the marriage proposal, then the withdrawal from college, followed by the loss of summer employment.

Margaret wanted desperately to speak with her father. She knew he would understand and help her get back on course. His health was improving every day, but her mother kept insisting she not talk with her father about the things that were troubling her. Margaret's faith in the Fourth Commandment was strong. She would never defy her mother and go behind her back to speak with him. She would remain patient and continue to pray for her father's full recovery.

When Mrs. Gabriel told her husband about Lewis's marriage intentions, she hadn't mention she planned to withdraw Margaret from Holy Trinity or that she'd prevented her from working over the summer. She led him to believe that these had been Margaret's decisions. Mrs. Gabriel wanted her daughter to remain at home with her. She didn't want to be left alone if her husband's heart failed him. The telephone call from Mrs. Barren to arrange her son's first date with Margaret, and then hearing Lewis's proposal, had been all the excuses she needed to keep Margaret home. Mrs. Gabriel figured if her husband didn't survive his bad heart, she could always live with her daughter and Lewis when they were married.

Margaret pushed aside her sadness and planned to have another pleasurable Saturday. She was also looking forward to seeing Lewis that evening. Margaret resolved to ask him to clearly state his intentions. She was convinced he did not want to marry her and was too respectful to say so.

Margaret pulled out of her driveway in her yellow VW Beetle. She was heading to Radnor Lake. She enjoyed the ride and would always go by way of Granny White Pike. She loved the tree-lined country road, but most of all she loved the name Granny White. The thought of the name Granny always made Margaret recall her grandmothers who had passed away and the comfort she'd always felt when visiting with them.

Her lunch was packed, and she had Erich Segal's novel with her. The radio was playing a new Ray Stevens' song, "Everything Is Beautiful." As the music filled the car,

Margaret hummed and sang along. She was enjoying the freedom she felt when driving her yellow car.

Margaret had chosen Radnor Lake for her Saturday excursion because she wanted to spend the afternoon reading her book. At the botanical gardens, she would often get distracted admiring the flowers, talking with the gardeners, or being absorbed in her own thoughts. At the lake, sitting on her blanket, she knew she would give the book her full attention.

The time passed quickly as Margaret read about the love story between Jennifer (Jenny) and Oliver Barrett IV (Ollie), the novel's two main characters. As Margaret started reading the book, she quickly realized she was entering a world very unfamiliar to her. The characters were bigger than life. The way they spoke, acted, and bantered with each other was different and unlike anything she'd been exposed to growing up.

Margaret thought of her relationship with her father as she read about Oliver's dinner with his father after a hockey game. She couldn't imagine thinking disrespectfully of her dad in the way Oliver thought about his; and she could never speak to him in such a way. Margaret felt like her father was her guardian angel. She could recall the dozens of times when he would magically appear when she needed him most, such as when she was a little girl who'd fallen off her bike, her first flat tire, or waiting for the bus in a downpour. Somehow there was her dad. He would care for her bruises and help her back onto her bicycle, fix the damaged tire, or drive her home in the rain. But they would never go directly home; they would always stop for either ice cream or hot chocolate.

Despite entering such a foreign world, Margaret loved the character Jenny. She felt she didn't have the confidence Jenny had, or the courage and wit. She couldn't help loving everything about her, though. Margaret knew she was smart and enjoyed life, but she feared she couldn't be an outgoing and assertive woman like Jenny.

Margaret could feel the love Jenny and Ollie had for each other, and she was excited when they got married. She knew that over the past decade other people, especially young adults, were changing their views about sexual relations. Margaret would never throw stones in the biblical sense, but she believed that sexual intercourse was an act of love reserved for marriage.

Thinking about this made Margaret sad. She did not love Lewis. A marriage and a sexual relationship with a man she didn't love made her feel cold.

Margaret smiled to herself, imagining Jenny telling Lewis, *Sorry, preppie, I'm not marrying you. I'm off to college.* She wished she were a character in a novel and was saying those exact words.

Margaret shed a lot of tears reading *Love Story*. She thought Jenny dying was one of the saddest stories she'd ever read. But it wasn't Jenny's death that made Margaret cry the most; it was when she thought about how Jenny had found and married the man she loved while, somehow, she was engaged to Lewis, a man she really didn't know and didn't love.

Despite reading such a sad story and shedding so many tears, Margaret had an enjoyable day. It was getting close to four o'clock, so she grabbed her belongings and headed to the parking lot. As she walked to her car she couldn't help saying to herself, *After reading about making love with a boy outside of marriage, and after calling Lewis preppie, my penance after confession might take a little longer than usual.*

Margaret left the park and drove to church to say her confession. When she reached home, what was waiting for her turned her lovely day to gloom.

12

*A*s Margaret approached her driveway she immediately noticed two cars blocking the entrance into the garage. She pulled her Beetle to the curb and parked. Margaret recognized Lewis's car right away. She did not recognize the other vehicle or know anyone who drove a large black car. The sight of Lewis's vehicle parked unexpectedly at her home gave her that awful anxious and nauseous feeling that had become much too familiar.

Immediately upon entering, Margaret was met with a chorus of greetings with everyone seemingly speaking at once. She thought she saw her parents, then Lewis, and Mr. and Mrs. Barren. The feeling of anxiety increased; she was lightheaded. Her heart started to race, and she could feel herself tremble as if she were hit with a sudden burst of frosty air. She felt she couldn't breathe and it was hard for her to focus. It seemed like her mind was suddenly engulfed in fog so thick she couldn't see.

All Margaret could hear were phrases. She couldn't tell who was talking, "Oh, Margaret, there you are." She wasn't sure, but she thought, *my father is speaking*. "How was your day, sweetheart? Isn't this a delightful surprise for you?" *Is that mother talking?* "Good afternoon, Margaret," *Mr. Barren,* she thought. Then quickly someone said, "Oh, Margaret, I just can't get over how pretty you are and so slim." She asked herself, *is it Mrs. Barren talking?* She didn't think she heard Lewis speak. She wasn't sure if she had really seen him.

The chatter and shock of what she was seeing and hearing destabilized her. It wasn't until Lewis stepped forward and said, "Margaret, you remember my parents, Isaak and Doris," that she gained enough presence to respond.

"Yes, it's nice to see you again, Mr. and Mrs. Barren." As Margaret said this, she was handed a narrow-stemmed glass with a small amount of liquid in it as Lewis's father asked for everyone's attention and announced, "A toast to the soon-to-be bride and groom."

Margaret, lightheaded, stood trembling until her mother said, "Drink up, dear, it's just a sip." Margaret could see the glass move to her lips, the vapor reaching her nostrils, then her head slightly repelled from the acrid smell. When the bitter taste of the alcohol met her tongue, she couldn't swallow the unfamiliar liquid.

As soon as the toast was over, the attention returned to the conversation that had been taking place before she'd arrived. Margaret stood perfectly still, trying to control her breathing. As she observed the lively activity, the only lucid thought running through her mind was, *I am now a stranger in my own home.*

Margaret was overcome by an exhaustion that forced her to a chair in the corner of the room farthest from the meshing of loud voices she was hearing. Lewis's mother, Doris, was the first to notice Margaret sitting quietly and said, "Oh dear, sweetheart, you look so tired. How are you feeling?"

Before she could respond, Margaret's mother said, "It must be the excitement of the engagement. Oh darling, you know we couldn't keep it a secret forever. My dear, look at you, you must be tired, all this celebration, and the champagne."

Mrs. Barren said, "Maybe a little rest will help her feel better."

Margaret's mother responded and said, "Margaret, why don't you go upstairs and lie down. You've had a busy day, and now with this special surprise you must be exhausted."

Margaret slowly stood up and started for the stairs that led to her bedroom. As she walked away she could hear her mother say to the others, "Margaret is thrilled about the wedding. She just can't wait."

Mr. Barren immediately responded with an enthusiastic voice, while putting his arm around his son's muscular shoulder and squeezing him, "Why, I'm sure she's thrilled. Lewis is a fine young man, a very fine young man."

Watching his daughter walk away, her father quietly said, "All I want is for Margaret to be happy." Speaking over her husband's words, Margaret's mother excitedly said, "They will make a beautiful couple."

As Margaret walked to her bedroom, she couldn't cry. Her despondency heavy, she could feel the tingling of her numbness. It had been nearly nine weeks since her father's heart attack. She'd hardly slept and was regularly falling to sleep during the day. Everything had happened suddenly — her father's illness, Lewis's proposal, and the loss of college and the summer job. Now the unexpected announcement of the engagement. It all combined to create a weight that was crushing her youth.

Margaret recognized her symptoms; she'd seen them in her mother. It frightened her. She desperately wanted to talk with her father and straighten out her life, but she was afraid for his health.

Margaret didn't remember undressing or reaching her bed. She lay shivering as she fell into a deep sleep.

Margaret slept for fourteen hours. She wasn't sure if she'd been dreaming or if her mother had come into her room to try to wake her. Her eyes were closed, but she was finally awake. Margaret didn't want to get out of bed. She thought about how anxious she'd felt the evening before, and it horrified her to think she could be inflicted with the same anxiety and depression as her mother. Margaret knew it was wrong, but she couldn't stop the overwhelming feeling of wanting to sleep and never wake up.

She wondered if everything that'd happened over the last couple of months had all been a bad dream. Margaret knew she was very fortunate. She'd grown up in a beautiful home with a loving family. Her parents had been financially secure, and she'd been given all she needed. She was committed to her faith and always tried to live a Christian life.

Margaret thought about the Old Testament and the story of Job. She felt as though she was being tested. Then she scolded herself for comparing her situation to Job and those who truly suffer. In stressful situations, Margaret regained a sense of calmness through prayer. She began to recite her prayers and tried to relax. She wanted to think rationally in order to come to grips with what was happening to her.

Margaret cleared her mind and thought about her circumstances. It was only then that everything came into focus. She spoke the words out loud. She wanted to be certain they were real. Alone in her room with a voice filled with melancholy, she said, *I am now engaged to a man I don't really know, a man I'm not in love with, a man who never asked me to marry him.*

Hearing her own words in her own voice, Margaret began to weep.

13

*M*argaret's mother had tried to wake her up, so she could attend Mass with her parents. Her mother was annoyed they had to leave without her. The Gabriels had been invited to brunch with Lewis and his parents, and Mrs. Gabriel didn't want to be late. She was not pleased; they would now have to make a special trip back to their house to pick up Margaret.

The location of the brunch was at the private club where the Barrens were members. Margaret's father had been there several times for business meetings and thought it was a very nice place but found the distance inconvenient. It was nearly thirty miles from his home.

The brunch was usually well attended by members of the club. The gathering of the Barrens and the Gabriels was to serve as an unannounced engagement party. Mr. Barren was certainly going to share the news with the members. He wanted to make his son the center of attention and receive the many well wishes and congratulatory comments. Isaak was proud of his son, but he also wanted to create a little envy among some members. He knew there were people at the club who were jealous of his family and their success. Isaak also knew human nature; some of these same people were greedy and would jump at the opportunity to be included in the Barren circle of friends. If he needed them, that's exactly what he would do.

Isaak Barren conducted a lot of his business at the club either while dining or playing golf. He had been taught by his father that to be successful in business, appearances were everything. Lewis Isaak Barren was the future of the family business. Isaak knew it was important that Lewis be seen not as his son but as a family man, a business professional, and a club member in his own right.

Barren was a family-owned communications company that had been started by Exuvial Barren in 1890 as a printing company. In the early 1900s, he'd expanded and bought a local newspaper. When opportunity struck he'd bought other similar-size papers, and in the 1920s he purchased his first radio station. Through the 1930s and '40s, he'd kept buying local radio stations when they became available. In the early 1950s, the company dumped their small newspaper chain and focused on local radio and television. They mostly made their money through advertising sales and investments.

The Barrens didn't get people to like them and do business with them simply because of money or the desire to make it. The Barrens got people to like them by deviously exploiting what they most value and love, and most times that was their faith and their family. The Barrens had no real religious convictions or affiliations. They used religion when it helped them land a big advertiser or secure financing from a banker or investor. Religion served a purpose but held no spiritual meaning to them.

Isaak would never forget his grandfather's words: "It was the serpent who was the most cunning of all." Young Isaak was told the saying came right from the book of Genesis and was the only religion he needed to know.

The Barren family also learned another important lesson that greatly contributed to the family's success. Exuvial told his son Vernon there was no place for love or emotion in a marriage.

Exuvial, his son Vernon, and his grandson Isaak were not romantic people. They'd grown up and survived during hard times when poverty was right around the corner. Love and emotion had never entered the equation when they'd selected a spouse. They had all married practical woman who sought companionship and would assist them in running their business and raising their children. It was a formula that had served the family through two World Wars and the Great Depression.

Isaak had no doubt; companionship with a practical woman was not a formula that would work for Lewis Barren now that he was of age.

Mrs. Barren had been the first to notice Margaret. She had attended a social function when she'd observed Margaret with her mother. Mrs. Barren had been struck by Margaret's presence, the way she moved, how she stood, her mannerisms, and her beauty. Margaret was shy, reserved, modest not elegant, but special in a way that was hard to describe. Mrs. Barren thought Margaret was extraordinary. This made her think of Lewis, her only son.

Mrs. Barren loved her son and saw in him all the qualities that made Barren men successful. Lewis was hardworking, respectful, mature, and committed to the success of the Barren family business. Looking at Margaret, she thought the young woman would make a very good partner for Lewis.

Mrs. Barren had quietly made inquiries about Margaret and her family. She liked what she'd heard and decided to speak with Mr. Barren. When she had the chance, she discussed the matter with husband.

As Isaak Barren listened to his wife speak about Margaret and their son Lewis, he couldn't help thinking about his father, Vernon. When Lewis was born, Isaak's mother had told him that his father had been abusive to her until he was born. His mother wasn't aware if Isaak had been violent with his wife, Doris, before she delivered Lewis, but she wanted him to know if he had been violent, he needed to stop now that Lewis was born. He'd assured his mother he hadn't but would never forget what she'd told him about his father.

Isaak's son Lewis had inherited Vernon's hate, and it had cost the family a considerable amount of money keeping his problems from reaching the courts and the press. He hoped his son's violence toward women wouldn't be directed at his new wife. Isaak wasn't going to take any chances. He needed to find a young woman for his son who would have a deep religious and sacred commitment to her wedding vows. Isaak knew the media world, and he didn't want his son's deviance to be a headline story blaring over the airwaves of one of his local television or radio stations.

He knew Doris had no knowledge of their son's earlier problems with women. Isaak had always kept her in the dark about Lewis's violence. He would only tell her if the time came and he needed her help to clean up a problem. Isaak knew Doris loved her son, and she'd do anything to protect him. As she continued to speak, he thought, *It's time for another long talk with Lewis about his aberrant behavior.*

Mr. Barren was pleased by what he heard and asked Mrs. Barren to arrange for Lewis's first date. Margaret's mother had been thrilled when Mrs. Barren called her. She knew Doris Barren in a casual way, but had never received a telephone call from her. Mrs. Gabriel had never been supportive of her daughter going away to college like her husband was. She'd wanted Margaret to stay close to home and find a young man who would provide for her and give her a good life. In her mind, there was no better family to marry into than the Barrens.

14

Margaret's parents arrived home after Mass, and when they did not find Margaret dressed and ready, her mother went up to her bedroom. The door was closed. She knocked, opened it, and stepped into the room. Margaret was lying in bed with her eyes closed. Hearing her mother, she opened her eyes and turned her head slightly to look at her. Margaret's eyes were red and moist. She fixed her gaze on her mother's face and said, "I don't love him."

Margaret's mother ignored the comment and said, "Margaret, you need to get out of bed and prepare yourself to attend a brunch with Lewis and Mr. and Mrs. Barren. If you don't hurry, we'll be late. We certainly don't want to insult the Barrens by having them wait for us; it would be very inconsiderate. They were gracious inviting us to the brunch, so we can all get to know each other better."

Margaret did not move. She continued to look at her mother as if she didn't hear what she said. "I don't love him," she said again, slowly enunciating each word.

"My dear, we have discussed this already; no one is rushing the wedding. You have the rest of the summer to get to know each other better, and if love is what you are looking for, well, I'm sure you'll love Lewis in no time at all. I have no doubt, darling; your wedding will be a glorious event. Now please, you need to get out of bed and get ready to brunch with the Barrens. You have thirty minutes to prepare yourself or we'll be late. Your father is waiting downstairs, and we don't want him to get upset. You know he has a bad heart. I don't have to remind you that he doesn't like us to be late when he's meeting people. Now please, you need hurry up and get ready." As Margaret began to rise, her mother left the bedroom.

Margaret hadn't known about the brunch. It had been arranged the prior evening as she slept. In her current state of mind, it was something she hadn't considered.

Before leaving her bedroom, Margaret stopped to look at herself in the full-length mirror. What she saw confirmed how she felt. Margaret had the look of total exhaustion. She'd lost a little weight, and with her small, slim frame, it made her look ill. Her eyes were still red, and her face had lost its sheen. As Margaret continued to look at herself in the mirror, she almost smiled at the words she was thinking, *No one would want to marry the withering teenager looking back at me.* She couldn't smile, though; she felt no joy, only sadness.

Margaret left her bedroom and went down to meet her parents. Her mother was no longer annoyed by the delay; she was angry. She'd rarely verbalized her anger, but even a stranger could see what her face was saying.

As Margaret's father drove to the brunch, she remained silent. Sitting in the back seat of the car, she once again began to think about Lewis and the wedding. She was finding it difficult to focus on her thoughts. Everything in her life had changed so fast. Margaret felt she was being pushed into a wedding she did not agree to. All these things happening at once made her feel anxious, exhausted, and unhappy. She felt it was her mother who wanted her to get married. She desperately needed to talk with her father, but her mother insisted he was still not well.

Margaret by nature was a happy, joyous young woman. She always tried to view difficult circumstances in the best possible light. Margaret then began to silently say her prayers, and as she did, something her mother had said that morning entered her thoughts. As she concentrated on her mother's words, they came to her. She'd told Margaret, *You have the rest of the summer to get to know each other . . . and if love is what you're looking for . . . I'm sure you'll find it in no time at all.*

Margaret, trying to see light in her darkening world, thought to herself, *Maybe Mother is right.* She knew she would always feel the loss of the opportunity to attend Holy Trinity and to grow into an independent, college-educated woman. She sadly admitted to herself that she would never be like Jenny Cavalleri as portrayed in *Love Story*.

She then let herself think about Lewis from a different point of view. She focused on the things she did know about him and not on how much she didn't know. *Lewis comes from a good family; he's hard working, always respectful, pleasant, five years older, and mature. He has a good position with the family business, and he's committed to it.* Margaret smiled for the first time since she'd arrived home last evening when she said to herself, *And not unattractive. After all, he is good looking.*

Margaret then thought about one of her favorite poems by William Cowper called, "God Moves in a Mysterious Way" and quoted to herself, *He will make it plain.*

The silence of the ride was broken when her mother said, "Joseph, please slow down, dear. We'll be arriving shortly, and we still have a few minutes to spare. You can drop us off in front, and then go park the car. I need to speak with Margaret before we go into the club."

As Margaret's father slowed down, she said, "Mother, I'm fine. I feel much better. I was just very tired. I'm looking forward to the brunch and seeing Lewis."

Margaret's father smiled and said, "I'm glad you're feeling better, sweetheart."

"Thank you, Daddy."

"Margaret, you're such a good girl. Thank you, my dear," replied her mother.

"Yes, Mother," responded Margaret without enthusiasm.

Margaret would never say it, and certainly not now that she was prepared to see if God's purpose for her was to find love rather than attend college, but the words ran through her mind: *Yes Mother, I am a girl, but just a girl. A girl too young to marry.*

15

*L*ewis watched Margaret and her parents arrive at the club while standing at a window with an obscured view, a perspective that provided those inside the club a perfect vantage point to view arriving guests. Whether by design or happenstance, it made timing the greeting of people natural, as if it were by chance. Lewis had been taught by his father to always seek the advantage when dealing with people, particularly in business; and for the Barrens, today's brunch was about business. He needed to close the deal for the wedding his parents wanted.

Lewis had been going to his parents' club since he was a little boy. His father had started schooling him to conduct business at the club the day Lewis could carry a set of golf clubs on his shoulder for eighteen holes. Lewis was taught how to speak the language of business and behave around the people his father was entertaining. He watched his father work and saw that he always found a way to wink at Lewis when one of his business acquaintances said the word *fair*. The Barrens were never fair; they always tried to subtly exploit those they did business with. The family's private joke was when someone said, "Isaak, you're a fair man."

Isaak had told his son his grandfather's favorite saying, "Always remember when dealing with people, it was the serpent who was the most cunning."

Lewis would always remember his great-grandfather's words, and the best place to practice them was when doing business at the club. He had to be subtle; Margaret was not yet receptive to the marriage. He wasn't ready to close the deal today; he was here to soften her resistance. Lewis knew Margaret would marry him. He could hear the words, *a little cunning always works,* run through his mind. The sly smile he was about to display came when he knew he was about to be cunning.

As Margaret and her parents approached the main dining area to meet the Barrens for brunch, Lewis surprised them from the opposite direction and said, "Mr. and Mrs. Gabriel, Margaret."

Turning, the Gabriels saw Lewis approaching with a welcoming smile that lit up his face. When he reached them, he extended his hand to Mr. Gabriel. As their palms connected and their grasp closed, Lewis said, "Good afternoon, sir. I'm very pleased you're looking well."

Mr. Gabriel, with a firm grip, responded, "Good afternoon to you, Lewis, and thank you. I'm feeling stronger every day."

Lewis then turned to Mrs. Gabriel, embraced her, and said, "I'm so glad you could make brunch today on such short notice. I know how much you love your Sundays to be family time. My parents are very appreciative of your sacrifice."

"Why, Lewis, that's so considerate. It's no sacrifice at all. It won't be long, and we'll all be family." After a slight pause, Mrs. Gabriel continued and said, "My, what a pleasant location for our little get-together."

As Lewis first approached them, Margaret watched him intently. She immediately detected a change in his behavior. He'd always been polite and gracious but most often reserved. Today, for the first time she was seeing Lewis with feeling. He was more outgoing and enthusiastic. She smiled. She liked the Lewis she was seeing. To her great surprise, when Lewis turned to her, he reached for her hand, held it, leaned forward, and gently kissed her on the lips.

Margaret could feel herself blush, but then she stiffened. She wasn't sure how her reaction appeared to Lewis or her parents.

Lewis, perceiving Margaret tighten, leaned back slightly and, still holding her hand, said, "Margaret, I'm very glad to see you. Last evening, I was very concerned for your health. However, your mother assured me it was only the excitement of all that's happening, and you just needed to rest. Now standing here, you look so pretty; actually, you look beautiful. I just felt a need to kiss you in front of your parents. Was that all right?"

Margaret was less surprised by the kiss on the lips than she was seeing Lewis showing true happiness and joy. Those were Margaret's traits, and she'd hoped more people would embrace them. Seeing Lewis in this new light made her happy and optimistic.

Still holding Lewis's hand, she said, "I'm very glad to see you, too, Lewis. Thank you for your concern. A little rest was all I needed." Margaret realized while she spoke she'd been looking down at Lewis's hand holding hers. She then looked up at his face, smiled, and said, "Your kiss was very welcomed, thank you."

"You're so sweet, Margaret." As Lewis said these words, he paused for a few seconds and looked directly at Margaret. He wanted her to feel his presence a little longer, to let her know at that moment she was the center of his attention. When he felt the timing was right, he turned his head slowly to look directly at Margaret's parents and said, "My gosh, I nearly forgot about Mom and Dad. Let's hurry to the table. They're just busting to see you." As he said these words, he guided the Gabriels toward the dining room and his parents' table.

16

*T*he meal the Barrens and Gabriels shared at the Sunday brunch brought the two families closer together. Isaak was in his element at the club. This was the one place he knew he had an advantage over those he sought to do business with. Since the first Sunday he had entertained Margaret and her mother at his home, Isaak had wanted Lewis and Margaret to wed.

He'd immediately seen Margaret from the same lens as his wife. She was a young woman who had all the qualities three generations of Barren spouses possessed, but in Margaret's case more beauty and grace. Isaak knew unlike previous Barren women, she was emotional and believed in all the love nonsense. With Lewis, he was convinced that was more of an asset than a liability. Once Isaak had determined that Margaret could help his son, he was cunning enough to believe they would marry.

Isaak knew the brunch was critical to bringing Margaret and Lewis closer to his goal. He carefully arranged and choreographed a performance designed to solidify the marriage in the eyes of Margaret's parents. He also wanted Margaret to see the Barren family as a loving one, similar to her own. Isaak did not just want to soften her resistance to the marriage, he wanted Margaret to willingly marry Lewis. He believed in time she would see the benefits of the marriage as a partnership, just as his wife had. He was leaving nothing to chance. That was the way Isaak Barren conducted business.

Isaak had long ago selected the table where he dined advertisers, bankers, and other business people. The placement was important to him. He wanted a view of the ninth fairway, with the lush green grass framed between two rows of pines sitting neatly on a blanket of dried needles. He also wanted one slightly removed from the other tables for privacy, and with just enough floor space around it to welcome guests. Isaak had paid all this attention to detail for one purpose, to disarm the client. He wanted them to relax and, however slight, drop their guard, and give him the advantage in negotiations.

Isaak did not want the best view because that could distract his target. He wanted something more subliminal. He wanted them to feel the view rather than see it. Isaak had selected a table location that provided natural light, creating the impression of dining outdoors in a beautiful setting. Isaak's plan was designed to provide his prey with a feeling of relaxing in a familiar, comfortable place.

Lewis and Mrs. Barren had attended many dinners with Isaak and had learned the importance of the role each played in entertaining people. For Isaak, it was an art form to master; he wanted to forge the illusion that the Barrens meant more to people than they actually did.

The Barren family had learned to be charming, gracious, and confident, but so had many other people in business. Isaak distinguished himself by knowing everything about those he did business with. He would dig into details about their faith and family. Isaak wasn't one to look for dirt; he knew that could cause problems. He wanted to know what motivated them. He wanted to exploit their goodness, the feelings in their heart, their faith, and their family. Once he knew their motivation, manipulating them was easy.

As Lewis escorted Margaret and her parents toward their table, that cued Isaak and Mrs. Barren to stand up and move to the area where they would greet the Gabriels. The Barrens had performed this scene many times. Smiling, they quickly pushed up against the space people reserve for very special friends or family. They had a unique way of doing it without making people uncomfortable.

Isaak extended his hand to Margaret's father, who responded in kind. Isaak said, "Joseph, it's nice to see you again. You're looking very well."

"I am doing well, Isaak, thank you, and thank you for inviting us to brunch today. We appreciate your hospitality."

"You're welcome. It's our pleasure and such a happy occasion. After all, we both want the very best for the young couple." Isaak kept his face relaxed. He was letting his eyes speak for him as he looked into Mr. Gabriel's eyes. He didn't wait long to hear the words he'd expected.

Mr. Gabriel slightly tightened his grip and gently nodded his head and said, "Yes, we do."

This confirmed all he needed to know about Mr. Gabriel. Isaak knew he would have to package the benefits of the marriage between their children in words about faith, family, respect, and security, letting Joseph know he would never have to worry about Margaret. With his bad health, it would comfort him to know his daughter would be well cared for with a secure future.

The two men broke grips; pleasantries were exchanged. Mrs. Barren performed as expected, gently embracing Mrs. Gabriel first, and then Margaret. She was pleasant and complimentary. As the two fathers separated, Mrs. Barren gracefully exchanged places with her husband.

She embraced Mr. Gabriel then gently held his hand and said, "You do look very well, Joseph. It's so nice we could get together on such short notice."

"Thank you, Doris," responded Mr. Gabriel. "I am, too." She squeezed his hand with hers and smiled. After a slight hesitation, she moved to his elbow and escorted him to his seat, all the time speaking softly and telling him how much she adored his daughter.

Mr. Barren extended his left hand to Mrs. Gabriel and his right to Margaret in an open, welcoming gesture. As the three held hands, he commented on Mr. Gabriel's health and made some other very complimentary remarks. He then turned slightly to face Mrs. Gabriel; this prompted Lewis to move to Margaret's elbow and escort her to her seat as Isaak accompanied Mrs. Gabriel.

The seating arrangement had been predetermined. The fathers sat across from each other with Lewis on Mr. Gabriel's right and Mrs. Barren on his left. Margaret sat between Lewis and Mr. Barren, and Mrs. Gabriel between Mr. and Mrs. Barren.

The Barrens kept the conversation going with Isaak always taking the lead. He spoke conversationally, but in reality, it was a well-prepared presentation he had used many times, changing his words only slightly depending on the motivation of his guests. Mrs. Barren and Lewis were playing their familiar subordinate roles.

Isaak began talking about his family's religious faith and, because the Gabriels were Catholic, he emphasized his

Catholic roots and how it influenced his life and the decisions he made. Isaak had no affinity for religion. He would claim allegiance to whatever religious denomination he needed as long as it helped him close a deal and make money.

Isaak credited his grandfather, Exuvial Barren, and his grandmother, Démon, who brought their work ethic and faith with them to America and started Barren Printing. He talked about the importance of family, without mentioning marriage. Isaak thought he'd already sold Mr. Gabriel, and he knew Mrs. Gabriel was lobbying for the marriage. Margaret, the most important, was not ready to agree to the marriage with Lewis, but Isaak was confident it was only a matter of time.

Isaak also spoke about commitment, hard work, and how being fair in business brought financial security. He was subtle, but he made his point by saying a man's first obligation is to care for his wife and children. While he spoke the words, he returned the nod he had anticipated Mr. Gabriel would deliver. Isaak learned from his wife that Mrs. Gabriel said her husband knew his heart was unhealthy and was very concerned about Margaret's future. She also informed him that Mr. Gabriel was reassured when his wife had told him that Margaret loved Lewis and wanted to get married and have children.

Isaak orchestrated a lull in the conversation about an hour into the brunch. He knew Margaret's passion for flowers, and as the quiet set in, he suggested Lewis show her some of the flower gardens surrounding the property. Margaret looked to her father, who gave his approval, and the two excused themselves and left the table.

As the young couple walked away and out of hearing range, Isaak said in a voice just audible enough for those sitting at the table to hear, "I believe this just may be a marriage made in heaven." He waited for the response he knew would come.

"I certainly agree. I couldn't be happier," responded Mrs. Gabriel.

"I do agree," said Mrs. Barren as she smiled and nodded agreement.

Mr. Gabriel watched with a woeful expression on his face as the couple walked away. He held the words he was thinking and only recited them to himself, *Margaret, darling, I pray you made the right decision to get married.*

Gazing at Margaret from her chair, Mrs. Gabriel smiled and thought, *Lewis will be a good provider for Margaret and give her a good life.* Mrs. Gabriel had once passionately loved her husband. Her depression had changed her feelings toward him. While there were moments when she would recall her love for him, mostly she had been content with knowing that he was a kind, compassionate companion and a good provider. Mrs. Gabriel wanted the same type of stable, secure marriage for Margaret.

Mrs. Barren, watching the engaged couple, smiled and said to herself, *Securing Margaret as a partner will guarantee Lewis's success.* She would never allow sentiment or the notion of love to influence a marriage decision. Mrs. Barren knew many people like herself, who had endured the hardship of the Great Depression and the rationing during a World War. Most had married for love; she had never considered love. She'd found and married a fine, agreeable man she was confident would provide her with a financially secure life.

Watching the two women, Isaak asked himself, *Do I love Doris on some emotional level?* He immediately discounted it. He knew that loving her wasn't important. She had proved to be an effective partner when he needed her, and more importantly, she'd given him a son. He wanted Margaret to do the same for Lewis.

As Lewis and Margaret walked out into the warm, fresh air of a late June afternoon, Lewis said, "Margaret, it would be nice if I could hold your hand."

Feeling somewhat enchanted by all she'd experienced since arriving at the club, she responded, "That would be nice, thank you."

"I'm so relieved your father is recovering from his heart attack. I know how difficult it's been for you these last couple of months. I hope the time we've spent together has provided you with some comfort as you've had to cope with your father's health. I wanted to be with you more, but I know how committed you were to your father's recovery. I really respect the way you cared for him, and I didn't want to intrude."

"Oh, Lewis, it had helped. Really it had. I appreciate your concern very much. I know I've been distracted, and I do apologize," responded Margaret with tears in her eyes.

"Margaret, there's no need to apologize. I surely understand your concern for your father," responded Lewis as he embraced her. Margaret then placed her face against his chest and began to cry.

Joseph Gabriel's heart attack had been an unexpected benefit the Barrens would exploit. Isaak had quickly learned from his wife that Elizabeth was having a difficult time coping with her husband's heart attack and couldn't imagine living alone. When Doris suggested maybe Margaret should forgo college, Elizabeth had readily agreed. She was relieved when Doris later told her that once Lewis and Margaret were wed, she would never have to worry about finances or living alone.

When Margaret stopped crying she said, "Thank you for holding me, Lewis. It was very comforting."

"You can always count on my support, sweetheart," responded Lewis as Margaret withdrew from his grasp.

Once separated, Margaret and Lewis strolled the pathways and enjoyed the flowers and the fresh air. Margaret shared her observations with Lewis, and he nodded with a smile or repeated her words as if in agreement. When Margaret pointed out the beauty or striking color of an azalea, Lewis would lean down and take in its fragrance. She would then point to a hydrangea or an iris, and Lewis would respond, "Yes they're very beautiful" or "The color is striking." He was simply parroting Margaret's words, a way to show his interest in her interest. Mostly, to the observer, the couple appeared to enjoy their private walk together.

When Lewis suggested it may be time to rejoin their parents, Margaret seemed slightly hesitant. He sensed she wanted a sign of emotional sentiment to convince her that falling in love with him was possible.

Lewis looked into her eyes and said, "Margaret, I've had such a marvelous time with you today. Listening to you speak about the flowers, the beauty you find in them, greatly affects me. You have a joy for nature I tend to overlook. Thank you for sharing today with me. You're always very generous."

Margaret returned Lewis's gaze, fixed her eyes on his, smiled, and said, "Thank you, Lewis. I had a very nice time with you today."

Still holding her hand, Lewis leaned his face downward and kissed Margaret on the lips. The kiss wasn't a slight peck or a passionate one; it was a kiss he held only long enough for her to sense love was possible. When their lips separated, Lewis locked onto Margaret's eyes, and he let his gaze tell her he would give her all the time she needed to fall in love with him.

17

*T*he Sunday brunch had been the turning point in the relationship between the Barren family and the Gabriels. Isaak's plan for July and August was to keep Margaret and her parents within their sphere as often as possible until the wedding. When the Barrens weren't entertaining business associates, they would schedule an event with Margaret and her parents. Lewis wasn't always present when the families were together. Mr. Barren had conveniently tucked him away on company business. He figured they couldn't fault a young man for working hard for the benefit of his family.

Isaak wanted Margaret to fall in love with the budding new relationship between the Barrens and the Gabriels. He wanted her to feel Lewis's presence whether he was there or not. The Barrens would create the illusion by sharing anecdotes of Lewis with Margaret. They were carefully creating a bond, implanting a sense the Barrens and Gabriels were two families with a long history together.

Mr. Barren also knew his son, and if Margaret were to be overexposed to Lewis, the marriage might never occur. Beginning in high school, Isaak had paid a lot of money to keep Lewis's personal problems contained. If the Barren family hadn't had the funds to pay for legal fees, settlement agreements, and to ship him off to another state or country when they needed to, Lewis would have a rap sheet blotted with sexual assault, rape, and battery. His volatility with women made him unpredictable. Isaak wanted Lewis married to a good woman in the hope he would settle down, mature, and control his deviant urges.

With the wedding planned for September, Isaak wasn't taking any chances with his son where Margaret was concerned. Isaak limited Lewis to seeing Margaret about twice a week and only once without his parents being present. When they talked or dated, Lewis was always pleasant, appeared happy, and Margaret thought he was a very good listener.

When Lewis telephoned Margaret, the calls lasted the usual ten to fifteen minutes. She became more animated as the weeks passed. Margaret would relay a story his parents had told her about his childhood. Lewis would always sway his responses between adding additional details to the story or feigning embarrassment. When the couple did spend time together, Margaret began to wonder if she was starting to fall in love with Lewis.

Isaak watched the relationship develop. It had reached a juncture where he wanted Margaret to feel Lewis's absence. He wouldn't make it a long one; it would be just enough time for Margaret to miss Lewis and feel a void. He wanted Lewis's return to captivate her emotionally. Isaak sent Lewis on a business trip that would guarantee the cancellation of their regular Saturday date. In Lewis's absence,

Isaak invited Margaret and her parents to his home. The gathering included friends and one very important advertiser, Mr. Barrow, who was a devout Catholic.

Mr. Barren had several motivations in his plan. He wanted Margaret and her parents to feel a part of his family. He also wanted Margaret to reflect on how much more enjoyable the evening could be if Lewis were with her. His more sinister motive was to wittingly use Margaret in Barren family business. Isaak knew Margaret would share her commitment to her Catholic faith if the topic came up conversationally. Margaret would never preach her beliefs to other people; she was always respectful of those who chose to worship differently.

When Isaak had the opportunity, he introduced Margaret to Mr. Barrow as his son's fiancée and planted the seed for a sharing of their faith. Margaret was becoming used to being called Lewis's fiancée, even though Lewis had yet to propose to her. She was starting to enjoy the sound of it. Isaak then excused himself to attend to other guests. Isaak watched closely as Margaret charmed Mr. Barrow. Later that evening, Mr. Barrow complimented Isaak, saying, "I see a fine young woman in Lewis's fiancée. It speaks highly of your son, marrying a woman with such a commitment to Catholic values. I look forward too many more years of partnership between our companies."

Isaak, not one to miss an opportunity to embellish on his faith, smiled and said, "We love Margaret. She's a fine young woman from a good Catholic family. Lewis feels blessed he has Margaret in his life."

"I'll certainly pray for their happiness. A September wedding, if I'm correct?" was Mr. Barrow's response.

"Thank you, yes sir. September . . . such a long way off," responded Isaak.

"Why, Isaak, it's the middle of July. The glorious day will be here before you know it."

Isaak didn't respond; he just let the words *here before you know it* settle in his thoughts.

When Margaret saw Lewis for the first time since his business trip, she immediately embraced him. She told him how much she missed him, and, surprising herself, said, "I love you."

Lewis replied with a broad smile, wrapped his arms around her, and lifted her off the floor. He said, "Oh, Margaret, I love you, too." Margaret was excited to see Lewis and hear confirmation that she was now engaged to the man she loved and who loved her back.

The remainder of the summer was a frenzy of activity attending to wedding plans, guest lists, dress fittings, flowers, and all the other details of a grand wedding. Mrs. Barren took charge of everything. She made Mrs. Gabriel feel like a true partner in the entire wedding production. Mrs. Barren was used to taking charge and convincing other people that the decisions were made by consensus.

With her mother and Mrs. Barren making most of the wedding plans, Margaret finally resigned herself to simply accept and appreciate the two mothers' indulgences.

18

*L*ewis had little interest in wedding planning. He did his best to avoid all conversations on the subject. When he did listen, he would act polite and appear interested. Margaret, with her enthusiasm, shared all the details. Lewis always made Margaret believe he cared and would thank her profusely for all the work she was doing to ensure a fantastic event.

Margaret was agreeable to all the arrangements recommended by her mother and Mrs. Barren. She expressed just a couple of matters she felt most important to her. None of her concerns were much of a surprise to Lewis or his father.

Margaret knew she couldn't get married at Holy Trinity; instead, she wished to marry in the Cathedral of Incarnation rather than her local parish. She loved the magnificent church with its Roman architecture. She had often visited the cathedral on class trips, and now hoped to stand on the beautiful altar and recite her wedding vows. Mr. Barren told her he thought it was a spectacular idea and would make the arrangements.

Margaret spoke with Lewis about finding an apartment close to her parents' house. She told him with all his business travels and long hours, she would like to live close to them. Lewis appeared open to her request, and she was satisfied.

Margaret would learn two weeks before the wedding that Isaak Barren had purchased a four-bedroom, brick-front Tudor-style home as a gift for her and Lewis. The house was located only two miles from the Barren family home. Showing Margaret her new house for the first time was well orchestrated. Lewis picked her up at six o'clock on Saturday evening with the pretext of dining with his parents at the home of a family friend. As soon as the couple pulled away from the driveway, Mr. and Mrs. Gabriel got in their car and drove thirty miles to meet Mr. and Mrs. Barren. They hid their vehicles in the double garage, entered the house, and waited for Lewis and Margaret to arrive.

When the engaged couple stood before the front door it was slightly ajar. Lewis pushed the door open and standing before Margaret were the four parents loudly exclaiming, "Surprise!" Margaret wasn't sure what she was witnessing. She was always happy to see her parents but wasn't expecting them at dinner. She also wondered what surprise they were speaking about.

Isaak had prearranged for Margaret's father to announce the gift as a present from both families. When Mr. Barren informed Mr. Gabriel he wanted to purchase a house for Margaret and Lewis, Mr. Gabriel asked if he could contribute to the cost by saying, "After all, Margaret's my only child."

Mr. Gabriel had been disappointed when Margaret withdrew from Holy Trinity. He knew she was distressed over his heart attack. He'd thought she wanted to remain close to home in the event he didn't fully recover. He felt responsible for Margaret's decision to abandon her dream of attending Holy Trinity. When his wife told him that it had been Margaret's decision to withdraw from college he'd been relieved. His wife told him Margaret had fallen in love with Lewis, even though they'd only dated for a short time.

Isaak accepted the contribution from Mr. Gabriel and was all too happy to let him break the news to his daughter. He knew she would never convey her true feelings about living so far away from her parents, especially when her father went to such an expense to buy her the most beautiful house.

As the news of the gift became real for Margaret, she began to cry. Her tears were of both joy and sorrow. She was happy about her beautiful new home but saddened by the distance to her parents' house. Margaret talked about the house becoming a lovely home and what a splendid place it would be to raise a family. She was happy that it was such a large house where their children could run around and enjoy themselves. Margaret wanted her children to have siblings and lots of them. Still in tears, she hugged and thanked everyone. She pushed aside her sadness at being so far away from her parents and let her love for her future family be her happiness.

Isaak could not have been more pleased as he watched Margaret express her thanks and appreciation for the house. He wanted to slowly isolate Margaret from her parents. He knew the Barrens could never replace them as Margaret's support system, but he felt it was important that he diminish her dependence on her parents and make her rely more on the Barrens.

On the drive home with Lewis that evening, Margaret expressed her concern with the distance between her new home and her parents' house.

"Lewis, the house is beautiful, and our parents are so generous. Between the expense of the wedding, and now the new house, we're truly blessed by the love they have for us."

"It's a fine house and Mother confirms what you told me about the wedding plans. Our wedding will be a terrific affair," responded Lewis.

Tentatively Margaret said, "The distance from my parents' house seems a bit far."

"Not very, Margaret, when you consider the drive to the club and the distance to my parents' house. You know how close our families have become, and how often we spend time together. You can be sure we'll always remain close," responded Lewis with enthusiasm.

"I guess I'm used to seeing them every day, but as a married woman, well, I think all new brides have the same thoughts."

"You'll love them no less by the distance or their absence. If you give it time, it'll seem like a short drive to travel for the joy of spending time with your mother and father."

"Oh, Lewis, you're so sensitive. Thank you."

"You're welcome, Margaret."

The couple drove in silence for several minutes as Margaret thought about the drive and the distance. When she spoke she said, "You know, Lewis, I truly do love to drive my little Beetle, and it's very good on gas."

When Margaret mentioned her Volkswagen, Lewis's hateful heart began to stir, and it was his good fortune that Margaret was not looking at him as she spoke. His facial reaction may have been momentary, but the evil he displayed was frighteningly apparent.

Lewis never knew what little issue might trigger his rage, but when one did, it gripped him in such a way he was no longer in control of his body. The physical reaction seemed independent of his thoughts and memory. In the aftermath of his violence, he would often look at the scene as if he were a spectator, gazing at the horror and wanting to know what happened. Lewis had learned to control his anger in the early stages through concentrated effort and discipline. He knew the common denominator was women. His misogyny intensified when he had a dating or sexual relationship. At work, Lewis was indifferent to women; to him, women simply didn't exist. While he didn't love Margaret, he was willing to please his parents and marry her. He viewed her beauty and innocence through the eyes of a predator and couldn't wait to violate her.

When Margaret mentioned her Volkswagen, Lewis took steps to control his rage. While he couldn't restrain his initial reaction, he was quick to extinguish it before he exploded. Lewis simply hated Margaret's car. He knew how happy Margaret was when she was in her yellow Beetle. She felt joy, freedom, and exhilaration, and Lewis couldn't stand it. Any woman he possessed would never have joy or freedom. He would control her and do with her as he wanted.

With his rage simmering but under control, he responded to Margaret and said, "I know how much you love your car, and I see how happy you are when you drive it. It makes me happy just thinking about your joy. I thought, and I hope you agree, that if you left the car at your parents' house, and I'm sure your father wouldn't mind, you could drive one of our family cars during the week. On Saturdays when you visit your parents, you can drive your Volkswagen to all the places you like to visit. Just think, you'll save on gas and wear and tear on your car, and it will last much longer."

"Lewis, what about the expense of another car? Certainly, you'll need one, and I'll need transportation," responded Margaret.

"Margaret, you're so practical; that's why I admire you. The car you'll drive and the gas you'll use during the week will be paid for by the company; it's not an expense we need to worry about. If you agree, you'll save us money we'll need for our future."

As Margaret thought about this arrangement, she considered its practicality. She knew in her own way she wanted to contribute to their future. She felt if she could help save money, she would not be thinking only of herself. Lewis always worked during the day on Saturday or golfed with his father and his associates. She was always free to visit with her parents on those days.

Margaret resolved that on Saturdays she would arrive early, spend time with her mother and father, and then drive her car to visit the places she enjoyed. She vowed to visit her parents, the lake, or the gardens and make Saturday a glorious day.

"That would be splendid. Thank you, Lewis."

Lewis caught himself before he revealed that sinister grin he let slip about a couple of months ago when Margaret had been pestering him about the wedding, how soon it was, or some other annoying thing he couldn't remember. He said, "Margaret, you know I'll do anything for you."

At that moment, Margaret felt truly blessed to be engaged to a wonderful man from a devout Christian family.

19

September had just arrived, and it was the last Saturday before the wedding. Margaret planned a special day for herself. She woke early and wanted to spend a little time with her mother at breakfast before heading out for the day. She planned to drive her yellow Beetle to one of her favorite places.

Margaret greeted her mother in the kitchen with an embrace and said, "Oh, Mother, I'm so happy. You and Daddy were right. I spent the summer getting to know Lewis just as you suggested, and I do love him."

"Darling, I'm pleased to see you're happy. We're very satisfied your future is determined. Lewis is a fine young man with lovely, generous parents. We take comfort in knowing you'll be provided with a very good life. I'm sure you'll quickly fill your new home with lots of children," said her mother.

Blushing from her mother's last comment, Margaret said, "Mother, we're not yet married, but we'll certainly have children in time. I do want a large family, a house full of happy and delightful children."

Mrs. Gabriel turned serious and said, "I'm sure you and Lewis believe you're in love, but remember you'll be a married woman. You will have an obligation to your husband. A duty, such as I had with your father."

"Mother, I know how much you and Daddy care for me. Lewis and I are truly in love, and I will be a good wife to my wonderful husband."

"You'll find, my dear, when you have a child, your burden will be lifted. You will not only be a wife, you'll be the mother of your husband's children. Lewis may still very well feel affection for you, but what's most important is he will respect and care for you as he would his own mother. Margaret, you're a beautiful young woman, and Lewis is a handsome man, but what you think is love is fleeting. I'm sure your relationship with Lewis will be exactly what I have with your father. A good man, a companion, a provider who gave me a very good and secure life. That, Margaret, is what matters most."

Margaret didn't agree with all her mother said. She knew she loved Lewis, and he loved her. *After all,* she thought, *isn't love all that truly matters?* Rather than respond directly, she said, "Mother, thank you for all you do for me. I love you and Daddy very much."

"We both love you too, darling."

Margaret knew her mother only wanted the best for her. Watching and listening to her mother speak, Margaret sensed the sadness that was often present in her mother. At times her mother's mood changes would lead to severe depression, and she would be hospitalized. Margaret's father would care for her when her mother was away for treatment. He became her confidant, but since his heart attack, Margaret had only her mother's guidance.

Thinking about her parents' relationship made Margaret pause when she recalled something her mother had said to her. It was the Monday after she'd first learned of Lewis's proposal. Her mother had startled her then, and now, as she recalled the words, *"I didn't love your father when we were first married . . . I'm not sure I ever loved your father; you can be content in a marriage with a man who cares about you and provides for you."*

Remembering these comments, Margaret asked herself, *"What's a marriage without love?"* She knew the New Testament. The letter to the Ephesians, chapter 5, said to love your spouse as you love yourself. Recalling these words, Margaret wanted to shout out loud, *"I do love Lewis as I love myself, and Lewis loves me as he loves himself."*

With these words echoing in her mind, Margaret kissed her mother on the cheek and left the house to enjoy her last Saturday as Margaret Elizabeth Gabriel.

Part Three

You restore my strength.
You guide me along the right
path for the sake of your name.

20

Franklin, TN—September 1971

*M*argaret was still sitting at her writing table, her letter to Nicholas barely started. She had just recalled the summer of 1970. She was overcome by her malaise; the thought of her wedding brought her back to the present. Margaret was trembling. Her mind and body were fatigued. She started to panic. *How long have I been sitting here? How much time do I have left?* She felt sick, nauseous; the terrible feeling from a couple of months ago was back. Margaret jumped-up, her chair tumbling over as she ran to the bathroom. Her mind was shouting the words she had wanted to say to her mother, *Lewis loves me as he loves himself . . . Lewis loves me as he loves himself.* The words were echoing, deafening. What little there was in her stomach ejected from her mouth; she was vomiting.

Margaret sat on the cold ceramic tile, hanging onto the porcelain bowl waiting for the last of the green and yellow bile to pass. When she felt as if she could, she stood up on her unsteady legs and inched her way to the sink. Margaret didn't recognize the pale ghostly reflection in the mirror. She closed her eyes and weakly gripped the handle. She groaned as the faucet turned slowly. The water trickled then flowed hot. With her hands cupped, she let the steaming water sting her palms as her face descended into the heat.

Her face searing, suddenly alert, she was fearful. Margaret needed to check the time. Lewis would be home at six o'clock. She had to finish writing the letter and mail it to Nicholas. Margaret labored toward the kitchen and checked the clock. There was still time, but she needed to pull her thoughts together.

Margaret had so much to say to Nicholas. She needed to explain. Something was compelling her to write to him. Her letter would crush his already broken heart. Margaret never wanted to hurt Nicholas. She loved him. She had no explanation, but she could feel a force telling her that writing the letter was the right thing to do. She had to finish; there was a purpose.

Margaret drank a glass of water from the tap. She could no longer drink anything cold. It would only remind her of her frigid, unloving husband and the life that had chosen her. She struggled as she returned to her writing table. The exhaustion from recalling the memories she'd long suppressed was draining her. She needed to find strength. Her life with Lewis had become hopeless. She had lost her way, her source of courage.

Lewis's anger, his hate for Margaret, was like a walk through a dark and frightening valley. She thought she should have been brave, but she felt so much fear; it was as if her faith had abandoned her. Margaret then thought if she could walk through the fear of her memory and fear no harm, maybe, just maybe, that was all the faith she needed to complete the letter.

Picking up the pen, Margaret would now let her mind focus on Nicholas. She needed to recall her memories of him in order to feel his strength and courage. These remembrances would surge through her and help her endure the fear of recalling Lewis's assaults. Margaret could then walk through that valley of fear and know Nicholas was at her side. She would fear no evil.

Margaret let her mind return to that warm May afternoon in 1971 when she'd found her wings and flew toward joy, happiness, and love, and the memories she cherished so very much. She recalled sitting at Radnor Lake when suddenly she began to feel overwhelming fatigue and drifted off to sleep. When she finally began to stir, she stretched her body without a conscious awareness of her movements. She was just waking, feeling foggy as she rolled onto her back, her eyes closed, directed toward the sky. The beam of sunlight was on her face, blinding her as she tried to open her eyes. She squinted at the bright rays.

Margaret could see movement in the sky directly above her, a circling motion. Something was gliding. The sun radiated off the object, creating a hallowed glow. It appeared white, its movement effortless. Margaret saw a dove. The dove was approaching her, getting closer, ready to land.

Margaret sat up quickly. She looked at the white bird that landed next to her. She stared intently. *A dove, no, not a dove*. It was an all-white seagull, greedily eating the remains of her lunch.

Margaret smiled for the first time in months. Since she had become a Barren wife, she had no happiness. She had lost her way, her faith. She no longer prayed; she felt such sloth. When she went to Mass or some other religious service she said the words but ignored the sound. They no longer held meaning for her.

Seeing the white bird as a dove, a message of hope, she felt her heart stir. The feeling was strange; she had felt so little, for so long. Margaret was nearly disappointed when she realized it wasn't a dove; except, standing before her was a dove-white seagull, five hundred miles from the nearest ocean and eating her lunch.

Margaret had a sudden thought of the novel she had read by Richard Bach, *Jonathan Livingston Seagull*. The seagull was an outcast that had mastered flying and could go wherever it wanted. As she continued to stare at the bird, she thought of the ocean she'd never seen and had hoped to explore when she was a student at Holy Trinity.

Margaret then thought of Holy Trinity and how much it had once meant to her. All these thoughts were racing through her mind when a sudden screech disrupted her thinking, and her attention was drawn back to the seagull. Margaret had to blink. She thought the seagull nodded to her as it slowly flapped its wings, lifted off the ground, and propelled itself upward into the air. Rising slowly, steadily, circling above, tipping its wing toward her, it moved away. With its wings fully extended, and gracefully swaying, the white messenger continued on its migration heading northeast.

Margaret watched the seagull disappear. She had a sudden insight; she wanted to fly, to soar like the seagull. She felt the energy and let it erupt. It was a feeling she didn't want to let go. She wanted to be reborn—to be happy, joyful, loving—the way she always was and wanted to be again. Suddenly, she saw her way clearly. She needed new memories, happy, joyful, and loving memories. Memories that would help her endure the life that had chosen her. She wanted to walk the campus of Holy Trinity, see the ocean, and walk the beaches, to visit all the places of her dreams.

Margaret stood up, grabbed her belongings, and started to run. She rushed to her yellow Beetle and drove to her parents' house. She was praying for the first time in many, many months that her parents had not returned home. When she arrived, she burst through the door, and ran up to her bedroom. She quickly packed some of her old clothes and threw them into her purple-and-pink paisley travel bag. She opened her small keepsake box where she'd left some money she had saved before her marriage. She placed a handful of the green bills into her purse, ran down the stairs, and headed out the door.

Within minutes Margaret was driving her Volkswagen toward Route 40 east, heading toward 81 north. She had studied this route many times when college seemed real to her. It was real now. She was on her way to visit the College of Holy Trinity.

Margaret knew she would never be a student, but it didn't matter. She was going to visit the beautiful campus. She would collect as many remembrances as she could for her memory scrapbook. She would recall those memories whenever she needed them, and she would need them if she was going to endure her barren life with Lewis.

Margaret would now turn her attention to Nicholas and think only of the five days she'd spent with him in May 1971.

21

*A*s Margaret recalled the first time she saw Nicholas, she felt a warmth in her body absent from her life since the last time he'd embraced her. Margaret had been drawn to Nicholas because of his easy smile, enthusiasm, and playfulness. Mostly though, it was the kindness he'd shown to the local children who'd come to watch grown boys play football.

Margaret had left the athletic field with a refreshing feeling about the goodness and kindness in people. She'd seen in Nicholas a person who had the confidence to wave away his friends for the simple purpose of giving joy to a group of youngsters. Nicholas seemed loving to her.

As Margaret walked to her car, she wondered what she would do now that she'd arrived at Holy Trinity and walked the campus. She still felt the same joy and happiness of being at the school as when she'd first arrived, but she didn't have a plan for where to stay or what to do next. She wasn't concerned; she only needed to figure it out.

When she'd pulled into a parking spot and exited her car, she hadn't noticed that one of the tires was nearly flat. Margaret had little experience dealing with her car. Her father, her guardian angel, had always been there to take care of her problems. She now had a flat tire to manage.

Margaret decided to walk back around the campus and try to find someone to help her. As she approached the athletic building, she saw a group of young men just leaving. They were moving in the opposite direction. She spotted Nick among them and, as a test of her new assertiveness, called out, "Nicholas."

On the drive up to Holy Trinity, Margaret thought about the characters Jonathan and Jenny. She was really learning to fly, to be free. She knew it wouldn't be easy for her. She needed to be brave and courageous if she was going to soar over Holy Trinity and Cape Cod.

Margaret also knew she needed to be confident and strong like Jenny. She could only do the things she'd hoped to do if she also had her same spirit. She'd wondered, *Did Jennifer need to transform into Jenny in order to be the person she was at college?* Margaret thought that in a way maybe she could be like Jenny if she had a nickname.

Margaret considered all of the diminutive possibilities, *Peggy, Maggie, Meg.* She'd liked them all and settled on *Meg,* the first initials of her full name, Margaret Elizabeth Gabriel. Margaret would now be called Meg and she would be bold, but she knew she would never be as bold, courageous, or strong as Jenny. Meg hoped a little boldness would be fun.

Nick turned when he heard his given name. The students on campus never called him Nicholas. He was taken by surprise when someone did. Seeing her cream-colored face and dark warm eyes looking back at him, he was stunned. The reaction from his friends had been more of a shock. A boisterous chorus of quips quickly flooded the air with his teammates seemingly talking at once, all loudly wanting to know the name of Nick's new girlfriend and why they hadn't met her.

Nick ignored his friends and gazed at Margaret. He knew he didn't know her. Nick was always too busy for dating or girlfriends. The slim, attractive girl with short dark hair and a warm, comforting smile couldn't be a student or his buddies would certainly know her.

Nick was nearly frozen in place until one of his friends pushed him from behind and said, "Hey, Nick, you're keeping your girlfriend waiting, or do you want me to take care of her." This evoked laughter from the group and embarrassment in Nick.

The momentum from the push sent Nick in the direction of Margaret, and he continued walking toward her. He tried not to stare at her face, but he couldn't resist looking. He was captivated by her appearance. She was very pretty, but it was much more than that; she had a dignity, a poise, a gracefulness. He could sense her warmth; it was compelling. Nick was trying to speak but was stumbling for words. Margaret, sensing this, saved him and said, "Nicholas, I'm very sorry for troubling you. I didn't want to embarrass you in front of your friends. It's just, I don't know anyone on campus, and I'm in need of assistance."

Nick's shyness was evident as he quickly turned red. He searched for a response then said, "How do you know me? I'm sorry to say I don't remember you."

"Nicholas, you don't know me," responded Margaret.

"But how did you know my name."

Margaret had an immediate liking for Nicholas. She decided to tease him a bit and said, "Well, Holy Trinity is a Catholic college, isn't it?"

Nick smiled and responded in a somewhat questioning tone. "Yes, it is, but I'm not sure how that helps knowing my name."

"I would think in a group of young men walking together on a Catholic college, one of the boys would certainly be named Nicholas. After all, I believe he is the patron saint of sailors, thieves, and students. I simply knew calling out the name Nicholas would get the attention of a good Catholic boy. I'm just not sure which of the three positions you hold," said Margaret.

Nick was taken with Margaret. He knew she was playfully teasing him and he was enjoying it. He thought for a moment then responded, "Well, Ms. . . . ?"

"Meg," said Margaret.

"Well, Ms. Meg, I am Catholic, I'll give you that. I am a boy; however, I'm soon to be a nineteen-year-old boy. It struck me, seeing a damsel in the compound of this luxurious estate, I must assume to be all three. I was a student. Now, seeing your beauty, I'm compelled to be a thief, and I will steal you away and make my escape as a sailor on a boat," said Nicholas.

Meg laughed and clapped her hands at Nicholas's response. She said, "Bravo, Nicholas, spoken like a struggling, or rather starving, playwright."

Nicholas also laughed and asked, "Meg, are you a student at Holy Trinity? I'm sure I would have remembered you and your voice; it has such a pretty, almost Southern sound."

Meg laughed and said, "The choirmaster wouldn't agree with your description of my voice. He wasn't impressed with my Nashville elocution. And no, I'm only visiting from Tennessee. I had planned to attend, but it didn't work out the way I'd hoped."

Nicholas was still smiling from the elocution comment and said, "I'm sorry the choirmaster was tone deaf, and I'm even more sorry to hear that it didn't work out. Holy Trinity is really a terrific place. I will miss it while traveling the high seas with such pretty cargo."

"You have a talented ear for sound and a very enchanting smile, Nicholas, and a very corny sense of humor," responded Meg jokingly.

"Meg, I do take great issue with being talented and enchanting; and I will always take greater liberties with the corny. After all, how could a student-thief-sailor maintain a buccaneer reputation with an enchanting smile?"

"Nicholas, as a court jester, you may be forced to walk the plank," said Meg.

Nicholas could feel his emotions in a way he wasn't used to. The only women he was comfortable speaking with were the sisters, and only on Saturdays when he was busy scrubbing their floors. He desperately wanted to keep the conversation going, but he wasn't sure what to say next.

Meg again sensed Nicholas's shyness. She knew from their short conversation that he had a sense of humor. She'd already witnessed his kindness and playfulness with the youngsters. She liked him, and more important, she felt she could trust him.

She was about to speak when Nicholas asked, "Would you like to see more of the campus?"

Meg paused then said, "Nicholas, I do appreciate the offer, but I've had a full day and I'm a bit hungry."

Nick, in the spirit of his Italian heritage, and without wanting her to leave, blurted out, "I can feed you."

Meg laughed at the way Nicholas's words spurted out and responded, "Why now, you have truly impressed me. You're not just a student-thief-sailor, you're also a cook. How very enchanting. Oh, I do apologize, your buccaneer reputation."

Nick said, "No really, I can take you to the cafeteria."

Meg thought for a minute. She enjoyed Nicholas's company, but she needed to have someone help her with her tire. She once again saw how truly bashful he was as his face flushed again, and his eyes looked down toward the ground. After a lengthy pause, Meg said, "Nicholas, I would very much enjoy dining with you. It's just, the reason I called your name was my car. When I arrived on campus this morning, I hadn't noticed the tire going flat until I was ready to leave. I was looking for someone to assist me, and well, I don't want to inconvenience you. I'm sure your friends must be waiting."

Nick immediately said, "Meg, I'm very happy to help you. It will add it to my resume with my other four qualifications."

"Nicholas, I'm grateful for your help, but as a damsel, and one in some distress, I have a bold request," said Meg as she let her soft dark eyes speak for her.

Nick with his heart beating rapidly said, "Anything, Meg."

"Henceforth, you shall be called Nicholas and not Nick. It is unfitting to be named after a saint who is now the patron of students, thieves, sailors, cooks, flat tires, and damsels," said Meg with a smile.

Nicholas responded, "I graciously accept your conditions."

22

*a*s Meg and Nicholas approached her yellow Volkswagen, Nicholas smiled and said, "I love the color. It seems to fit your personality."

"I love my Beetle; it's such a joy to drive. When I sit behind the steering wheel, I feel so free and happy. Every Saturday I drive it to my two favorite places, then spend a wonderful day enjoying all the beauty of nature. Oh, and the color, I love yellow, it reminds me of a yellow rose, a most joyous flower."

Nicholas was surprised by Meg's enthusiasm for her car and driving. He didn't drive or even have a license to drive. There really was no point. His father needed the station wagon for work, and there was no money for driving school. Nicholas never thought much about it; he'd always seemed to get where he needed to go without driving.

"Well, Meg, the color certainly conveys happiness. But, I'm not sure how much driving you're going to do. The tire is nearly flat," said Nicholas as he motioned to her tire.

The tire had just enough air to slowly drive the car down the hill to a local garage. Nicholas gladly offered his assistance. He was enchanted by Meg, and he didn't want her to disappear.

Meg quickly accepted his help and was thrilled she'd found a friend at Holy Trinity. Nicholas threw his vinyl gym bag in the back seat and sat on the passenger side. Meg drove cautiously down the hill to the nearest gas station.

When they arrived at the service station, Nicholas spoke with Christopher, the mechanic, about the tire and was told it would take about an hour to repair. Nicholas knew Meg was hungry, and he was always ready to eat. He told her about the wait and suggested they eat lunch at the Howard Johnson's. The restaurant was a short walk from the garage, and it was a warm, sunny spring afternoon. Meg was pleased by the suggestion and readily agreed.

Meg and Nicholas sat in a booth with orange seats and ordered their meals. Nicholas looked at her and thought how pretty she was and how odd it was for him to be sitting across from a girl eating in a restaurant in the middle of the day. He was nervous and searching for something to say. He then recalled Meg telling him how she would drive her car to her two favorite places to enjoy the beauty of nature. Nicholas spoke first and said, "Meg, if you wouldn't mind, would you please tell me about your two favorite places. They must be very special to you."

Meg smiled when she heard the question from Nicholas. This was the type of sharing she'd hoped to have with the person she fell in love with, the little bits of personal information you want to know when you care about someone. Meg thought, in another time, she would love to take Nicholas to the lake and gardens, but she stopped herself from thinking about her previous life. As long as Meg was at Holy Trinity, she was determined she would have only beautiful thoughts. She would do her best to keep her regrets and Lewis from entering her mind.

Meg said, "Nicholas, Radnor Lake Park and Cheekwood Botanical Gardens are in Nashville and are the two most glorious places. I love the botanical garden for the spectacular flowers and the peaceful walkways where you stroll through all the beauty. You can always find a quiet area to read a book or just get lost in your thoughts. Radnor Lake Park is quite different. It has a natural beauty with trees, flowers, animals, and birds and, of course, the lake. It's as if an artist painted a hundred different, wonderful pictures. You can walk the trails around the lake, pick any spot, look through the greenery, and see the water framed in God's natural beauty looking back at you. It makes my eyes well with joy at how beautiful it is."

"They sound like fabulous places, Meg. I'd love to see them one day. I grew up in the city and, well, we have some very nice parks, but most of the time we played sports in the street on the asphalt. Even our school yard was blacktop," replied Nicholas.

"You must have a special place you keep in your heart, a memory you recall when you're sad or lonely," said Meg.

Nicholas hesitated. He was grateful their food came, and their conversation was interrupted. A silence occupied the air, not for a loss of words but because both were reflecting on the places they each held close to their heart. Meg was thinking of the joy, freedom, and happiness she'd felt when visiting her favorite places. Nicholas had a place so fixed in his mind, a special place he'd never shared with anyone.

Nicholas broke the silence when he found the courage to talk about his most cherished place with another person. He couldn't believe he was doing it, especially with someone he'd just met. He looked at Meg and thought, *this is a person who makes me feel like I've known her my whole life. Someone who's been dormant in my heart since my mom died.* Thinking all these thoughts, Nicholas could feel his eyes water and wasn't sure he could speak.

Meg noticed Nicholas's eyes after she asked him about his special place. She hadn't intended to make him uncomfortable. Seeing his emotions surface, she wanted to reach out, touch his hand, and comfort him. Meg didn't have the courage; her scars were too deep. She longed for the warm, sensitive touch of another person. Meg wasn't ready, not even for light contact on the hand to comfort someone she had started to like and who needed it.

Nicholas began to speak hesitantly and said, "Meg, my mom, her name was Peggy, died when I was little and, sometimes I thought I had memories of her, but then I wasn't really sure. I've always had this one beautiful vision of my mom. We're sitting on the beach, just her and me, wrapped in a blanket. The breeze is coming off the water and the green beach grass is swaying. The evening air is chilly, and my mom's warmth is comforting me while her arm is around my shoulder holding the blanket. Out over the horizon the evening sun is setting, slowly settling into the water.

"That's my only memory of my mom, so beautiful and loving. It sustains me and gives me courage when I need it the most. I've carried the image with me for so long; it started to feel as if I'd imagined the whole thing because I needed something of my mother that was real and only mine.

"Then one day a couple of years ago, my dad was working late, and I was doing my homework. I needed to look up a word and had forgotten my dictionary at school. My father had this old beat-up, faded blue Webster he kept by the side of his chair in our parlor. I'd never touched it before; it was old, and I was afraid it would fall apart. He bought it when he went into the Navy and had kept it with him on the ship during the war. He's had it ever since, always looking up words he didn't know or understand.

"When I gently picked up the dictionary, there was a corner of a photograph sticking out between the pages. Without really thinking, I opened the book to look at the picture. The photograph was face down and there was writing on the back. It must have been my mom's. She'd written, Rock Harbor, summer 1957. I turned the picture over, and there was my vision—my mom and me on the beach, her wrapping me in a blanket to stay warm, watching the sunset. It made me cry. I'm not sure how long I held that picture in my hands, but when I heard the door start to open, I closed the dictionary and ran to bed. I pretended to be sleeping and cried myself to sleep."

Meg was in tears listening to Nicholas, the sensitivity of the story, how personal and emotional. He was sharing it with her. She looked deeply at Nicholas, trying to touch his soul. She saw in him such a good, caring, sensitive boy. Something reached her, and without thinking, she let her hand gently touch the back of Nicholas's hand. Meg thought she was comforting him, but it was his warmth that was penetrating her, soothing her anguish, and comforting her. She felt an energy bringing them together that made her feel safe.

Meg, her sensitive soul searching for words, said, "Nicholas, you have a beautiful memory with your mother, and you know it's real. She loved you very much, I can hear, I can see how much you loved her and miss her. It breaks my heart to think you lost a mother's touch, her warmth, and her comfort at such a young age. I'm so very sorry for your loss."

Nicholas strained to hold back his tears said, "Thank you. As much as it hurt to see the picture, I'm grateful for it. Now I know for sure I remembered my mom holding me close, protecting me from the cold, and at the same time showing me the beauty of a setting sun. It's a memory I keep close to my heart, and not one I ever spoke about before today. I can't explain why I wanted to tell you. I felt like I needed to, as if it was important."

"Nicholas, thank you for sharing such a cherished part of your life with me. I'll always treasure your trust."

"I've never opened up to anyone like I did with you today. You are a very special person, Meg."

"Thank you, but I'm reluctant to extend the same compliment to you; after all, you must protect your buccaneer's reputation," said Meg, giving them both a smile and lightening up the emotional mood of the conversation.

When the check came, Meg wanted to pay, but Nicholas resisted and negotiated a Dutch treat. As they walked back to the garage, Meg said, "Nicholas, you must visit Rock Harbor often to watch the sunset and think of your mother. What a lovely thought."

Nicholas had always wanted to return to Cape Cod and Rock Harbor in Orleans, but he never had the opportunity. After his mom died, his father never brought him back to the ocean; it was Nicholas's plan to visit when he graduated from college and had a job.

"My dad and I never went back to Cape Cod or Rock Harbor," said Nicholas.

When Meg heard Nicholas say Cape Cod, she stopped and said, "That's one of the places I've always wanted to visit. I dreamed of going to Cape Cod and seeing the ocean for the first time while attending Holy Trinity. I had planned it all out in my mind, all the beautiful places that I would visit on school breaks and long weekends. You must have loved the beaches, the ocean, seashells, and seagulls."

"I don't remember much, Meg; my mind is fixed on the picture in the photograph. I think I've pushed out all the other memories," said Nicholas.

Meg asserted her new boldness for the second time and said, "Nicholas, if you're not too busy, I propose I take you to Cape Cod."

Nicholas, not thinking Meg was serious, said, "That would be great. When would you like to go?"

"I would like to go now. I suggest the buccaneer Nicholas I met before our delightful lunch, who claims to be a student, thief, and sailor, board my yellow vessel and leave immediately," replied Meg.

"Are you serious?"

"I'm most definitely serious. I believe it's a two-hour drive to Cape Cod. We can sit on the beach, watch the sunset, and return directly. I'll have the opportunity to see the ocean, and you'll get to return to Rock Harbor. We will look out over the water with the memory of your mother in our hearts."

Nicholas had been chilled by Meg's words and the thought of returning to Rock Harbor. He responded in a hesitant tone, saying, "I'm not sure I can."

Meg sensed she'd imposed herself on Nicholas's private remembrance and said, "I'm sorry, I shouldn't have suggested it, something so personal, and we've just met. I'm sure there's someone special that you would want to go there with. I don't know what I was thinking, or hoping."

"Meg, it's not that. I don't know if I have the courage to return to Rock Harbor and sit on the beach and watch the sunset. The memory of it breaks my heart. I know how much it will hurt being there and remembering my mom sitting next to me, hugging me, imagining her touch."

Meg reached out and held Nicholas's hand and said, "You told me a very personal story of your mom, and of all the boys on campus, we somehow met. I can feel it in my heart and in my soul our paths crossed for a reason. If my presence helps you return to your special place and watch the sunset with your mom in your heart, I feel blessed I was chosen for this kindness. I don't quite understand it, but I feel it's important that we go and do this together."

Nicholas, holding back tears, nodded in agreement. As they stood on the sidewalk and faced each other, their embrace was mutual. Meg could feel Nicholas's strength through the gentleness of his hug. She felt comforted, secure, and safe wrapped in the arms of the boy she chose.

23

$\mathcal{W}$ hen they arrived back at the gas station, the tire was fixed. Meg paid Christopher, and they got in the Beetle. Just as Meg was about to start the car, she suddenly remembered the College of Holy Trinity decal she'd bought for her Volkswagen. She had planned to put the sticker on her car while she was visiting the campus and Cape Cod. She'd intended to visit and see the ocean on her own. She had wanted to look at the HT sticker and forge a memory connecting her Beetle with the college and her travels. Meg knew she would need to remove the decal when she returned home. She didn't care; she wanted the memory.

She now felt having Nicholas with her would make the trip more enjoyable and meaningful. Meg asked Nicholas if he would put the sticker on her car. Smiling, he readily obliged and placed it in the corner of the rear window. When Meg turned to look at the purple and white decal her eyes became misty. She was doing one more thing she'd always planned to do as a student at Holy Trinity. Meg knew her dream of attending the college would never come true. She would take special joy in the decal and the Holy Trinity sweatshirt she'd bought at the college bookstore. Meg had planned to keep the sweatshirt at her parents' house and wear it on Saturdays when the weather cooled and she visited her two special places.

The VW Beetle was on the move and the car was quickly out of Worcester, Massachusetts, the home of the College of Holy Trinity. They were traveling on Route 290, heading to 495 south toward Cape Cod.

Meg turned on the radio, and the car was soon filled with the music of some of her favorite artists. On her seventeen-hour road trip from Tennessee to Massachusetts, she'd listened to many different radio stations, and heard new and interesting songs. Meg loved the music, the lyrics, and the sentiment. Some made her cry, and when she started learning the words, she would sing along with the music playing on the radio.

During the drive, she'd fallen in love with the songs of Carole King and her new album, Tapestry. She told Nicholas it was her favorite. Meg's other special artists were James Taylor and Judy Collins. She loved Simon and Garfunkel's "Bridge over Troubled Water" and told Nicholas it was another song that made her eyes tear every time she heard it.

When one of Meg's favorite songs came on the radio, she would look at Nicholas and start singing.

Nicholas smiled and said, "Meg, you have a beautiful-sounding speaking voice, and I love your accent. I hope you don't stop the car and have me walk the plank when I admit my error and say your choirmaster had a fine ear for music."

Meg laughed and continued to sing and gave it her best effort. When she didn't know the words, she would hum.

Nicholas told her she hummed like a hummingbird and sang like a seagull. Meg responded in a serious tone and said, "Thank you. Seagulls are a most majestic bird."

Nicholas thought she was joking and, remembering one of his favorite books, *Jonathan Livingston Seagull,* said, "You're so very welcome, Jonathan."

Meg turned and looked at Nicholas. She immediately thought of the dove-white seagull that changed her life and the book by Richard Bach. She said, "Jonathan is my second favorite character from a book. You must have read it."

"Yes, it was excellent. The part that really had an impact for me was the desire to be the best and not for selfish reasons, but to teach and to help others achieve success."

"I loved the book because it inspired me and gave me the courage to visit Holy Trinity and now Cape Cod."

"Well, *Jonathan Livingston Seagull* is now my favorite book. I'll credit the seagull for bringing us together," said Nicholas.

Meg smiled and thought how wonderful this trip was turning out to be.

During the two-hour ride to Orleans, Nicholas kept his eyes fixed on Meg's face and smiled at how pretty she looked. He couldn't believe the day he was having. He had earlier thought the highlight had been when the neighborhood kids tackled him after football practice. Now, sitting next to Meg driving to Cape Cod, he felt this was the best day of his life.

Meeting Meg seemed unreal to Nicholas. He was amazed he'd told her his most personal and guarded memory of his mom; and now, he was driving to Rock Harbor for the first time since 1957. He wasn't sure how he would react when he was sitting on the beach, watching the sunset, and recalling the small boy cuddling with his mom. Nicholas knew he was very happy he would be with Meg when he did.

The time passed quickly and before they knew it, they were on Route 6, traveling along the Cape Cod Canal approaching the Sagamore Bridge. When Meg saw the steel gateway over the water, she said with excitement ringing in her voice, "Look, Nicholas, the glorious bridge, and right across the canal is Cape Cod. How welcoming."

Nicholas, filled with gratitude, said, "Thank you for taking me with you. I'm really not sure when I would have made this trip on my own. It always seemed far away. It was part of what made me think my vision, my memory of my mom, never really happened." Pausing and reflecting, he continued, "Now, driving to Cape Cod seems such a short ride." Finishing with emotion, Nicholas said, "Meg, I'm just grateful that when I watch the sunset tonight, I'll be watching with you."

Meg looked at him with tears rolling down her cheeks and, in a tone, barely audible said, "I am, too, Nicholas. I am, too."

The last forty-five minutes of the drive Meg and Nicholas mostly remained silent. They were both reflecting on how much this day meant to each of them. When their thoughts intersected, they turned their heads, looked into each other's eyes, and saw all that was good.

Meg thought she was blessed to have met Nicholas. She was doing something good and kind for another person. Meg felt helping Nicholas to sit on the beach, recalling the only memory of his mother, was an honor. She knew being with Nicholas remembering his mom as she'd hugged her little boy, sharing the beauty of a sunset, would be a powerful memory.

Meg had tried not to think of Lewis. She'd told herself she wouldn't, but she couldn't stop the thoughts from entering her mind. She silently spoke to him and said, *Lewis, I will use this memory to block out your violence.* With these words, she knocked him out of her thoughts.

Nicholas was thinking of his mom and his only memory of her. He was going to pray. He would ask for her help in lifting the weight of her death and the pain that was crushing his father, a heartache so powerful his father had lost his will to enjoy life. Nicholas's dad blamed himself for the cancer that took his wife's life. He'd wanted to die for her. He had prayed to die for her, but in his heart, he knew he couldn't have died so she could live. Nicholas's dad had listened to the Gospel according to John, and he'd heard the words, "To love one another as God loves you . . . no one has greater love than this, to lay down one's life for one's friend."

Nicholas had felt the same hurt as his father and sometimes when the loss of his mom was too heavy a load for him, he would have the same thoughts. He would have died for her. But Nicholas knew cancer hadn't picked him, and it hadn't picked his dad; with all its evil, cancer had chosen his beautiful, kind, loving mother, and there had been nothing he or his dad could do to change that.

24

*T*he parking lot at Rock Harbor was relatively small, but on a cool May evening well ahead of the tourist season, there were plenty of places available for the yellow Beetle. The sun was already dropping, taking its time on a steady course to seemingly slip into the ocean.

Meg was chilled and put on her new Holy Trinity sweatshirt. Nicholas opened his gym bag to retrieve his heavy practice jersey to keep warm. As they started to walk along the pier overlooking the boats, Meg remembered the blanket she always kept in her car. She would bring it with her when she visited her favorite places. She'd sit on top of it while reading a book, eating her lunch, and sometimes on a warm clear day, she'd drift off to sleep on it.

Nicholas waited at the dock, looking out over the jetty that extended into the bay from the end of the harbor. When Meg returned a few minutes later, she was holding her checkered red-and-charcoal-colored blanket. When Nicholas saw it he said, "That looks like my mom's blanket. You couldn't tell by the black-and-white picture, but our blanket looked just like that, with the little red and dark-gray squares. It reminded me of a checkerboard, and Mom would play checkers on it with me. We found small rocks and shells on the beach and used them for checkers. Wow, I can't believe I remembered that."

Meg, her emotions always on the surface, looked down at her blanket as Nicholas spoke. When he finished speaking, she looked at his face and said, "I knew there was a reason we came here together. You'll remember your wonderful vacation. If my old blanket can help you recall the past, surely sitting on the beach and watching the sunset will, too." Meg paused and again looked down at the blanket. When she returned her gaze toward Nicholas, her eyes were moist, and she softly said, "I would like to sit close to you with the blanket wrapped around us. I know it won't be the same for you, but it would make me feel a part of something very special to you, and I would like that very much."

Nicholas reached out and put his hand gently around Meg's and without speaking the couple walked slowly past the boats. They could see out over the water as the sun continued to set. They walked the sandy path and weaved their way through the knee-high beach grass flowing rhythmically in the breeze. The beach was nearly deserted as Meg and Nicholas continued their hike until they found a secluded spot encased by the lush green grass of the bay. They rested their young bodies on the soft sand, felt the contact as they wrapped the checkered wool blanket around their shoulders, and felt comforted in their loneliness.

The wind off the water cooled the evening air, creating the invitation for Meg to lean against Nicholas and feel his warmth. He gently pulled her toward him, the physical connection strong, the heat of their bodies merging, getting hotter, their emotions sizzling. They felt the same glow of the sun as it illuminated the water and melted away in the distance.

They remained motionless staring out over the bay. The human comfort that had long evaded them was overwhelming. Neither wanted to move, neither wanted to speak. They didn't want to break the bond that was building between their two lonely souls, Nicholas from the loss of his mother and a father too broken to comfort him, and Meg from the abuse of a man who never loved her and took pleasure in hurting her.

Nicholas interrupted the stillness when he said, "I remember the fire."

"There was a fire?"

"Yes, when we sat on the beach we had a small fire in front of us. I remember when we first arrived we gathered driftwood and built a small fire. I'm sure it had been my dad who lit it after the sun disappeared. We stayed on the beach until the fire went out. I think we must have gone back to the cottage after that; I just don't fully remember."

Suddenly, Nicholas scrambled up and started to gather some driftwood. Meg smiled as she watched him scurry around to collect what wood he could. When he'd sat back down, he asked, "Do you have matches?"

Meg, laughing, just shook her head.

They could see a fire burning farther down the beach. Nicholas said, "Don't move, this buccaneer is off to get something to light the fire." He then sprinted down the beach. When he returned he was juggling more wood, a small bundle of dry kindling, and some reliable stick matches. Meg was genuinely impressed with his resourcefulness.

Nicholas said, "I didn't realize starting a small beach fire was such an art. A nice couple laughed when I asked them for help. They gave me proper instructions, and said,

'All you city kids are the same.' I thanked them profusely, then they started laughing again and told me not to burn down the beach."

Meg sat with her arms wrapped around her knees, bringing them toward her chest as she watched Nicholas start the fire. She was wishing their incredible day would never end.

When the fire was glowing, Nicholas sat back down and once again wrapped the blanket around their shoulders. The physical contact that would have been improbable hours earlier now seemed natural as they relaxed their bodies against each other.

Nicholas again was the first to speak and asked, "If Jonathan is your second favorite character in a book, who's your first?"

Meg was moved by the question. She knew she'd told Nicholas that Jonathan was her second favorite, but was surprised he'd thought to ask about her favorite. "Jennifer Cavilleri, but she was called Jenny. She's a character in the book *Love Story*. I just love the novel. I keep it in my car and always take it with me when I visit my favorite places. Holding it in my hands and thinking about the love the characters had for each other brings me to tears."

"It must be a beautiful story."

"You haven't read it?"

"No, I haven't had time."

"Oh, you must."

"I will, but I'd like you to tell me about it."

"It's a beautiful story of two college students who fall in love. They struggled to pay the bills and lived in really cheap apartments. Jenny worked to put Oliver, her husband, through law school, and when he graduated he found a good job. Everything about their future seemed bright until

Jenny was diagnosed with cancer and died suddenly. She was brave, and she helped Oliver have the courage to deal with her death."

"That's such a sad story," replied Nicholas.

"I know. Every time I think of it, I want to cry. What is really sad is that in all the great love stories, it seems the woman always has to die."

"Even in real life, they die, too," Nicholas responded mournfully while thinking of his mom.

"Oh, Nicholas, I'm very sorry. I should have considered your mom."

Nicholas gently squeezed Meg and brought her a little closer to comfort her and said, "I only meant to say that so much of fiction is based upon real life. There's nothing sadder than when two people love each other, and one dies, especially when the death occurs and they're young. The heartache always seems much greater. Listening to you speak about the book makes me want to read it. I promise, I'll find the time to read *Love Story*."

"I think of the pain you must have felt when your mom died. I imagine your dad was deeply hurt by the loss of the woman he loved. When you look at the picture of you with your mom, it must have been your dad who took the photograph. I think if your father had kept it to himself all these years, it's very meaningful to him. I see a beautiful, loving family enjoying a special time together. The photograph your dad keeps to himself, the image he sees, shows me how much he cherishes the memory."

"You know, I never considered my dad's feelings. As a boy, I felt the loss of my mom and lived with my father's distance. You're right, my father truly loved my mom, and her death took his love of life right out of him."

"It's just heartbreaking to think about."

"I do love my father. He works hard and he made sure I had a good parochial school education. I owe a lot to the sisters who taught me, and I have wonderful memories I will always keep in my heart. One of my favorite nuns was Sister Mary Mark Damon. We would have all these interesting conversations every Saturday when I was scrubbing the convent floors."

Meg interrupted Nicholas and said, "You scrubbed the convent floors?"

"Yes, it's sort of a long story."

"I'm happy to hear about it."

"When I was younger, I think I wanted to get punished by the nuns. I would sometimes be disruptive or get into an occasional fight in the school yard. I would do all these things to get attention, and even though I was punished, I felt the love of the sisters. They would discipline me and then take the time to talk with me and pray with me. Our Mother Superior, Sister Mary Anne Donovan, gave me a picture of Our Lady of Perpetual Help with her prayer on the back. She had me pray to her three times every day. It was comforting, so I kept misbehaving, and the sisters continued to punish me and then console me. One day, I really think Mother Superior figured me out and decided to make me scrub the convent floors on my knees every Saturday."

"That must have changed your behavior."

"Well, it did, but not because of the punishment. I had the opportunity to see the sisters in their home when they were relaxed and funny, and they would speak to me with kindness. I looked forward to Saturdays. Then one day Sister Mary Mark told me Mother Superior said my punishment was complete, and I didn't have to come back anymore."

"You must have been relieved."

"Actually, I wasn't."

"What did you do?"

"I told Sister Mary Mark, I would be back next Saturday and every Saturday until I graduate. My grades and behavior improved, and I was accepted to Holy Trinity. Now I'm sitting on the beach with a beautiful girl and a blazing fire, so it doesn't look like we'll be leaving soon."

When Meg heard Nicholas's last words about not leaving soon, she was very happy. She really liked him and didn't look forward to dropping him off back at Holy Trinity. Nicholas was thinking much the same thing as he continued to gently hold Meg close to him.

It had been an improbable day, mysterious in many ways, as if their two hearts were destined to be united. One broken by the loss of his mother, and the other abused and battered by an evil nearly biblical in its description. Yet when one's trajectory was altered, a force had intervened and united them on the grounds of the College of Holy Trinity, leaving their destiny in each other's hands.

As they sat watching and staring at the fire, they both fell silent. The air was getting colder, but the warmth from the fire, their bodies touching, was keeping them warm and comforted.

Nicholas, thinking of Meg and how pretty she was, slowly turned his head to look at her. Sensing his movement, she turned to face him, their eyes locking. Nicholas slowly moved closer and gently pressed his lips to Meg's, emotions surging through them. They held the kiss, then slowly pulled apart and looked into each other's eyes. As they held their gaze, Nicholas squeezed Meg gently as she inched closer. They remained silent and faced the fire and let the warmth from the blaze cool the heat of their bodies.

25

The Tuesday morning air had turned cold and only moist ashes remained where the warm fire had burned brightly the night before. Meg and Nicholas lay fully clothed, sleeping on the sand with the blanket covering their shivering bodies. It was too early for light, and the air was heavy and wet. A morning fog had drifted in from the waters of Cape Cod Bay. The sun would burn away the haze, brighten the skies, and warm the mid-May afternoon; but that was hours away.

Gall was hauling his seventy-six-year-old body over the sand with his fishing pole in one hand and a small tackle box with the few lures used by the local anglers in the other. Over the years, he'd seen any number of sights on the beach or in the water near Rock Harbor. Gall wasn't at all surprised to see two young people sleeping on the beach, their fire had long burned out and a damp blanket barely covering their bodies. Most times they were naked; seeing the fully clothed teenagers made him smile.

He'd seen the little yellow car with the Tennessee license plates parked in the lot and couldn't help noticing the Holy Trinity decal. Gall knew the two-young people would be chilled and damp from the morning brume. They would probably catch a cold if they didn't get a hot shower, dry clothes, and some of Maggie's warm cranberry muffins to eat.

Over the past fifty-four years of marriage, Gall had brought home to his wife all kinds of things he'd found on the beach. On several occasions, when he'd come across good people who needed a helping hand, he would bring them home, clean them up, and sometimes provide them with a warm bed for the night. Maggie was always prepared for it. Gall had been named after Saint Gall, the patron saint of birds, so she called them his broken-winged gulls.

Gall wasn't exactly the shy type; he figured why should he be? He was getting up there in years, and besides, he'd given the lower half of his right leg fighting for his country. As Nicholas and Meg lay sleeping, he shouted to them, "All right, you tenderfoots, time to get up and get off this darn cold beach."

Meg and Nicholas were startled out of their slumber and scrambled to their feet, not knowing what to expect. When their eyes focused, they saw a lean but strong-looking man with a white beard, wearing a fishing hat and displaying a great big smile. With an authoritative voice he said, "You," pointing to Nicholas, "Pick up that blanket, and you and the little lady follow me."

Nicholas did as he was told. The man had a certain type of commanding presence you just didn't question. Meg looked at Nicholas, and they exchanged a glance that said, *Do what he says.*

As they started walking, the stranger in the lead and the first to speak, said, "I'm Gall, and this here's my beach. I've been fishing these waters since 1899 when I was four years old, and ever since 1919, I fish here most every day."

"My name is Nicholas, and this is Meg. We're sorry for trespassing on your property, sir."

"Nicholas, well that's one fine name. It ain't my property, but I treat it like it is. I don't suspect that's your yellow car parked in the lot now, is it?"

"Sir, that's my vehicle. I apologize for leaving it there. You see we were watching the sunset, and we had a nice fire, and we were talking. Well, we fell asleep."

"Why, I detect a slight, welcoming Southern accent you've got there, young lady. That sure explains the Tennessee license plates. But no apology is necessary, though. You're lucky old Gall found you or you two youngsters would have caught a humdinger of a cold. You two lovebirds wouldn't have wanted that. Would ya now?"

"No, sir," responded Meg and Nicholas in unison.

"If it's all the same to you, just call me Gall, like in, you got a lot of gall, mister." And then he laughed at his own joke.

For a seventy-six-year-old, his six-foot frame was moving at a powerful pace, one that left the athletic Nicholas and the slender Meg scurrying to keep up. Once they were off the sand, they walked a short way down Rock Harbor Road. When they came to a small opening between a row of hedges, they turned onto a driveway covered in crushed seashells. Facing them was a small, two-story, Cape Cod–style house with weathered cedar shakes.

As they entered through the front door, Gall yelled out, "Maggie, my love, you won't believe what I found on the beach this morning."

"Well, it better not be a pretty young girl, that's all I have to say, Gall, or one of your broken-winged gulls." As Maggie walked into the front room, she saw Meg standing in front of her with Nicholas blocked out by Gall.

Meg, shivering in her damp clothes and her small frame looked like a lost, but a very pretty young girl. Maggie said, "Oh my dear, look at you. You're freezing, you poor soul, you must've gotten lost, sweetheart."

"No ma'am, I, me, well we, Nicholas and I fell asleep on the beach, and Gall woke us up and brought us here. I'm so sorry for the intrusion."

"Well, there's no intrusion at all. Old Gall's been sheltering strangers ever since Henry David Thoreau walked the beaches and back roads of Cape Cod."

"Now, Maggie, you know I ain't that old."

"Well, you sure move like you are."

Gall quickly approached his wife and hugged and splattered kisses over her face, saying, "I'll show you how these old bones move."

"Gall, you get away from me. Not in front of the pretty young girl."

Meg was laughing and thinking what a marvelous loving relationship they had. She couldn't help to remember a time when her parents behaved in such a relaxed and loving way. That had been before her mother's moods had started to change and she'd been hospitalized.

Nicholas was lost behind Gall, and with all the fun-loving antics finally stepped forward and said, "Good morning, Ma'am."

"Now who's this handsome young man?"

"Ma'am, my name is Nicholas."

"Well, Nicholas, you're a guest in my house, so please call me Maggie. Now get out of those damp clothes."

Nicholas froze. He wasn't sure what to do.

Maggie said, "Well, not here, go upstairs. The first door on the right, that's the room where our summer ballplayers stay. There are plenty of clothes to choose from. Every year these college kids just leave behind all types of clothes and such. Then you bring your wet things down to me. I'm going to wash them for you. You can shower after that.

Meg, darling, you're going to take your shower inside and get warm. I'll find you some of my granddaughter's clothes to put on. Now hurry, I don't want you catching a cold."

Nicholas went upstairs and did as he was told. Maggie brought Meg to the bathroom and showed her everything she needed. When Nicholas came down from the bedroom, he was wearing sweatpants and a sweatshirt. He was carrying his damp clothes and clothes to put on after he showered. Gall told him to leave the wet ones with Maggie and follow him outside.

The two walked out the rear door leading to the backyard. Gall showed him a small, enclosed wood structure attached to the house. He said, "The cold water is on the left and the hot is on the right. You can shower outdoors. I'll go hang your blanket on the clothesline to dry."

Nicholas did as he was directed. He opened the wooden door and entered the outdoor shower stall. He'd never seen anything like it before or at least that he could recall. If there had been one in the house his parents had rented when he was only five years old, he didn't remember.

He undressed and stepped under the spray. The hot water was comforting, blocking out the cool air and quickly warming his body. He couldn't believe how refreshing an outdoor shower was or how long he stayed under the steaming water until he heard Gall laughing and yelling,

"Nicholas, after Maggie's breakfast, you're going to be chopping wood to pay for all the hot water you're using."

"I'll be right out, sir."

"*Gall.*"

"Yes, sir, sorry. Gall." All Nicholas could hear was laughter coming from the other side of the shower stall. He quickly dressed into a pair of straight-leg khaki chinos, a blue button-down shirt, and a pair of white low-cut Converse sneakers that were left in the bedroom by young men who'd played baseball in the Cape Cod summer league.

While Meg was in the shower, Maggie had found some of her granddaughter's jeans and a sleeveless top. When Maggie knocked on the bathroom door, Meg quickly covered herself as best she could and told her to enter.

When Maggie walked in, she noticed the bruises on Meg's upper arm and welts just below the towel she had wrapped around herself. Mrs. Barren had seen Meg's battered face, but no one other than Lewis had ever seen the damage he'd inflicted, and Maggie was only seeing a very small portion of his brutality.

Maggie quickly closed the door and said, "Nicholas?" as she pointed to the bruises.

Meg shook her head to signal no and began to cry.

"Gall will beat that boy."

Still crying, talking fast, Meg said, "No, honestly it wasn't Nicholas. We just met yesterday at Holy Trinity. He's a wonderful, kind person. He helped me with my car, and then we had lunch. He told me about his mom. Her name was Peggy, and she died when he was five years old. He has a memory of sitting on the beach at Rock Harbor, with a fire in front of them, just his mom and him, wrapped in a blanket, watching the sunset. We came down yesterday afternoon to watch the sunset and remember his mom. Nicholas is good and kind and caring. He would never hurt me. He doesn't know about my bruises. He must never know."

Maggie had seen many abused women over her seventy-five years. As she looked hard at Meg's face, she knew she was telling the truth about Nicholas. Maggie thought about what Meg had said when she mentioned Peggy, her five-year-old, and Holy Trinity, and asked, "Was Peggy from Worcester?"

Meg was surprised by the question and said, "Yes, they came to Rock Harbor in the summer of 1957. Nicholas found a picture his father kept of him with his mom on the beach."

"Oh my! I remember them. They stayed in a small cottage we rent down the road a ways. I remember Peggy, now that I look at you and see your reflection in the mirror. You remind me of her a bit. It's like looking through a window to the past. She was slim like you, about your height, very pretty, and she had a nice way about her, hard to describe. As young parents, Peggy and her husband, they were proud of their little boy and happy all the time.

"The reason I remember is one morning I was bringing over some of my cranberry muffins and with it being summer, the door had been left open to the cottage with just the screen door closed. I heard Peggy crying, so I gently knocked on the door, being concerned, I asked if everything was alright. She just cried and said she was very ill, and I mustn't say anything.

"I felt so bad. I hugged her and cried with her. I'm sorry to hear of her death. It must have been hard on her husband. He loved her very much. A lot of folks pass my way down here. I see the ones who are truly in love, and they were. That's so very sad."

Meg with tears still in her eyes looked at Maggie and quietly asked, "Do you think you have something with longer sleeves?"

"I'm sure I do, sweetheart. You just wait here, and I will be right back. When you come out, we're going to have a nice breakfast, and I believe I have something to show Nicholas," said Maggie with compassion as she embraced Meg and went to find her another top.

26

*W*hen Meg was dressed, she walked out of the bathroom with that fresh shower look, wearing blue jeans, a white top with three-quarter length sleeves, and flip flop sandals. Nicholas was sitting at the kitchen table with Gall, and Maggie was working by the stove.

Seeing Meg, Nicholas immediately stood up and said, "Wow, you look beautiful." He walked over to her and gave her a gentle hug. Meg smiled, and to her surprise as well as Nicholas's, she gave him a quick kiss on the lips.

Smiling, Maggie said, "Hey, hey, we'll have none of that lovey-dovey stuff. I don't want old Gall getting any ideas. I'm too busy making breakfast for that sort of thing."

"Don't you worry, Maggie; there's always later," said Gall.

Maggie had indeed fixed a fabulous breakfast for her guests, complete with large cranberry muffins, scrambled eggs, and thick slices of Canadian bacon. They ate mostly in silence, except for the constant compliments and gratitude extended by Meg and Nicholas in appreciation for the food and hospitality. Gall had been advised by Maggie, "Not to ask too many darn nosey questions," in her words, and promised to fill him in later.

"Nicholas," said Maggie as she looked at him to get his attention.

"Yes, Maggie?"

"I was talking with Meg earlier this morning, and she mentioned your mother. I'm so sorry to hear of her death. When you were a boy, your parents rented our small cottage down the road. Your mother had confided in me at the time and told me she was very sick. One morning, I'd brought over some of my muffins and heard her crying. We spoke, and she told me of her illness. It was so sad. You truly had terrific and loving parents. I watched the three of you for nearly a week and saw the happiness. I could see how much your father loved you and your mom."

Nicholas's eyes began to water as he held back his tears. Meg's had started the moment Maggie said "Nicholas." She'd anticipated what Maggie would say. Gall hadn't yet connected the couple. He would wait for his wife to explain.

"If you're up to it, we can all walk over to the cottage. I'd like to show you something you may remember," said Maggie.

Nicholas couldn't speak. He was desperately trying to hold back his tears. Meg looked at him, sensed what he wanted to say, and through her tears said, "We would like that very much, thank you." Nicholas simply nodded his head in agreement.

When breakfast was finished, everyone pitched in to clean up the table. Maggie and Meg took care of the dishes, and Gall said, "About that firewood, Nicholas," as he motioned for him to follow.

Once outside, Gall gave Nicholas space to be alone and went off to do some chores until the ladies were ready. He was trying to recall Nicholas's parents. He'd remembered his wife telling him about the pretty woman she'd found crying at the cottage who was very sick.

When he recalled the Holy Trinity sticker on the yellow car, he fixed his memory on the city in which it was located, a place he knew well. He then began to recall Nicholas's father. Now he remembered, he was a good man, and one night the two men had spoken over a couple of beers. They were both veterans of foreign wars and Gall had thought of the words they hadn't spoken, the silence that'd said more than the words they had.

When Maggie and Meg came out of the house, Gall appeared as if by signal. Nicholas stood up and the four headed over to the small beach house. The cottage was plainly furnished with the basic accommodations needed to satisfy weekly summer renters. The sunroom was wood paneled with an orangey-yellow-colored knotty pine. When it had been first rented out, the guests had inscribed their names into the wall. Rather than repair it, a tradition had been started and everyone who'd rented the cottage over the past twenty years had left their name and a short message. It gave the cottage character; everyone wants a memory and to be remembered.

Nearly two hundred families had left an inscription memorializing the week they'd spent vacationing at Rock Harbor. Over the years there'd been plenty of repeat renters, and they'd never failed to leave their mark and date the visit. When Meg and Nicholas walked into the room they were amazed. They immediately started searching the walls for the message his parents had left behind.

Nicholas found the marking on the right side of the double-hung windows. He stood motionless when he saw the inscription. Meg quickly went to his side and held his hand. Etched into the pine was written, "The Avellino Family, Peggy, Andrew, Nicholas, summer 1957." Nicholas ran his fingers over the engraving; he could feel the grooves. With his index finger, he traced the words, and as he did, his reflection was captured in the glass. Looking back was the image of Andrew, as if transformed back to that wonderful summer, carving their names and marking their visit into the wall.

Nicholas had a sudden vision of his mom and dad smiling as the family imprint had become part of the beach house, but he wasn't sure if it was real. He saw them hugging and kissing, and the five-year-old boy who was part of their joy and happiness and love.

"I want to remember. I can feel their presence, the three of us together in this room. I'm just not sure."

Meg whispered, "You see it now, Nicholas. The words, your names, you feel your parents, their love for each other and for you. Maybe it's enough to know it's all real."

Meg squeezed Nicholas's hand, and he turned to look at her. They both had tears in their eyes. Meg and Nicholas embraced, the water slowly trickling down their cheeks. Nicholas always tried to hold back his tears, but now in Meg's presence, he lost his inhibition. He felt a freedom to express himself without embarrassment.

With his arms wrapped around Meg, he cried all the tears he'd struggled to hold back since his mom had died. He could feel his love for Meg grow with every tear he shed. They stayed in the cottage most of the afternoon and hadn't noticed Maggie and Gall leave. They'd quietly left to give the young couple their privacy. They could see Nicholas needed to mourn his loss.

When Meg and Nicholas were ready to leave the cottage, they held hands and walked back along Rock Harbor Road toward Maggie and Gall's house. Neither wanted to discuss what was on their mind—returning to Holy Trinity. They knew they wouldn't be able to stay in Rock Harbor much longer. They felt blessed by the kindness of Maggie and Gall, but they didn't want to impose upon their generosity.

When they arrived back at the house, the decision had been made for them, at least for one more night. Gall asked Meg if she could retrieve her car from the harbor parking lot and leave it in the driveway.

He also said, "Maggie decided to cook supper for us this evening, so I got some fishing to do or we won't be eating. No need making excuses like you have to leave, it's already decided. She's feeding her guests. I know you're going to ask, but no, we won't be needing any help getting ready, just with the cleaning up."

As Gall was walking away he said, "Maggie made up the beds in the spare rooms for you to sleep in tonight. She told me to tell you there'll be no hanky-panky in her house. I don't know what she means; there's always plenty going on when we're alone. But you best listen to her." As he continued walking, he was laughing as usual at his own words.

Nicholas turned to Meg and with affection said, "I know the time will come, but I never want this trip to end. I care so much about you and all we've shared. You make me feel, really feel, and able to express my emotions. It's all new to me. I've always held my feelings closed up, never wanting to express myself. You're teaching me what's important in life: caring for another person, being with them in their need, comforting them, and expressing your feelings. You've done all this for me, and we hardly know each other. I feel like you've been with me, hiding in my heart, waiting to comfort me."

"What you've allowed me to do, to be a part of something so intimate, is just special. If I could have one wish, it would be that we never leave Rock Harbor. We'll watch the sunset every evening, including the days there's no sun. The two of us will sit on the beach in the rain, the snow, the windiest days, and let our imaginations create the sunset. Our bodies touching, we'll wrap ourselves in a blanket and snuggle. We'll feel the warmth of each other, the beating of our hearts, the joy and happiness of just being together," responded Meg as if she were creating the life of her dreams.

"Believe me, I wish, I want the same as you."

"Nicholas, it's just a fairy tale; you have college and football, and an incredible life ahead of you."

"I find I'm telling you everything I've held locked up in my heart for so long. The only reason I play football is so I can go to college. If I didn't play, I wouldn't be at Holy Trinity. I have no love for the game. When I'm with you, I'm beginning to feel how you feel. You show your emotions when you're happy, or joyful, or sad. You don't hold back. You cry when you want to cry and laugh when you want to laugh. It's all beautiful."

Nicholas paused. He was saying so much. They were too serious, and Meg looked sad. He wanted her to smile so he said, "I have only one more wish." He paused for a moment then said, "I wish you'd hum when you want to sing."

Meg laughed and gave him a big hug; the tension broke. Nicholas then gave Meg a tender kiss on her lips. When they separated, the couple walked to the harbor holding hands, and drove the car back to the house. They would spend one more night together in separate rooms. Maggie would not permit hanky-panky in her lovely home.

27

*T*he evening was cool but comfortable, with a slight breeze blowing off the water. Maggie had decided to serve dinner outside on the picnic table. Gall loaded a bundle of dried wood into the stone fire pit he'd built for nights spent outside with family and friends. He planned to light it once the darkness set in and their meal was finished.

As they sat down to eat, Maggie asked everyone to hold hands, and she thanked the Lord for the food and said a prayer for Peggy. The four sat quietly for a few moments until Gall broke the stillness and said, "*Let's eat.*"

Maggie told Gall earlier about the bruises she'd observed on Meg. She assured him they hadn't come from Nicholas and that he didn't even know about them, and Meg didn't want him to know.

Once the food was served, and the conversation began, Maggie was the first to speak. She kept the conversation general, talking about food, her garden, and the weather. Gall talked about the harbor he loved and the beach where he'd been fishing since he was a boy. Nicholas talked about school and sports, while Meg was mostly vague but enthusiastic about all she'd experienced since arriving at Holy Trinity.

When the meal ended and the dishes were washed, Gall lit some kindling and the logs started to ignite. They watched the flickering as it quickly rose and the fire began to burn steady. They all sat in silence with their own thoughts. Nicholas and Meg were sitting closer than they had been during the meal, holding hands.

Gall looked at Nicholas and said, "I remember your father. It took me a while to recall, but I remember him well. We had your parents over for an evening meal, much like tonight. You were sleepy, so your mom brought you in the house and settled you on the couch where you fell asleep. Maggie and your mom stayed inside to talk.

"Well, your dad and me, we'd both served our country during wartime. Your dad was in the Navy during World War II, and my service had been in the First World War. We got to talking in general, and I asked him where he did his duty. He told me he'd been assigned to a patrol craft in the Pacific. I think he said his ship's number was 1260, but don't quote me; it's been a few years. I'd read once in an old edition of the *Stars and Stripes* newspaper they'd nicknamed those tough little vessels the Bronco Navy.

"The patrol crafts were part of the seventh fleet and had been used to help guide small boats landing on the beaches. We all knew when our boys hit those shores, it was like fighting to get into hell. Well, these ships, they'd been used in every combat zone worldwide under extremely dangerous conditions. They'd helped capture all the important islands spread out over the Pacific.

"Your dad and me, we weren't talking war stories. We'd both seen too much fighting and death for that, but your dad, he did tell me about the time his ship got rammed, and he ended up getting wet.

"He'd been a signalman waving his flags, sending a message, and the next thing he knew, he was overboard in the water. He told me all he could think about was getting home to Peggy. There he was, in the Pacific Ocean, not sure if his ship was going down, and all his thoughts were of the woman he loved. That's a powerful incentive to live. Your dad, he really loved your mom. I'm sure her death has been hard on him."

Meg was silently crying, squeezing Nicholas's hand, as Gall told his story. Nicholas, with his eyes tearing, sat silently listening then softly said, "My dad never spoke about the war. I don't even know much about my mom. I'm learning more about him and my mom now than I've ever known. I'm just so grateful to Meg for giving me the courage to make this trip, and to you, Maggie and Gall. I appreciate all your generosity. Thank you."

Nicholas couldn't believe he was actually visiting with two strangers who'd known his parents. They were good people who'd rented them a cottage and had them over to eat, whose couch he'd slept on as a boy. He then turned and looked at Meg and saw such a special person. He knew he owed her so much, and he didn't want her to ever leave him. She looked at him, sensed a need, and gave him a light kiss on the lips.

Meg with all sincerity then said, "Maggie, I want to thank you and Gall for all your hospitality, and please know that Nicholas and I, well, there will not be any han-ky-panky tonight."

"Hanky-panky! What? *Gall*! Did you tell these two lovely kids that? I have a good mind to lock you out of the house tonight. Fifty-four years I've been married to this man; I don't know how I do it. Hanky-panky, I'll give you hanky-panky."

"That's just what I wanted you to say, Maggie. Now come over here and give me a big kiss."

"I'll give you no such thing."

Gall quickly stood up and showered Maggie with kisses.

"No more of that. Now you say you're sorry to Meg and Nicholas."

All four broke out in laughter as Maggie and Gall bantered back and forth while he continued to hug and kiss her.

"You really do love each other very much. It's so wonderful how much you care about each other," said Meg.

"Maggie is the love of my life, my savior. I could never repay her for all she's done for me."

"Gall, I love you, too, but you know I don't like to hear I'm your savior and you can never repay me. You are a good, good man."

"Wow, fifty-four years, and you love each other so much," said Nicholas.

"When I look at Maggie, I still see the beautiful and sweet twenty-one-year-old girl I married. And, you never really think about fifty-four years; it's like having one beautiful loving year fifty-four times. We never get old, our bodies age, but in our hearts and in our minds, we're still the two kids who fell in love and never fell out of love."

"I love you, you old grump," said Maggie, her eyes tearing.

Meg was listening intently to Gall and Maggie speak about love in such an open and honest way in front of two people they hardly knew. She thought of her mother's comment about not being sure she ever loved her father, the man she married. Meg knew it had been a long time since there had been any overt expression of love between her parents. She then thought of Lewis; he had no love.

Meg heard about Peggy and Andrew and how much they'd loved each other and how much they'd loved Nicholas. She could sense that when Peggy died, Nicholas's father loved him but in a sad, silent way. Listening to Nicholas words, she felt his father had lost his will for joy and happiness. Meg thought how sad it was that he'd distanced himself from Nicholas and hurt him unintentionally but, still, he'd hurt him.

Meg could feel her love for Nicholas building. She did love him, but she needed to contain it. She had another life and knew she couldn't escape. Lewis would find her, and her parents wouldn't be safe. Meg wanted a life like Maggie and Gall with fifty or one hundred times of one beautiful, loving year with Nicholas.

"Meg and Nicholas, you two are still young. I want to share our love story with you. Love is hard; it takes courage, and sacrifice, and tolerance, and forgiveness; but the reward is joy, happiness, love, and a beautiful life together."

"Gall —" but before Maggie could finish speaking, Gall interrupted her.

"Maggie, I love you dearly, but I want you to sit quiet and let me tell our story. You saved me. You're my savior and the love of my life. It's a story I'm going to share with our new friends."

As Gall started telling his story everyone sat quietly, listening. Maggie knew it well, she'd lived it; she was Gall's hero. He would tell his tale, a story to test any marriage, but it was one with a happy ending. They loved each other and loved the wonderful life they'd carved together, despite all its early hardships.

Gall indeed knew the College of Holy Trinity well. He'd graduated in May 1917, and a few days later he'd married Maggie. Their country had been at war for just over a month, and Gall didn't wait to be drafted. With his college degree in hand, he'd enlisted in the army and received a commission as a first lieutenant. Gall left his new bride and shipped out for boot camp. He would serve in the infantry and lead his men into hell.

Gall had been sent to France in July 1918 as part of the 79th Division, under the command of Brigadier General W. J. Nicholson. His infantry division was made up of mostly draftees from some of the East Coast states. Gall, as a junior grade lieutenant, would lead his brave, good men into combat many times and was proud of their service.

By early September, Gall was preparing the soldiers under his command for their role in a major military offensive across the entire western front. The 79th had been ordered to drive the strongly fortified German army out of the township of Montfaucon with its sweeping view of the entire area. The Germans would not easily retreat from such an important strategic position.

On the 26th of September, three hours after Allied forces bombarded the German lines, Gall was leading his men into combat under heavy fire. Enemy machine guns protected by reinforced bunkers had his unit frozen in place. Gall had his orders, and they were clear: keep pushing uphill at all costs. He knew what that meant; he could see the bodies mounting. He was now fighting two battles—powerful enemy resistance and geography. The incline was an obstacle course of rocks, soft muddy dirt, crater holes, and streaming bullets.

Gall would never forget that day; it was an explosion from one of the enemy's heavy guns that nearly severed his right leg. He would always remember the sound of the shell as it propelled toward his location. He felt as if time had frozen until the pain set in.

He would always credit the brave men who risked their lives carrying bandages, tourniquets, and morphine with saving his life. He would blame himself for succumbing to his depression over the loss of his lower right leg and his addiction to morphine, cocaine, and any other drug that would deaden his pain.

Gall was one of the lucky ones. He'd been shipped home, and Maggie was waiting for him. She was one hundred and ten pounds of strength, toughness, and love. She deeply loved Gall, and she would not give up on his hopelessness and despair, or his addiction. It took her nearly four hundred days, she'd marked the calendar every day, before she could defeat "Goliath," and the man she'd married returned to her emotionally, spiritually, lovingly, and addiction-free.

Maggie and Gall had been married fifty-four years, and every day since the day his soul returned to him, he has told Maggie how much he loves and appreciates her for all she did to save him from himself.

Meg was crying throughout the story, and Nicholas's eyes welled as water slowly dripped down his cheeks. Maggie had heard Gall tell this tale many times over the years, and it never failed to bring her and Gall to tears. Her husband shared his struggle and all she did for him out of his love for her.

Gall told them that he shares his story to teach others a lesson about life, with all its struggles and challenges, its hopes and dreams, but mostly it's a message about the kind of love the Bible says there is no greater love than. Only when you have that kind of love can you overcome the struggles and challenges of life, and realize your hopes and dreams.

"I love you, Maggie," said Gall.

"I love you, too."

Meg stood up and hugged Maggie then Gall. Nicholas couldn't move at first. He was thinking about his dad and how he'd lost the love of his life. He thought it would take a new love, someone like Maggie, to nurse his father back to the loving man he used to be. It saddened him as he realized his dad would never open his heart to the possibility of having it broken again. It was only when Maggie spoke that he finally moved.

"Well, it's getting late, and I suspect you and Meg will want to get an early start in the morning."

Nicholas and Meg thanked Maggie and Gall for their generosity, kindness, and friendship. As they entered the house, they all said good night.

Meg and Nicholas walked up the stairs to the second floor. When they reached the landing, the lights on the first floor went out, and the house was quiet. They stood silent, facing each other, and kissed passionately. The connection penetrated their hearts and settled into the depths of their souls. They held each other tight and felt the comfort of love. When they loosened their embrace, they lingered, looking into each other eyes, not wanting to move. Separating slowly, hands still held, their fingers touched as they moved apart, and finally they said good night.

It had been only thirty-five hours since they'd met, but they had already shared more of what was in their hearts than most people ever do. Their love for each other was building, getting stronger, wanting to bond, but not knowing how.

These were their thoughts as they prepared for bed, their emotions charged. Neither wanted to sleep; neither could sleep. Nicholas was thinking of knocking on Meg's door when he heard the light tap on his. He opened the door, and there stood Meg in her Holy Trinity sweatshirt and pajama bottoms. Without speaking, she walked into his room.

She told him she wanted to watch one more sunset before leaving Rock Harbor. Meg removed the blanket from the bed and laid it on the floor. She motioned for Nicholas to sit. The shade was up, and they looked through the window at the darkness of the night. They let their imaginations create the image of the setting sun from the night before.

Meg began to speak contemplatively and said, "I see a love in Maggie and Gall that's special. It's the kind of love I always believed was real. I wanted it to be real.

"My mother and father love me, and I can feel their love. With my mother, it's no longer an expressive love; it's subtle and distant. She suffers from depression, and it changed her. It makes me sad to think of how she used to be. My father has always been special to me. He was there when my mother couldn't be. He expressed his love through hugs and kisses. I kiss my mom and dad. I hug them as often as I can, and they accept my demonstration of love, and I feel it in their words, so much love for me." Meg paused; she took a moment to wipe a tear from her cheek.

When she continued, she had sadness in her voice and said, "I can't remember the last time my parents expressed their love for each other. It's sad to think when two people marry their love fades, or something changes like with my mom and dad. Or, for some people, there was never any love.

"My mother told me she didn't think she ever loved my father. She said it didn't matter because they had companionship, and marriage was a duty to each other. I don't believe her. I remember how they used to be together, and then sometimes, I'm not so sure, maybe companionship could be better if there was no love at all.

"When my father had his heart attack, I was frightened. The thought of him dying and the loss of his love, his touch, it crushed me. I have so much to tell him, but . . ." Meg couldn't finish her sentence. She didn't want to reveal any of what she desperately wanted to say to her father and how it would affect his health. She paused as she collected her thoughts then continued. "I watched and listened to Maggie and Gall. I now know love is real; it matters. A marriage needs love; it sustains it, makes it strong and unbreakable. Love gives you a youth, a vibrancy you lose if you lose your love."

Nicholas sat quietly, listening to Meg as she shared her personal story of her parents. He said, "I'm sorry about your mom and dad. I'll pray your father fully recovers, and you can once again tell him all you have to say."

Nicholas took a moment and then said, "My dad lost more than my mom when she died; he lost his will to express his love, his feelings. I never thought he didn't love me, I just never felt his love. I'm sad for my dad, and I'm sad for your mother and father. I want a love like Maggie and Gall, and I want to always express my love."

Meg snuggled up against Nicholas as he pulled her closer. Gazing through the window, imagining the sun gently dipping into the ocean, and for the second night, they fell into a slumber under the comfort of a blanket and remained fully clothed.

28

eg was the first to wake; the sun had yet to rise. She quietly left the bedroom while Nicholas slept. She went into her room, removed her pajamas, and changed into clothes. She kept her Holy Trinity sweatshirt on to keep herself warm against the early morning chill. Walking down the stairs, Meg could see the light from the kitchen. She entered to find her hosts drinking their morning coffee and said, "Good morning."

When they looked up, Meg smiled then gave them both a big hug. She said, "Thank you for such a lovely time. I'll really miss you when we leave."

"You're most welcome, and good morning to you," said Gall.

"Good morning, sweetheart. We'll miss you, too. It's been our pleasure to have you and Nicholas as our guests," said Maggie.

"You look like you're ready for the road. I hope you don't plan to leave Nicholas behind when you go. You ain't sneaking out on us all bundled up with your sweatshirt on?" said Gall as he laughed.

"No, I'm going to try to keep Nicholas with me a little longer. At least until we get back to Holy Trinity. I suppose I'll start back to Tennessee after that. But I did have a lovely time and met some wonderful new friends. I was just going out for a walk."

"Well, keep warm, there is a chill out there. The sun's just coming up, so you won't be getting lost."

"Thank you, Gall. I just love being outside in the early morning; you do find the most interesting things," responded Meg with a wink.

The three laughed as Meg stepped outside to meet the rising sun and the morning chill. She was warm and comfortable in her sweatshirt with the Holy Trinity emblem. She felt it was her shield from all that was cold.

Meg was looking for something unusual to seal the memory of this special place. She walked down Rock Harbor Road toward the docks. Meg could see the fishermen loading up their boats. She stopped to watch some of the old, sea-worn trawlers slowly floating along the jetty, making their way toward the deep. She then moved in the direction of the beach. She wanted to walk along the shore with her feet in the water in search of a little treasure from the bay.

As she strolled along the water's edge, Meg picked up a variety of empty shells of different sizes and colors. On the wet sand, she examined the little prizes the receding tide had left behind. She held the weathered stones and the colorful, polished sea glass in her hands. But it was the fully intact sand dollar that would seal her memory of the early morning stroll on the beach at Rock Harbor.

Meg hurried back to the house. She was hoping to return before Nicholas was awake. She wanted to show him her treasure. As she entered the kitchen, neither Maggie nor Gall was in sight. She hurried up the stairs and saw the bedroom door was slightly ajar just as she'd left it. She peeked through the opening and could see Nicholas was still asleep. Meg quietly approached him then sank to her knees. She gently touched his shoulder. Nicholas, barely awake, turned to face her. Meg smiled and started to quietly sing her own rendition of one of her favorite songs, "You got to wake up every day . . . With your happy face on . . . And tell me how much you love me," while holding the "me" sound.

Nicholas smiled when he saw Meg. He listened to her sing as he thought about the happy face button on the visor of her car. She always pointed toward it when singing along to the radio version of the song. Nicholas couldn't wait to respond to her. He wanted to tell her he loved her, a love that had been building from the first time she'd called his name.

"I love you," said Nicholas. He'd tried to wait to see how long Meg could hold the "me" sound, but he couldn't. He'd wanted so desperately to hug her and kiss her.

"I love you, too," responded Meg.

They said the words, and the two broken-winged gulls meant it with their hearts and souls. The love they felt at that moment was built on kindness, affection, compassion, and the comfort they had provided each other. For Meg, it was a big step; she had to put aside the dark cloud of her other life, open her heart, and risk trusting another person. The distance she'd created between the prison where she lived and the loving home of Maggie and Gall loosened the viselike grip Lewis held over her. Every day she spent connected to Nicholas, with all his love and goodness, pulled her from that grip. It brought her closer to freedom and the life she'd always wanted.

Nicholas longed to love and feel loved. He had been waiting for Meg. He had needed her since the loss of his mom. When she sang her song and asked him to tell her how much he loved her, he knew she loved him, and he loved her. It scared him, not because he didn't love her; he thought of his father and what the loss of love did to him. Nicholas didn't want a life absent of the will to love. He didn't ever want to lose Meg and suffer the same loss as his dad.

After speaking their words of love, Meg's excitement burst, and she told him about her early morning walk. She showed Nicholas the sand dollar she'd found on the beach. Meg told him about all the other shells, the different-colored stones and beautiful small pieces of smooth sea glass that had washed up onto the shore. She told Nicholas about all the beauty of her treasures, the keepsakes that she would store in her memory scrapbook. His eyes filled with tears from the sheer joy of Meg simply sharing her newest discovery with him.

Gall interrupted their moment of tenderness when he called up the stairs to say Maggie would have breakfast ready in thirty minutes. He said Nicholas could shower outside, while Meg could use the inside bathroom. Their clothes were washed and ready for wear. Nicholas and Meg kissed, then hurried to shower and dress so they wouldn't be late for breakfast.

With their bags packed, they walked down the stairs to the kitchen, and the four new friends ate breakfast, cleaned up, and said their good-byes. As Nicholas and Meg were about to walk out of the house, Maggie said, "I didn't want to trouble you because it would be out of your way, and I wasn't sure if you had time. But, I wanted to send some of my cranberry muffins to my good friend Jeanne. I was hoping you would have the time to do this for me."

Gall knew what his wife was up to and added, "You'd be doing us a big favor. We don't get out to Truro often. When we do go, Maggie just criticizes my driving."

"If you stopped looking around and paid attention when you drove, I wouldn't need to."

Smiling, Meg said, "Oh, Maggie, I would be pleased to bring your delicious muffins to your friend Jeanne. I'm sure Nicholas won't mind."

"It's the least we could do after all you've done for us, plus I get to spend a little more time with Meg," said Nicholas.

"Thank you. Jeanne will be thrilled. I'll call her and let her know you're coming."

Maggie and Gall watched the little yellow car as it pulled out of the driveway and onto Rock Harbor Road. Meg and Nicholas would soon be on Route 6, heading to Truro, doing an errand to repay the hospitality of their new and very loving hosts.

Earlier, Maggie had called her friend Jeanne, the former Sister Mary Jeanne Marie de Maille. They'd discussed the physical marks of abuse she'd seen on Meg's thin body. Jeanne had lived on Cape Cod for twenty years, helping victims of spousal abuse. Maggie was hoping Jeanne would get Meg to open up to her and accept an offer of help. Jeanne would never push the women who were abused. She knew it wasn't her decision. Jeanne didn't live in constant fear of the abuser and didn't experience the isolation, loneliness, subtle threats, overt intimidation, and the beatings.

The law—the courts—were deaf to spousal abuse, battered women, and wife abuse. They couldn't even agree on a name, or call it what it truly was: a crime. It was a crime of violence with very real injuries and very real pain. Jeanne would wait a long time to see the changes that made it possible for women to escape their abusers and for abusers to be punished for their crimes. In the meantime, she would do what she could to help those who'd risked so much to be free from the evil and cancer of violence.

Maggie had sent Meg and Nicholas to Truro for Meg's benefit. She had no idea that Jeanne was also prepared to help Nicholas learn of the love between Peggy and Andrew Avellino.

29

*T*he yellow VW Beetle headed down Rock Harbor Road and back toward the rotary, where the third exit would take them to Route 6. They would soon be entering Eastham, on their way to Truro. The day was still early, and Meg and Nicholas had decided to take their time driving to Jeanne's house. They wanted to see as much as they could on the way. There would be beaches, lighthouses, cranberry bogs, and marshes. The scenic and beautiful sights of Cape Cod were all new to them.

Meg had seen the water running through the canal and the bay capturing the sun on a clear evening, but it was the Cape Cod National Seashore and the Atlantic Ocean that had captured her imagination.

When they saw the sign for Nauset Light and Coast Guard Beach, Meg turned the Beetle right. They were leaving the state highway and were on their way to the historic lighthouse, the first stop on their journey. The young couple walked around the old keeper's house and admired the unique tower with its bright red chest, wedged between

a white base and a black crown. The once all white structure of brick and cast iron stood tall facing the ocean winds.
The stately appearance of the one-hundred-twenty-foot
maritime beacon had all the dignity of a Queen's Guard.

A short drive later, they arrived at the parking lot
of Coast Guard Beach. Once Meg parked her car, they
walked to the far end of the lot and were introduced to
one of nature's treasures. Holding hands, standing against
a wooden railing, Meg and Nicholas gazed out over the salt
marsh with its varying shades of color, and took in the com-
plex ecosystem protecting and supporting the habitat and
wildlife that made up its natural community. The sun's rays
reflected off the cobalt-blue ocean. The calm waters gently
brushed against its winding perimeter. Meg, captivated by
the beauty that lay before her, created an imaginary photograph for her scrapbook.

Meg and Nicholas were like many other couples visiting Cape Cod for the first time. They were enjoying their
time together while seeing the simple beauty of water, sand,
vegetation, and the pale blue sky with puffs of white clouds
spotted along the horizon. They were in awe, admiring the
priceless art of nature's paintings.

When they decided to walk the beach, Nicholas
retrieved his gym bag from the car. He went to the bathhouse to change into his athletic shorts. Meg had on a pale
red sundress with a calico print of small white flowers. The
hem of the dress fell just below her knees, and she wore a
white, open-front cotton cardigan with three-quarter length
sleeves. Despite the warm weather, Meg was comfortably
dressed. She was wearing clothing that would conceal the
scars of her physical abuse.

Meg told Nicholas she would wait for him on the beach.
She strolled toward the stairs just beyond the bathhouse

where he was changing. She looked out over the ocean, closed her eyes, and let the soft breeze massage her skin. Meg then walked down the steps and, once on the warm sand, she noticed the beach was nearly deserted. She stopped halfway between the stairs and the water to wait for Nicholas. It wasn't long before she spotted a lone seagull flying toward her.

In the couple of days since Meg had arrived on Cape Cod, she'd seen seagulls but always off in the distance. Meg wasn't surprised by the sight. She was expecting it and, frankly, thought she would see many more of the beautiful birds.

As she stood watching, enthralled by the gracefulness of the lone gull slowly circling overhead, she sensed the bird was communicating with her. Meg was fixated on the sight, not noticing the arrival of the other seagulls. Suddenly she was alerted by the familiar screech. Meg looked down to find herself amid a flock of the friendly birds. She was captivated as the gulls surrounded her, welcoming her. It was as if they were forming a circle to protect her. Meg felt a surge of hope, feeling she'd arrived at a place where she would be safe and protected.

Meg heard Nicholas calling and turned in his direction, the seagulls seemingly holding their ground as if ready for battle. Meg opened her arms in a welcoming manner. Nicholas moved toward her, and they embraced; it was only then that the birds began to drift away slowly, as if waiting to be convinced Meg was indeed safe. As the couple held hands on the sandy beach, with the sound of waves washing ashore, the serenade of the sea, the last of the flock flew away.

"Oh, Nicholas, did you see the seagulls? They were amazing. I can't believe how many there were. It's as if they were welcoming me, speaking to me, and protecting me. They made me feel like this is the place I should be, a place to be happy, a place where I belong."

"It was indeed a sight. From the top of the stairs watching, it appeared as if you were a part of them. It was mystical to experience; you seemed to be one of the flock, but the prettiest seagull of them all," said Nicholas as he embraced her. When he released her he said, "I love you."

"I love you, too," responded Meg as they strolled hand in hand along the beach, lost in all its wonder and mystery. Meg was shadowed by the watchful eyes of a lone seagull during their walk. She would later recall the presence of a guardian gull always close by, always vigilant during the remainder of her time on Cape Cod.

It wasn't long before they were back in the Beetle, continuing their trip, driving along Route 6 heading into Wellfleet. When Meg saw signs for wildlife or a scenic viewing area, she would follow the directions and take the time to admire the view, looking for birds and other creatures. They saw ospreys nesting, red-tailed hawks soaring, and numerous small, colorful birds. They were fascinated by it all.

Back on the road, with the ever-present sound of music, Nicholas suddenly said, "Meg, take this next right onto Cahoon Hollow Road."

Meg negotiated the turn and asked, "Did I miss something, Nicholas?"

"No, I'm not sure why I said to turn. I guess I just felt we should."

"That's why I love you, Nicholas. You told me you were a buccaneer when we first met, and you do have that spirit," said Meg as she smiled.

"I just hope I don't get us lost."

"You must have a sailor's sense for direction," said Meg with a laugh.

"I do, until we get lost."

"I trust your instincts; we've had a delightful time so far."

"Now who's the buccaneer?" asked Nicholas while laughing.

As they continued down the road, they came to a large body of water surrounded by native pines. Meg pulled into the small parking lot, and when they got out of the car, they saw a sign for Great Pond. The tree-lined pool was a large body of freshwater too shallow to be called a lake, but certainly big enough. Old wooden steps led down to a narrow strip of sandy beach.

Meg and Nicholas walked down the cranky stairs, took off their shoes, and enjoyed the rush of cold water as they stepped in ankle deep. The day was warm, and Nicholas couldn't resist a plunge into the clear, refreshing water. Still wearing his gym shorts, he dove underwater as Meg watched and waited for him to surface. She counted the seconds, and two minutes later Nicholas suddenly burst through the water with a smile on his face as he shouted, "Meg, it's fantastic, you can see the bottom of the pond as if you're looking through a glass."

Meg stood smiling and laughing as Nicholas began to swim back toward shore. He was keeping his head above water; he wanted to take in her beauty. Meg was standing in the shallow water just above her ankles, the sun shining on her. She was waving to him and smiling. She then brought her hands up, cupped her face, held the pose, and continued to smile.

When Nicholas saw her stance, his mind flashed, and he had an image fixed in front of him. He broke his stroke, started to tread water, and looked closely at Meg. He was stunned by how she appeared. In a flash, he returned to the summer of 1957, but when he blinked, the vision was gone. Meg was again waving and smiling. Nicholas swam to shore, increasing his strokes. He had something to tell her.

As he stood in the shallow water, he reached out and held both of Meg's hands. He faced her, and with excitement ringing in his voice, he spoke quickly. "I remember this place, I came here with my parents. My mom was standing right where you were, her hands to her face like you had them. She was smiling and then waving. I was in the water with my dad. He was swimming with me on his back. I was excited to be out in the deep part of the pond with him. I was waving to my mom, and she was waving back. The pose! I remember clearly. The sun on your face, the way you held your hands, it framed your smile. I thought you were my mom, the posture, your height, your presence."

"Oh, Nicholas, that's wonderful. You must be happy to have these memories come back to you," responded Meg as she reached up, wrapped her arms around his neck, and hugged his wet body.

Nicholas was suddenly chilled. He wasn't sure if it was the burst of a breeze or the remembrance, but he needed to get out of his wet shorts. They walked back up to the car, and Meg waited by the stairs to stand watch as Nicholas returned to the water's edge to dry off and change his clothes.

Feeling refreshed, they were once again back in the car and heading to Highland Road in Truro. When they came to the intersection of Route 6 and South Highland Road, they took the right turn off the Mid-Cape Highway and continued on their adventure. As they drove down the narrow two-lane road, they came upon the grounds of the Highland Lighthouse and decided to stop.

After parking the car, they walked by the small nine-hole links golf course that shared the scenic area with the proud old lighthouse. They enjoyed the thrill of entering the tower and taking the sixty-nine steps as they spiraled to the top. Gazing through the narrow windows, they viewed the majesty of nature: the landscape of pines, heath, Scotch broom, and the seemingly infinite blueness of the ocean.

Meg and Nicholas lingered, not wanting to leave. They held each other's hand, kissed, and whispered, "I love you." A slight breeze swept between them, and for briefest moment they felt as if they were two different people transposed back in time.

As they strolled toward the car, Meg remembered the food Maggie had prepared for them. It was well past lunchtime, and they were hungry. Eating on the beach would be pleasant, and on a map at the keeper's house next to the lighthouse, Nicholas located one just down the road. Meg drove the VW back onto South Highland Road and continued toward the soft sand of Cape Cod.

It didn't take long before they reached the end of the asphalt, and arrived at Highland Beach. The few parking places available were completely empty. They were thrilled to eat their lunch alone with a view of the Atlantic Ocean and a light, cool breeze off the water.

Meg carried their lunch and Nicholas the blanket as they walked toward the water and onto the sand. They noticed a spot next to a high sand dune that looked perfect. They took the narrow path through patches of withered grass to reach the soft sand where Nicholas spread the familiar checkered blanket.

"Thank you for inviting me to come to Cape Cod with you to watch the sunset and remember my mom. It's hard to believe it's Wednesday already, our third day. It feels as if we've known each other forever," said Nicholas.

"I've had such a lovely time. I've not had this much enjoyment since maybe I was a little girl."

"I would've liked to know you when we were children."

"I would have liked that, too, but there is a reason for everything. I would like to think it's all God's design."

"What do you think God was planning when you called me Nicholas the very first day we met?"

"When you look at the time we've spent together, it's been such a blessing for me. All the happiness, love, and memories. It's exactly what I was looking for and never would have thought possible when I'd first drove to Holy Trinity. My expectation was to walk the campus and experience in my own way what being a student could be like."

"Why didn't you go to Holy Trinity?" asked Nicholas.

Meg had to think before she spoke. She now realized she'd earlier said more than she planned. She'd let slip the comment about the seagulls protecting her, but Nicholas hadn't picked up on it. She felt guilty about not being honest with him; she knew it was wrong, but she couldn't help it. She desperately needed his love and the memory of it. The life she would return to had none of the kindness and love she'd received from Nicholas. He didn't know how much he was helping her. Meg would later recall Nicholas when she needed to. She would think only of him when she let her mind and body go numb to the brutality and violence that was waiting for her when she returned home.

Nicholas's mom had died from a cancer so vile it destroyed her body, and Meg's cancer was a human being doing the same thing to her. The two beautiful, loving women were linked by evil so deadly there was little hope of survival.

Meg wouldn't lie, she just wouldn't tell the whole story. She said, "My father had his heart attack, and my parents decided it was best for me to remain at home and not go to school so far away."

"You'd have loved the college, but in a way, I'm glad you didn't come. You would've been an excellent student and popular, and we wouldn't be sitting on the beach right now. You would not be getting this kiss from the boy sitting next to you who loves you," said Nicholas as he leaned forward and let his lips enjoy the warm softness of Meg's sweet lips.

Meg returned the affection with a big hug and another kiss that reached deep into their hearts. Not wanting to have to explain anything else, Meg said, "I think it's time we go deliver Maggie's muffins to Jeanne."

30

he yellow Volkswagen drove slowly down Highland Road in Truro looking for the home of Maggie's friend Jeanne. The day had slipped away, and it was late in the afternoon. Meg and Nicholas wanted to finish their errand after spending a breathtaking day exploring Cape Cod. Their ride back to Holy Trinity would be a long one, and while they never wanted to leave, they knew it was time.

The couple located the house on their second pass down the lightly traveled road. Jeanne's home was a ranch-style dwelling, tucked away neatly behind a row of high hedges. They could see a small cottage about thirty feet beyond the ranch. Meg turned her car into the driveway and parked. She then walked with Nicholas to the front door and knocked. They waited for several minutes and, when there was no answer, decided to explore the property and look for Jeanne.

The house was quaint and well maintained, with window boxes filled with small delicate flowers of red, yellow, and white. In the rear of the house was an enclosed stall for the outdoor shower. The cottage behind the house was similar to the small beach house that Maggie and Gall rented. They could see, off to the side of the cottage, an open area with a scattering of grass, small greenish shrubs, and large groupings of wildflowers. In a small gap through the shrubs, there was a walking path leading into the scrub pines. It seemed as if a forest of varying shades of green had corralled the rear of the property.

Seeing all the wildflowers, Meg said, "Look at the flowers, the yellow, pink, and violet." She had a smile on her face and the same excitement she'd always shown when viewing the simple beauty of nature, she loved.

"They're all very colorful," said Nicholas, as he handed her a small, white starflower and continued speaking. "I wish I could have found a yellow rose for you."

"Thank you. It's lovely and so delicate," said Meg as she gave him a soft kiss on his lips.

Their exploring was interrupted when a tall, slender woman with wavy reddish hair approached from behind and called out, "Meg, Nicholas?"

As they turned around, Meg and Nicholas were met by a welcoming smile as the woman said, "Good afternoon," and before she could say her name, she stopped speaking, and looked intently at Nicholas. Staring, Jeanne was recognizing Andrew Avellino, Nicholas's father, as a nineteen-year-old about to marry Peggy, her childhood friend. She was struck by the face, the resemblance, the same lean, strong body. If Maggie hadn't told her his name, she might have run toward him, and hugged and kissed her old friend as if it were 1957.

Composing herself, she continued speaking and said, "I'm Jeanne. You must be Meg and Nicholas, friends of Maggie and Gall. They spoke as if you've known each other for years, instead of two sleeping teenagers Gall found on the beach a couple of days ago. You certainly made a very good impression on them. Maggie said she wanted to adopt you two."

"Jeanne, it's very nice to meet you. We loved spending time with them. They are truly a very generous and welcoming couple," said Meg.

"Nice to meet you, too. We did have a great time with Maggie and Gall," said Nicholas.

Jeanne then walked over and hugged Nicholas, to his and Meg's surprise. She then said, "You don't remember me, but I made your acquaintance a very long time ago."

Nicholas looked at Jeanne as he tried to recall her. "I apologize. I don't remember meeting you."

"I'm sure as a five-year-old boy visiting Cape Cod for the first time, you only remember the fun things and not one of your mom and dad's old friends."

"You were friends? You knew my parents?" asked Nicholas with astonishment in his voice.

"We were very good friends. Your mom and I grew up together, and I met your dad when they were dating. The last time I saw the two together was in the summer of 1957. When your mom passed, I went to the funeral, and that was the last time I saw your dad. I'm so sorry about your mom. We were very close, and I miss her dearly. Your dad was greatly affected by the loss. How's he doing?"

"Thank you for your condolences. My dad's doing fine. He does miss my mom. He seems sad all the time."

"I can understand his sadness. He was at his best when they were together. They loved life very much and were always doing fun things. They were two city kids, but they loved the outdoors, hiking, swimming, or just going to a park to enjoy the day. Both of your parents were so loving and caring. I'm sure you have all their finest qualities."

"Thank you. I'd love to hear more about my parents. If it's okay with Meg, I'd like to stay for a little while."

"Well, let's not worry about that now, I'm sure you have enough time for supper. Then you can decide when you need to leave."

"We could drive back later if you like, Nicholas. It would be nice for you to learn more about your mom."

"Thank you, I really would like that."

"Well, that settles it, we'll have a nice meal. Francis will be home shortly, and you can meet him. We can talk further, and I can get to know this pretty young girl you found for yourself."

"Actually, Meg found me walking on campus."

"Is that so? Well, I recall your mom found your dad, too. They'd always joked about how he was walking with friends and heard someone calling out his name. When he turned, there stood Peggy, he said, and she was the prettiest woman he'd ever seen. Peggy always claimed she hadn't called for him. I knew she did, though; your mom wasn't shy. It was something she had the confidence to do, especially if she liked a boy."

"Nicholas's mom must have been an incredible woman," said Meg.

"She was and so happy, loving, and a great mom. Peggy was brave and so strong when she became ill. You knew she was suffering, but you could never tell by looking at her. Her death came very quickly; it was all so sad."

Meg's and Nicholas's eyes became moist as Jeanne spoke. He was hearing for the first time just how fast cancer took his mom's life. His dad had never talked about her death or the way she'd died. Nicholas knew it had been cancer, but it was something they never discussed.

"Why don't I show you around the place, and then I'll leave you two alone while I prepare something for dinner."

Meg and Nicholas asked if they could help with anything. Jeanne said she appreciated the offer but didn't need help. She pointed out the path between the pines and suggested they take a short walk after she gave them a tour to get acquainted with the property.

Nicholas went to get the muffins from the car and walked into the house with Jeanne and Meg. The home was cozy with a living room, a large kitchen, and a sunroom that served as a dining area. Located at one end of the house was a large bedroom with a bathroom. A second bedroom was used as a study and furnished with a set of oak desks and shelves full of books. The main bathroom was located in the hallway off the kitchen leading to the rear door.

Jeanne said they would eat in the sunroom with the windows open because it was such a pleasant evening. She offered them the choice to sit in the living room and relax or take a walk through the woods. She told them the trail was easy to follow, and if they continued, would eventually take them to the ocean. Meg and Nicholas decided to go for a short walk before cleaning up for dinner. They wanted to find a quiet place to talk and discuss what Jeanne had said about Nicholas's parents.

The young couple left the house holding hands and strolled toward the path until they reached the opening through the trees. They stopped abruptly and watched a large family of wild turkeys casually walk in front of them. The largest of the group stood staring back, as if to say, you're trespassing on my property. They laughed at the boldness of the birds and gave them time to pass by before starting on the trail.

About forty yards in, they came to a well-maintained grassy area. Before them were two green Adirondack chairs, a granite garden bench, several bird feeders and small, colorful bird houses, and a birdbath. There was also a three-foot statue of Our Lady of Perpetual Help. An assortment of flowers decorated the base of the stone figurine. The place was sunny and secluded. It was quiet and appeared to be a private sanctuary for praying, reading, or discreet talking. Meg and Nicholas sat down on the smooth surface of the stone bench, admiring the interesting little habitat.

Meg said, "What a splendid setting. I could bring my book and sit here all day."

"Do you think it belongs to Jeanne? I wonder why she didn't mention it."

"I'm not sure if it belongs to Jeanne. Maybe she didn't tell us because it's a pleasant surprise to come across while on a walk."

"I agree. It's a lovely place."

"The statue of Our Lady of Perpetual Help is beautiful with the colorful flowers all around it. It's an interesting choice for such a solitary place. People have prayed to her for centuries, seeking help and intercession for their difficulties. I don't imagine many people pass by this area. It must be a special place for Jeanne and Francis."

"I know how many times the nuns made me pray to Our Lady of Perpetual Help, and it certainly felt like centuries kneeling on hardwood floors."

Meg laughed and said, "I would love to know more about Jeanne. She seems very interesting, but we don't have much time. I think with her being close to your mom and dad, you really should try to learn more about them."

"It's funny how some things are coming back to me, but with Jeanne, I'm drawing a blank. How different life would have been if my mom had lived. My dad would be happy and fun loving. It's hard to imagine because he's been sad for as long as I can remember."

"It's hard to recover from the loss of someone you truly love. I was frightened when my dad had his heart attack, the thought of losing him and the sadness I'd felt."

"I couldn't imagine being my dad or being without him. The shock and sadness of losing the woman you love, your wife, the mother of your only child. I know he felt helpless not being able to protect my mom from the evil that entered her body. I would feel the same way, and I would rather it had been me that died."

"It must be very hard to be left all alone."

"But he wasn't alone; he had me."

"I'm sorry, Nicholas, I didn't mean that. I was only thinking of your mom."

"I know you were; it's just my dad couldn't see that."

"I'm sorry he couldn't. You and your dad deserved to be happy. A child to love should be enough to sustain you and give you hope."

"I don't blame him. I think I know how he feels."

"I know you don't blame your father. My mom changed so much after she was hospitalized. Sometimes she seems cold and distant, but I know it's not really her. There are times when she hugs me, and I feel her strength as if she is trying to speak to me and tell me her sorrow. I could never fault my mother when her illness is to blame. I will always love my mom just as you will always love your dad," said Meg as they turned to embrace and felt the firming of their love.

31

*F*rancis was home when Meg and Nicholas returned from their walk. He was tall and slender with light olive skin inherited from his Assisi ancestors. His black hair and beard were neatly trimmed, and his warm brown eyes were shielded behind tinted glasses. He was dressed in tan bell-bottoms, a white button-down shirt, and a brown corduroy sport jacket with patches on the elbows. He had the distinguished look of a college professor.

They sat in the living room, getting to know each other, until it was time to eat. Francis told them about his position teaching history at Cape Cod Community College. He said he commuted forty-three miles to work and didn't mind the drive. He loved teaching, his students, and Truro. The long ride was just the cost of loving where you work, what you do, and where you live.

Once they sat down at the table, Jeanne asked, "How did you enjoy your walk along the trail?"

Meg looked at Nicholas before responding. She wanted him to have the opportunity to talk about his mom and dad.

She could see he was deferring to her to answer, so she said, "We had an enjoyable walk and came upon the most peaceful setting in the woods. It was such a beautiful place."

"We enjoyed our time there; I wish we could have stayed longer," said Nicholas.

"Or brought a book," said Meg.

"I'm glad you enjoyed our little nature reserve. It's a special place where we appreciate the solitude. Francis loves the small animals and the many native birds that we've observed while spending time there. When we have guests they, too, find the peace and bits of nature it offers comforting," said Jeanne.

"When we first purchased the house nearly twenty years ago, Jeanne wanted a guesthouse and an area in the woods where we could sit and enjoy the outdoors. As a bird-watcher, it gives me great pleasure to sit quietly and enjoy the sight of the small local birds such as cardinals, blue jays, or hummingbirds grazing at one of our feeders. When we do spend time there, it's as if we're in a different place and not just our backyard, where oftentimes you can hear the traffic, especially during the summer months," said Francis.

"That's wonderful. I too love nature and spending time outdoors," said Meg.

"I'm glad you had the opportunity to experience our private reserve," responded Jeanne.

"Do you have neighbors in the cottage behind your house?" asked Nicholas.

"No, the cottage is usually occupied with guests. Rarely is it ever vacant, so we don't rent it out," said Jeanne.

"You must do plenty of entertaining," said Nicholas.

"In a way, but it's mostly for the work Jeanne does," responded Francis.

"You must be very busy," said Meg.

"In some ways, I am, and in others, not enough," responded Jeanne.

"How so?" asked Meg.

Jeanne considered her response. She hadn't expected to see Nicholas Avellino and she had so much to tell him about his parents. Maggie had called her about Meg, and she wanted time to speak with her about the bruises and scars. Jeanne needed time to build trust with her. She knew from experience it was the only way Meg would confide in her.

Jeanne wanted to share with Meg and Nicholas some of the work she'd done helping women who were battered and abused. Instead, she thought it best to speak generally until she had the opportunity to talk with Meg privately. She decided to start by telling them about herself, and hoped Meg and Nicholas had time to spend a day or two as her guests. Jeanne felt knowing her background could make it easier for Meg to confide in her.

"To fully understand my work, and to some extent Nicholas's parents, I need to tell you about my background."

Meg felt a strong, unexplained urge to know more about Jeanne and said, "Yes, thank you." She then looked at Nicholas and said, "Is that okay?"

"We'd like that, thank you." responded Nicholas as he smiled at Meg.

Jeanne began her story. When she'd been a little girl growing up, her two best friends were Peggy and Francis. They lived near each other and went to the same parochial school. Once in high school, she and Francis started dating, and by their senior year, they'd fallen in love. Jeanne had also felt a calling to become a Catholic nun. She would speak with the sisters about her desire, visit convents, and attend religious retreats. She was doing all the things that were recommended when considering the commitment required to join a religious community.

Jeanne had been conflicted; she had two loves: Francis and the church. Her decision was not easy. Francis had been sensitive to her situation, and he'd spoken with her about it. They'd agreed dating would need to stop, so Jeanne could be sure her decision would be the right one. Jeanne found a mentor who would pray with her, guide her, and who introduced her to a religious community.

By September, Francis was away at college, and Jeanne had made a firm decision to become a Catholic nun. She started the formal process and over five years moved through the required steps. She went through them all, starting with Aspirancy, followed by Postulancy, Novitiate, First Vow, and then her Final Vow.

A year later, Jeanne was working in the community when doubt set in. In the short time, she'd spent as a sister, Jeanne was helping victims of spousal abuse. She was also working with people who loved their faith but were alienated from the church. This was a troubling reality for her. These were good people who wanted to receive communion and not be judged as sinners because of who they loved. Jeanne also began to have recurring thoughts of Francis.

On a sunny spring morning, Jeanne went for a walk at a local park. She wanted time alone to reflect on her changing views and examine her feelings for Francis. More and more he was in her thoughts, and she'd started to yearn for a loving relationship with him.

As Jeanne strolled about the park that day, she saw families with their children and couples enjoying themselves. She imagined Francis at her side, holding her hand and kissing her like he had in high school. She also thought about those who were abused and the people who had a desire to participate in the entire Mass but were not allowed.

It was nearly a week after her morning walk when Jeanne decided the only way to satisfy her love for her faith, her work, and Francis was to resign. She would always love and practice her beliefs and serve those who felt alienated from the church. She would always love Francis, and she hoped he still loved her.

When Francis learned of Jeanne's decision, he immediately asked her to marry him. He had always loved her, and he'd hoped someday they would be together. Jeanne said yes, and they had been married for over twenty years. After the wedding they moved to Truro, where Jeanne started working with victims of abuse. She also started meeting people who had been excluded from receiving all the sacraments of the Catholic faith, or who had chosen to live in conflict with the church.

Jeanne paused in her story, reflecting on the last twenty years and the people she'd served. She also thought of the love these good people have in their hearts.

"When Jeanne left the convent, I was very sad for her. She had always spoken of being a nun and I knew how difficult of a decision it was for her to leave the convent. I fell in love with Jeanne as a little boy in elementary school and never stopped loving her. After six years she came back to me, and I love her more every day," said Francis.

Meg and Nicholas took in all that Jeanne revealed. They'd both grown up believing the church was infallible and that you didn't question the doctrine. They each had so many questions, but they weren't sure where to begin or how to ask them. They knew the importance of keeping a vow; on that the Bible was clear.

"Leaving the convent, and your vow . . ." Meg couldn't finish the sentence. She wanted to ask Jeanne about making a vow to God and not keeping it. But she stopped herself; it seemed too personal a question.

"I struggled with my decision, and prayed for guidance. In the end, I let my conscience guide me. My love for Francis would not allow me to remain a nun. Seeing those who love excluded from the church conflicted with my personal beliefs. There are more references in the Bible compelling us to love than there are to keep a vow. Both are sacred commitments, and in my final judgment, it will be known that I broke a vow, but I also loved very deeply," responded Jeanne.

Listening, Meg would have liked to discuss her marriage and the vow she'd promised to fulfill. She wanted to ask Jeanne for guidance, but she couldn't. She would never risk Nicholas finding out about Lewis. He could never know about the abuse and the assaults. Meg knew she would be judged for her deception and the consequences of her behavior; it was a price she was willing to pay.

"I would rather love and be judged for love. I've watched my father suffer the loss of my mom, the woman he loved. I know he loves me, but it's a sad love. He lost his will to show his love when my mom died," said Nicholas.

Meg became teary eyed as Nicholas talked about his dad. She spoke through her tears and said, "I was taught to be obedient. We weren't allowed to question our teachings. We did what we were told and believed what we were told. Listening now, it's so confusing."

"I didn't mean to upset either of you. You're two wonderful young adults. I would never try to persuade you to question your faith or the church doctrine. It would be wrong for me to do that. We all need to make our own decisions. Maggie told me how much you love each other. When I look at the two of you, I can't help thinking of Peggy and Andrew at your ages. I want to tell you about the goodness and love in their hearts. It was important that you understood something of my work to fully understand your parents," said Jeanne.

"I would love to know everything about my mom and dad, but I don't want to upset Meg," responded Nicholas.

"I want Nicholas to know everything about his mom and dad. He deserves to know. I'm sad about his mom's death, and his father's loss. And I love Nicholas so much. I only wished Mar, oh, never mind." Meg nearly said that she only wished Margaret had questioned her mother and her obedience to her. She had desperately wanted to talk with her father, but with his heart attack and slow recovery, she couldn't. Then when she'd fallen in love with Lewis, there was no reason to bring up not attending college and upsetting her father.

After a pause, Meg said, "Would you please continue."

"Thank you, Meg. In my work, I try to help those who need help. I sometimes offer spiritual guidance to those who ask, but I don't impose my faith; that would be disrespectful. Mostly I work with those who have suffered from abuse."

"My mom and dad knew all this about you?" ask Nicholas.

"Very much so. They came to me for help, not for themselves, but for a very dear friend. It's a longer story, and one that should wait for tomorrow. It's getting late, and we haven't even left the table, I do apologize. If you can stay the night, I would love to have you as our guests," said Jeanne.

Meg had tensed when Jeanne first mentioned spousal abuse but relaxed when she quickly moved away from the topic. When she later heard Jeanne say, "Those who have suffered from abuse," she could feel her anxiety rising. She wasn't sure what Jeanne would say next. She was relieved when Jeanne said it was getting late and they could continue talking tomorrow.

Meg felt the need to hear more of what Jeanne had to say, so she said, "I would like to stay and hear more as long as Nicholas agrees."

"Thanks, Meg. Yes, we'd like to be your guests, thank you," said Nicholas.

"Jeanne, if you want to get Meg and Nicholas settled in the guesthouse, I'll clean up in here," said Francis.

"Thank you, Francis," said Jeanne as they all stood up from the table.

Jeanne waited for Meg and Nicholas to get their bags from the car and then walked them over to the cottage. They were given separate bedrooms and shown the bathroom. Jeanne gave them a choice to use, either the inside shower or the outside one. While they were unpacking their bags, she told them she would be right back with extra blankets.

When she returned, Nicholas was in his room with the door partly opened. Jeanne knocked, and when she handed him the blanket, Nicholas said, "Thank you. May I please ask you a question about your work?"

"Of course, you may."

"When you said you work with those who suffer from abuse, what did you mean?"

"Mostly my work involves women who have been physically and emotionally abused by their husband, and sometimes a boyfriend, or another family member. I try to get them the help and support they need and a safe place to live. We wanted this cottage where you're staying to be a temporary home until we could find them something more permanent."

"Thank you. It's nice to know my mom had good friends like you and Francis."

"Thank you. I loved your mom. She was a lovely person and a special friend. I have much more to tell you tomorrow. Good night."

"Good night," replied Nicholas.

When she left, she shut the door. Meg's door was closed, so Jeanne knocked. It took Meg several minutes to open the door as she hurried to conceal the bruises Maggie had seen on her body. When she did open it, she apologized for taking so long.

Jeanne asked if she could help spread the extra blanket over the bed. Meg said yes, and as they laid it over the mattress, Jeanne said, "Maggie tells me you like to get up early and love to go out for a walk in the morning. She also said you always find the most interesting things."

"I do, yes. I teased Gall about it after he found us sleeping on the beach. I love the early morning coolness, waiting for the sun to come up. It's always peaceful, and I just love being outdoors."

"I'm also an early riser, and I'd love to go for a walk with you in the morning. I don't want to intrude on your private time; it's just that I do love the company."

"Oh, I don't mind. I think it would be fun. I don't have many friends or at least, well, they've mostly gone away to college, and I find myself alone so often. I do get lonely."

Listening to Meg was breaking Jeanne's heart. Meg was such a young, vibrant girl and so isolated. Jeanne knew all the signs. Maggie had spoken with her about the bruises and welts. She knew Meg was abused and forced to conceal her physical and emotional pain. Jeanne wanted so badly to help Meg, but she couldn't push. She had to be patient, build trust, and gain her confidence. She felt maybe then she could help her, but she knew that often it wasn't enough. The fear, retaliation, lack of a safe place to go, and having little money were real barriers that kept so many in violent relationships.

Jeanne was grateful they would talk more in the morning. Always hopeful she'd be able to help, she said, "Thank you. I will look forward to the morning. Just come into the kitchen when you get up. I'll be waiting for you."

Once Jeanne left, Meg put on her pajamas and Holy Trinity sweatshirt, and then walked across the hall. When she knocked, Nicholas opened the door. Meg laughed and kissed him when she saw the blanket already on the floor. The window shade was up and the sky dark. They would watch another imaginary sunset together on Cape Cod.

As they sat on the blanket, they could feel the warmth of their bodies touching. The physical connection was comforting; it was a feeling that had been building since they'd first met. Neither wanted to lose the affection, and both couldn't help thinking time was running out.

"I like Jeanne and Francis very much. Imagine Francis had waited all that time for the woman he loved. It's such a happy story," said Meg.

"I like them, too. They really love each other. I was concerned Jeanne was upsetting you."

"No, I was emotional thinking of your mom and dad, and the pain you felt when she died. It all makes me sad. Jeanne is a good and caring person, but she was a nun and took a vow. I don't understand it. You're told the rules, and you try to follow them. When you break them, you're bad and you get punished. Jeanne broke her vow, but she's good and caring and loving. How could that make her bad?"

"I know it's complicated. Young adults really started questioning and challenging their faith and authority when we were in grammar school. We sort of missed all that, but even in my freshman class, there are students whose values and beliefs conflict with Holy Trinity and the church," said Nicholas.

"I've always loved my faith and the values it teaches us to live by. It just—it gets so hard to stay committed when sometimes everything gets so confusing. Things happen and you question your beliefs."

Meg, you are the kindest, sweetest, most loving person I know. We all have doubts. You just try to be your best."

"That's just it; I always did my best." Meg's tears began to flow.

Nicholas, not knowing the depth of Meg's pain, said, "It's strange. I always tried to be the best in football, and now I have no love for football. When I was younger, I never tried in school, and now I want to be the best student I can and football gets in the way of achieving that."

"When my mother told me, I couldn't go away to college, it broke my heart. I love my parents and felt obligated to obey them. Now, I'm just not sure," said Meg.

Nicholas held her closer and said, "I love you. I know we've only known each other such a short time, but every day together seems like a year. I have friends I grew up with that know nothing about me. You know everything."

Meg cried a little harder. She was feeling the pain of guilt. Nicholas could never know everything about her. Meg through her tears whispered, "I love you."

Nicholas kissed the tears from her cheeks, and then softly pressed his lips against hers. They held each other closer, as if trying to merge two broken hearts into one big, strong, healthy loving heart that would guarantee their happiness. It was getting late, and they were both tired. They fought off the fatigue, trying to stay awake, not wanting the day to end and not knowing if tomorrow would be their last together.

32

*M*eg was the first to wake and sat quietly watching Nicholas. She loved him and wanted to tell him everything about her past. She never wanted to leave him, and if she could, she would spend all the days of her life with him. Meg wanted to tell Nicholas about her marriage and the violence, to show him her scars, and let his love comfort her. She knew he would accept her, protect her, and keep her safe. Her only hope was that somehow fate would show her the way.

Thinking these thoughts, she quietly stood and went to her room. She changed out of her pajamas. She kept her Holy Trinity sweatshirt on and dressed for her walk with Jeanne. Meg could see the light in the kitchen when she knocked on the door. Francis had early classes, and he was just leaving the house on his way to work. He kissed Jeanne, and then told Meg to enjoy her day.

Jeanne asked Meg if she wanted something to eat or drink before their walk. Meg said she was fine, and the two women headed out the door. Outside, the moon was full and the early morning gray made it light enough to see but made the presence of company welcomed.

As they walked along the path, Jeanne led the way, and the two remained silent until they reached the open, grassy reserve among the pines. They stopped, and Meg commented on how peaceful it looked in the morning. Jeanne said it was one of her favorite places to spend time. She then asked Meg if she would like to walk to the beach and watch the sunrise. Meg was overjoyed by the suggestion, and they resumed their hike through the pines.

As Meg followed behind Jeanne, she had her eyes focused toward the ground adjacent to the path. She was looking for a keepsake to show Nicholas. It wasn't long before she noticed two brown cones hanging from the branch of a pitch pine that appeared to be stuck together. Meg stopped momentarily to examine them, and discovered they were connected along the sides. When she pulled them from the low hanging branch, she could see that they formed the shape of a heart. She immediately thought of Nicholas's smile, and was excited to show him her treasure.

Meg quickly caught up to Jeanne, and they continued walking along the single lane path. When they reached the asphalt, they crossed Coast Guard Road. They located the narrow foot-stamped trail through the wind-worn shrubs that led to the soft sand of the beach. There they were met by the always-present and welcoming seagulls. They alerted Meg to their presence with their familiar screech. Meg smiled and waved to her old friends. She looked out over the water and saw a family of seals swimming. They were moving slowly, parallel to the shore, their heads bobbing, occasionally submerging, as they searched the cold blue waters of the Atlantic for their morning feed.

Meg commented on how beautiful nature could be.

"Would you like to sit for a bit? The sun should be peaking at us shortly," said Jeanne.

"That would be lovely."

As they sat on the sand, Jeanne said, "I hope I didn't cause you to be uncomfortable last evening when I was discussing my past."

"No, it was confusing, but I think you're wonderful, and you and Francis seem to be deeply in love."

"We, I, never stopped loving him. I hid it for a while. When I felt it again, I knew we had to be together. Francis was waiting all that time, hoping I would return to him. He never pressured me or made me feel guilty. He accepted my decision to be a nun even though it hurt him."

"He does truly love you."

"Yes, and I love him." Jeanne paused before continuing, then said, "I felt that speaking of my past, as a nun, would be reassuring to you and Nicholas. I wanted you to understand that part of me is still a nun, and part of me is a loving wife. I know it sounds confusing, but for me it's natural, and helpful in my work."

"I do understand. It's just the vow. What I mean to say is, a vow is something you keep."

"Oh, Meg, sweetheart, I wish that were so. It seems easy when you read it in a book. People, circumstances, and situations change, and bad decisions are made. There's conflict to be sure. How do you stay true to your vow when the agreement that binds changes?"

"I don't know. I used to pray every day, go to confession, and attend Mass. I would ask for guidance when I was troubled, and my prayers were always for those in need of God's help. Then I stopped praying; I lost my will to pray. Now I want to pray but only for myself. I feel so selfish. I no longer pray."

"When I was speaking of my work, I tried to be vague. I didn't want to make you feel uncomfortable. I thought it best to wait until we could speak in private."

Meg began to tense up. She wasn't sure what Jeanne would say, or if somehow, she'd seen the bruises on her body. Jeanne could see her reaction; she needed to reassure Meg.

"Do you trust Maggie?" asked Jeanne.

"Yes, very much. She's a lovely person."

"Maggie knows me from church but also from my work. She and Gall have opened their house for me when I needed them. They're very gracious and generous. When I was a nun, the work I did was with women who were abused, physically abused."

Jeanne had to stop speaking as Meg began to cry. Meg turned to face her, and the sadness was heartbreaking. Jeanne hugged her and held her close. The firmer Jeanne's hold, the greater the tears. She could feel Meg's small body shaking, as if trying to loosen all of the pain that had been crushing her. Jeanne held her arms around Meg until the last tear flowed.

When Meg stopped crying she said, "I'm sorry."

Jeanne held back her own tears and said, "Meg, you never have to say you're sorry. You did nothing wrong."

"I don't know why I always cry."

"When you're in pain, it's all right to cry. You need to cry."

"No, it's not all right to cry. I was bad for crying."

"Meg, I want to help you. I can help you. I know you trust Maggie, and I trust her, too. She confided in me. I know about the bruises on your body. If you let me, I will help you."

"I'm so ashamed; I know I could be better."

"You're a good person, Meg. You're loving and kind, and I see how much you care for Nicholas. You're also strong and brave. You carry the bruises and scars from the violence you suffered, but all you think about is helping Nicholas learn about his mom and helping him to overcome his pain and sorrow."

"I love Nicholas."

"I know you do, and I can see he loves you, too. I want you to believe, just as you are trying to help him, I will help you."

"I don't know what to do."

"If you let me, I will help you."

"I don't know. I'm so scared."

"It's scary, Meg, I would never say it's not. You're not alone. All the women I help are scared. Many are still scared; for some, they will always be afraid. So many live with fear and the threat of fear, but for some, their lives are changing, most often slowly but changing. There is hope."

"You're such a caring person. I've met the two most wonderful women, you and Maggie. I know you want to help me, I'm just not sure you can."

"I want you to think about it. You don't have to decide now, but I would like you to please think about it."

"You won't tell Nicholas, will you?"

"Meg, I promise you, I will never speak to Nicholas about what we've discussed. You'll always have my full confidence."

"We missed the sunrise," said Meg as she tried to smile.

"Would you like to go back to the house?"

"Yes, I want to wash my face before I see Nicholas. I'm hoping he's still asleep. I love to wake him and sing to him and tell him to wake up smiling."

"Meg, you are an amazing young woman—you truly are. You deserve to be loved; we all deserve to be loved, just as the Lord commands in the Bible.

33

*M*eg was shaken by her conversation with Jeanne. Having to recall Lewis with all his hate and violence was upsetting. She blamed herself for letting Maggie see her bruises. Now Jeanne also knew about her scars. Meg felt Jeanne's sincerity. She could see she was a good person who wanted to help. Meg just couldn't see a life free of Lewis's grip. His clutch had loosened by the love of Nicholas, the distance created by driving to Holy Trinity, and the time she had been away from him. Meg wanted to believe it was enough to protect her. But she had started to feel that every day spent in the loving arms of Nicholas was no longer freeing her. She now began to feel the squeeze of Lewis's powerful hand starting to pull her back. She just didn't know if the love she shared with Nicholas was strong enough to resist Lewis's evil.

When Meg returned to the cottage after her walk with Jeanne, she needed time to wash her face and settle her emotions, but she needed to hurry. Nicholas would be waking soon. She didn't want to miss singing to him when he woke up. When she thought she was ready, she quietly entered his bedroom.

Meg sat on the floor watching Nicholas, staring at his face. She gently touched his cheek and felt the warmth. He looked so peaceful. She thought, *How comforting it would be lying next to you, feeling your strength and gentleness, every day of my life. The love I would feel, and the love I would give to you, sweet Nicholas.*

Nicholas moved, and it broke her concentration. He began to stir but remained asleep. Meg didn't want to wake him just yet, she wanted to keep watching him. She whispered, *I love you.* Meg imagined Nicholas's smile, and his words saying, *I love you, too.* She made herself feel his embrace. Her thoughts were saying, *Tighter, hold me tighter.* In her mind, she was yelling, *Use all your strength and never let go of me.*

Meg finally felt calm, her anguish passing. She watched Nicholas's eyes flicker. They were opening; he sat up, gazed, and saw only love. Meg threw her arms around his neck and clutched him with all her strength. When she released her grip, she smiled, and with the voice of a one-hundred-and-five-pound girl said, "Now get up, and let's have a magnificent day."

Nicholas gave her a quick kiss, grabbed a change of clothes, and ran to the outdoor shower, while Meg readied herself in the bathroom. After Nicholas had dried off and dressed, he waited in his room with the door open. He could see Meg enter the hallway and thought how beautiful she was. She was wearing aqua-colored slacks and a pale-yellow top with three-quarter length sleeves. Her white cotton sweater hung over her shoulders. Nicholas quickly walked to Meg and they kissed.

He could see her happiness and said, "You must have had a very nice walk with Jeanne."

"I did; we had a splendid time. I found you a present walking along the path," said Meg. She showed Nicholas the two connected pinecones that formed a rough heart shape, and said, "It's for you. You won my heart, and I love you."

Nicholas let his imagination turn the pinecones into the shape of a Valentine heart and smiled when he thought he didn't need Cupid's arrow to fall in love with Meg. He then said, "Thank you for opening your heart to me. I'll always cherish your gift." He kissed her, and asked, "What else did you do with Jeanne?"

"She brought me all the way to the beach. My seagulls were waiting for me, and I saw a family of seals."

"Which did you adopt, the seagulls or the seals?" asked Nicholas as he smiled.

"It's almost mystical. I feel as if the seagulls have adopted me. I find their presence so comforting."

"I like to think my presence is comforting."

"Oh, it is when you finally wake up. I'm fortunate to have my seagulls watching over me while you are sound asleep and dreaming."

"I'm dreaming of you."

"They must be wonderful dreams. You sleep so soundly."

"I think it's the fresh sea air, and the peace I feel when you're around me. I've never slept better than I have these last few days. At school, I hardly ever sleep. I have to stay up late to study. In the morning, I'm up early for class or more studying. When you play a sport, you're always trying to catch up. If you want, you can wake me when you get up. I won't mind. I'll be with you."

"No, you should sleep. I love to watch you when you're dreaming. My early morning walks give me time alone and are peaceful. Most of all, I like to sing for you when you first wake up. Plus, I love the hug and kiss you give me to make me stop."

"I never want it to end, us together on Cape Cod."

"Neither do I, Nicholas," said Meg with sadness.

"I suppose it has to. We'll have to think about driving back to Holy Trinity today. I was wondering if we could take our time and enjoy our last day on Cape Cod."

"I would really like that. We'll have a splendid day. Jeanne said she wanted to talk to you about your mom and dad."

"Let's go speak with her and then plan our last day in paradise."

Nicholas clasped Meg's hand and held it as they walked to the kitchen to see Jeanne.

Meg and Nicholas entered the kitchen through the rear door. Jeanne was waiting, and they exchanged good mornings. The breakfast was already prepared, and Meg and Nicholas served themselves. Jeanne left them alone while they ate, saying she would return in about thirty minutes.

As Jeanne sat at her desk in her study, she couldn't help thinking about Meg and Nicholas. She saw Meg had already transformed into the happy, carefree young woman her exterior presented. She knew it was merely a façade peeling away. Jeanne could see the volatility of the fusion of Meg's emotions with her memory of the abuse she'd suffered. She knew Meg was struggling to contain her feelings. The mention of her work with abused women caused an eruption of the pain Meg had tried desperately to conceal.

Jeanne heard Meg's words; she'd listened to similar words many times. *I'm alone—so lonely—I no longer pray—I'm sorry—I'm so ashamed—It's not all right to cry—I was bad for crying—I'm so scared—I don't know what to do.* These were powerful words of pain, despair, isolation, and loss of hope. Jeanne felt powerless. She didn't believe she'd have enough time to reach Meg and give her the help she needed. Jeanne knew it was help that could save her from the violence that hurt her so badly.

Jeanne believed Meg's only hope was Nicholas. She thought to herself how it was remarkable that with all Meg's pain and sorrow and the physical abuse, she'd found a way to love. She could see the love was strong; Meg only thought about protecting Nicholas from his loneliness and sadness. Jeanne felt certain if Nicholas knew of Meg's abuse, he could reach her with his love and give her a path away from the violence. Jeanne would never tell him. That was a vow she would never break. She wished she could keep them together for another day or two, and just maybe Meg would confide in him.

Jeanne was struck by how quickly Meg and Nicholas had fallen in love. She also thought about how they'd met when Meg called out his name without knowing him. It had been mysteriously similar to the way Peggy had first met Andrew.

She thought about her impressions of Nicholas. She could see he was good, kind, and loving. She believed Meg felt safe with him. Jeanne knew she didn't know Nicholas well enough to assess his personality or his feelings. She couldn't help observing that when he was with Meg, he appeared happy and in love. She'd noticed last evening when she'd been speaking that he had been protective of Meg when she became emotional. She was convinced their love and affection for each other was real.

Jeanne liked Nicholas. She saw his father's compassion and his mother's sensitivity. But she felt there was something there that she couldn't quite grasp. Jeanne saw on the surface that he was happy and carefree. He made the same overt impression that Meg displayed. But she could detect a sadness about him that was subtle. She knew the loss of a mother, for a five-year-old, would have greatly affected him.

Jeanne had an odd feeling Meg and Nicholas knew something of their futures and they weren't happy ones. Jeanne shivered when she thought how similar it was to the aura of hopelessness and sadness she sometimes detected in many of the women who came to her for help.

Jeanne dismissed her thoughts to a kind of weary frustration caused from working hard to help the battered and abused—and making little progress. Support for Jeanne's efforts was always lacking. She sometimes felt physically fatigued. It was as if at one hundred and eight pounds, she was David in the first book of Samuel, facing Goliath. Many of the women who came to her were still trapped in abusive relationships. Jeanne prayed for the kind of change that would make it easier to help those in need. But her prayers remained unanswered. She would continue to pray for change and for Nicholas to reach Meg so they could save each other.

When Jeanne walked back into the kitchen, Meg and Nicholas released their embrace. She could see from the entrance that they had been kissing and laughing. Jeanne noticed the table was cleared and dishes were washed. She asked who did all the cleaning. Meg smiled and pointed at Nicholas.

"My father was on a small ship in the navy, and he said everyone washed dishes. He started me young, washing them. He just forgot about the everyone, so I always washed the dishes at home," said Nicholas as they all laughed.

Jeanne asked Meg and Nicholas if they would like to sit down. She then said, "I think it's time we talked about your parents."

Jeanne began by telling them about growing up with Peggy, attending school, and some of the fun things they'd done as kids. She told them two stories of when they'd attended parochial school together. The first was from the second grade, and Jeanne said, "It was the middle of the morning, and Sister Mary Therese Aloy was talking to the class, when suddenly an arm goes shooting up, and a little hand starts waving. Sister looked at your mom and held her gaze. It was very intimidating for us second graders, but not for your mom. We didn't think Sister Mary Therese was going to say anything, until she finally said, 'Yes?' Your mom stood up. She was all smiles and said, 'Sister, I think you and I should be in charge of the class.' Well, we all looked at your mom and thought for sure she would end up in front of Mother Superior. Instead, Sister Mary Therese just smiled and made your mom her little helper."

The second incident occurred when they were in the sixth grade. Jeanne said it was when Nicholas's mother announced she was no longer going to be called Margaret.

Jeanne said, "We were in class when your mom raised her hand. When Sister Mary Brenner recognized her, your mom stood up and said, 'Sister, would you please call me Peggy from now on.' The Sister looked at her, and after a long moment, politely said, 'Peggy, why that's such a pretty name. Would you please go to the chalkboard and write Peggy twenty-five-times? I want to be sure of the proper spelling.'

"Your mom was all smiles and said, 'Oh yes, Sister, I would love to.' From that moment on, Margaret was known as Peggy. When I asked her why she'd changed her name, she said, 'I just love the sound of Peggy.' Your mom always made these types of proclamations."

Jeanne then told them how everyone had liked his mom and how the nuns had loved her. She said there had been a way about her that was appealing, and no one could've said or done the things Peggy would without getting into trouble. Jeanne thought it was a kind of polite boldness, if there's such a thing. She said that's why she'd known it was Peggy who called Andrew's name when they'd first met.

She then talked about high school, sleepovers, and class trips. She was rushing through the years. Jeanne knew what Nicholas really wanted to hear. He wanted to know his mom and dad when they were married and he'd been a little boy.

"The first time I met your dad, I knew it wouldn't be long before he married your mom. He was kind and caring; he adored Peggy. Your dad also had a shyness about him. Your father was brave but never would have had the courage to ask your mom for a date.

"Those were the war years, when engagements were short. Before your father enlisted in the Navy, he asked your mom to marry him. They had only a few days before he had to report for basic training. They married as quickly as possible and had an overnight honeymoon at the Parker House in Boston. The next morning, your dad was on a train and off to war. Your mom became a war bride.

"I didn't see your mom much after her wedding. I was away most of the time, preparing for my vows. We stayed in contact as often as we could. We would occasionally exchange letters, but, well, money was tight during the war. Your mom would use her extra money to buy the three-cent stamps needed to send her letters to your dad. After a while, we started to lose touch. Then when I resigned from the convent and married Francis, we moved to Truro. Well, by then, we were both married and, for whatever reason, stopped telephoning or writing regularly.

"Then in 1951, I received a telephone call from your mom. It was like she'd never changed and we were back in high school. When I picked up the receiver and said 'hello,' she said, 'Jeanne, Peggy, I need a favor.' Just like that, just like when we were kids. You'd think we'd spoken every day. I started to cry, I couldn't believe it was Peggy. She said, 'Jeanne, stop crying; no one died,' then I started laughing. She said, 'Jeanne, what are you laughing for, I need a favor.' I said, 'Peggy, I miss you, too.' Your mom was so special. She said, 'Jeanne, I love you too, we'll have time for that later. I need a favor. I'm sending Andrew down to see you with a friend who needs your help. He'll explain everything. I'll call tomorrow.' That was your mom. I would do anything for her, and she would do whatever she could for a friend. I loved her very much."

It hadn't taken long for Nicholas's eyes to water and for Meg to shed tears, their emotions always on the surface and easily released. Nicholas was learning from Meg that love was feelings, and when you love, you laugh and you cry. She wasn't embarrassed to show her emotions, and he was learning that when he released his, it felt good. He no longer struggled to hold them in, and he was no longer embarrassed.

As Jeanne paused in her story to give Meg and Nicholas time to collect themselves, Nicholas asked, "What happened to Mom's friend?"

Jeanne continued and said, "I would like to tell you, but it's not my story to tell. I am sure their friend would be happy to see you again and would readily tell you the story. It's just not for me to tell. I will say, there was a happy ending to the story, and one that brought your mom and dad to Cape Cod in 1957. That was the last time I was with your mom. She'd confided in me and told me how ill she really was. She was so brave and courageous. It breaks my heart to think about it."

Nicholas's mind was racing; he had so many questions. He wanted to know more about his mom and dad. He composed himself then asked, "My dad drove my mom's friend down to Truro in 1951?"

"Actually, your mom and dad's friend, a neighbor named Toni who'd been very close to them, especially during the war when your dad was away. So yes, your father drove to Truro for a friend.

"Your dad had been working a second job a couple of nights a week when your mom called him at work. She told him to come home right away. Your dad left work, and drove home not knowing what to expect.

"When he got home, your mom handed him a thermos of hot coffee and told him he had to go to Truro to see Jeanne. She told him Toni needed a ride, and she told him to hurry back because he had to work in the morning. When he arrived, he stayed only long enough to give me a hug and a kiss and then he was off again. He returned home about four in the morning, and three hours later he was back at his regular job. Your mom called me the next day to check on Toni, and every day after that for several weeks. We spoke regularly until she died."

"You said their friend would be happy to see me again. We met?" asked Nicholas.

"Yes, I'm sure you don't remember. It was when we'd last seen each other, and you don't recall me."

"We visited Toni?"

"Yes, it was an enjoyable time for your parents. They were finally visiting Cape Cod. They were on vacation as a family, and a friend had invited them to their friendship ceremony in Provincetown. I'd been asked to perform the ceremony, and your mom and I had the chance to spend time together."

"What's a friendship ceremony?" asked Meg.

"A friendship ceremony is an opportunity for those in love to share their joy and happiness with friends and family. What binds the unity is the public expression of the love they have for each other. For many it's symbolic, but a very important and personal ceremony."

"Where do you do them?" asked Meg.

"I've performed the ceremony on the beach, in the park, and at our little reserve in the woods."

"I think that's lovely," said Meg.

"They are wonderful expressions of love," said Jeanne. Then she continued talking about Nicholas's parents, saying, "I invited your mom and dad to Truro regularly, but in the early 1950s, working people didn't have the money or the time off to go away on vacation. Your dad worked two jobs, and your mom would spend all her time with you. I think the only time you weren't at the park was at night to sleep. She had you outside in all kinds of weather. Your mom loved the outdoors. She said she would find the most interesting things. Meg's a lot like her in that way."

Meg and Nicholas held each other's hand a little tighter. Nicholas could feel the spirit of his mom and her love. He looked at Meg and saw the woman he loved. She had the same joy, happiness, and love as his mother. He vowed he would marry her, love her, and honor her all the days of his life.

Meg didn't show her surprise to learn Peggy's given name was Margaret. Peggy had been one of the names she'd considered on her drive up from Nashville. She knew it was a diminutive version of Margaret, but still it had startled her to hear the name. She was hearing from the people she'd met, and even from Nicholas, that she resembled his mother, and there were other similarities.

The coincidence of how Peggy met Andrew by calling out his name, and how she would find unusual things often overlooked was startling. Meg was beginning to feel like she and Nicholas were back in time, and it was 1957. She thought of Peggy dying from cancer shortly after leaving Cape Cod. Then Meg considered Lewis's violence and what would happen when she left this safe and wonderful place. She suddenly felt the same cold breath of Lewis as she felt when she was in his presence.

"I would like to meet Toni, if that's possible," asked Nicholas.

"I could give you the address if you have time to visit," said Jeanne.

Nicholas looked at Meg and noticed her vacant stare. He said, "Meg, are you okay?"

"I'm sorry, I must have been day dreaming," responded Meg.

Nicholas had never seen Meg with a blank, hollow expression of her face. He looked at her with concern as he repeated his words, "Do you think there's time to go visit Toni?"

"Oh yes, I'm happy to go, Nicholas," said Meg. As she responded to Nicholas, she smiled. Seeing her expression change, Nicholas returned the smile.

"It's still early enough in the day for you to drive to Provincetown. I'll let them know you're coming, but on the way there, you should think about spending a little more time seeing the area. The beaches, the dunes, and the lighthouse at Race Point are all wonderful to experience. That way, you can arrive after they close their shop for the day. The address is on Commercial Street and easy to find. They have a quaint apartment over their store. You can park your car down by the wharfs. It's a short walk to their shop and a very nice area to stroll. There are street vendors, and you can window-shop."

"Thank you," said Nicholas.

"Don't worry if you stay late. You can always spend another night here."

Nicholas stood, hugged Jeanne, and said, "Thank you."

"Thank you," said Meg.

"I'll help you get your things together and make the telephone call," said Jeanne.

As they walked toward the cottage, Jeanne said, "Why don't I give Meg a hand stripping the bed, since I'm sure your dad taught you how to strip and make a bed the Navy way."

They all laughed as Nicholas said, "Every week, I had to wash and iron the sheets, and make our beds. The corners had to be tightly pulled and folded on a forty-five-degree angle. Everything had to be neat and tucked in properly. When I was small, my dad would drop a quarter on the bed, and if it bounced, he would give it to me as a reward."

"You must have gotten a lot of quarters," said Meg.

"My dad thinks so. Every time I ask him for money he says, 'What do you need my money for, you still have all those quarters I gave you for making up the beds,'" said Nicholas, and they all laughed as he entered his bedroom.

Jeanne followed Meg into her room and closed the door. She said, "I just want you to know before your visit to

Provincetown, Toni was hurt very badly. Peggy knew my work when she called me and asked for help. I wanted you to know before you arrived, just in case you needed to prepare yourself."

"Thank you, I will. I want you to know, I'm thinking about what you said. I love Nicholas and feel safe with him. I know how much he loves me."

"I'm sure you will do what's best. Only you can decide if you're ready," said Jeanne as she embraced Meg.

34

*J*eanne wrote down the address on Commercial Street for them. She said Toni was thrilled they were coming to visit and would be expecting them in the late afternoon. Jeanne provided a list of places to see on the way. She prepared a lunch for Meg and Nicholas and said to take their time and enjoy the grandeur of the Outer Cape. It would be a delightful Thursday, their fourth day together.

Meg and Nicholas thanked Jeanne once more. The little yellow Beetle was back on the move. After turning right off Highland Road, they were quickly on Route 6, heading toward Provincetown. The traffic was light, and the windows were down. The salt in the air and the blue water of the bay gave them a sense of freedom. Their faces beamed; they would have another day together to explore. As Meg drove they could see the bright sun and feel its heat warming the air. A perfect day for their last special adventure.

The approach into Provincetown captivated them. They could see the salty sea waters of the bay on their left, and

Pilgrim Lake in its calmness was on the right. Beyond the lake, the lush green vegetation merged with the rising sand, then the dunes, small hills, and slopes nature created to shield the outermost tip of Massachusetts from the harsh wind and water of the Atlantic Ocean.

Shortly after entering Provincetown, they turned right onto Race Point Road. As they drove along the narrow lane, they admired the scenery. The wind-worn shrubs and trees, the sand dunes with spots of green, the little craters and bowl-like nooks all created the texture of the landscape. It was beautiful and unique and nothing like they'd ever seen. Each felt the joy of the other's presence; surrounded by land so inspiring, it sparked a feeling of hope and a desire that there would be more days like this ahead, and somehow, they would find a way to stay together.

Meg followed the road to Race Point Beach and parked the VW in the lower lot nearest to the dunes. It was getting close to mid-morning, and there were already about thirty cars in the lot when they arrived. They left the Beetle and walked toward the beach. Meg carried the blanket, and Nicholas carried the lunch Jeanne had prepared for them. They spread the blanket on the sand and rolled over one of the corners to protect their food from the sun's rays.

Meg slipped off her sandals and rolled up the bottom of her slacks. Nicholas took off the borrowed Converse sneakers and rolled up his pant legs. Holding hands, they walked to the water's edge and began to stroll along the shore. Meg, always attentive to her birds, waved at the flock of seagulls passing overhead.

The waters of the Atlantic were cold in the month of May, and they could feel the sting of nature's reminder. As they casually moved along the shallow water, they slowly adjusted to the temperature. Looking out over the horizon they admired the illusion of a painter's canvas with specs of white sails and fishing boats off in the distance.

"What a beautiful day. I'm happy we have this extra day to spend together," said Nicholas.

"It's lovely. We'll have to thank Jeanne." Meg paused as they walked a few more steps before she said, "How long ago it seems, we were driving to Rock Harbor."

"It does seem that way. But this morning when I was showering, my thoughts were just the opposite. I was thinking our time is over, and it just started."

"I know what you mean. I guess it's been all the memorable places and people, and all we've done together that makes it seem so long ago," said Meg.

"To think we met by chance. If your tire hadn't gone flat, you would've driven away. If my name was Andrew Nicholas like my dad instead of Nicholas Andrew, I wouldn't have stopped and turned around when you called my name."

"We met for a reason, Nicholas, I know it in my heart. I don't know the reason, but I feel I will know. I really believe our paths have crossed for a purpose."

"I don't know why we met. I love that we met. I love you for calling my name. I love you for driving me to Rock Harbor. I could list many more reasons why I love you. What I love most is you, your kindness, the joy you have every day, and how happy you make me. I never want you to leave."

Meg was smiling while Nicholas listed the reasons why he loved her, but she turned serious when he said, 'I never want you to leave.' Meg wasn't ready to explain her past or explain why she couldn't stay. She wanted to stay with Nicholas and be protected. Her heart said stay, but her thoughts were of her parents, her vow, and what Lewis might do to them. After a long, thoughtful pause, she said, "I love you, too, and I don't want to leave you, either, Nicholas. It's just that you have school and football. I'm sure you can't miss many more classes or practices."

"Meg, the semester is over, I'm not missing any more classes. All my coaches and friends say the same thing about football. It's your ticket to college. You'll get a great education; all you have to do is play football. I don't want to play football, but I can't go to college without playing. That doesn't make it fun; it makes it a weight I can carry, but I just don't want to.

"My dad went into the Navy during World War II. He could have gone to school with the GI Bill because of his military service. I was thinking of doing that before we met. Then when Gall spoke of the brave men carrying bandages, tourniquets, and morphine who'd saved his life, I thought maybe that is something I could train to do. I could learn about medicine and have my college paid for when I'm discharged from the service."

"You would leave school and give up football?"

"The only thing holding me back was not knowing what I would do when I enlisted. I had no idea you could train to learn about medicine and help the wounded."

"You would surely leave me then."

"That's just it, Meg, I would, but I wouldn't. My mom and dad only dated a short time before they fell in love and married. When Dad went to war, he supported Mom while she waited for him to return. Maggie and Gall did the same thing.

"You heard Gall say my dad thought only of my mom when the collision knocked him into the ocean. We could do the same as them. I know it sounds impulsive, but I love you, and you love me." Nicholas paused, he knew he had spoken fast and his proposal was sudden. He didn't want to lose Meg, but he also didn't want to pressure her. He continued thoughtfully and said, "All I'm saying is there may be a way for us to stay together. We should think about it while we still have time."

Meg stayed quiet, her expression hopeful, and she gave a little smile when she thought of Jenny. She almost felt like her. She had picked Nicholas, the boy she'd fallen in love with and who loved her back, and he had proposed to her. Then she remembered Jenny's death, and her own comment, *it's always the woman who dies in great love stories*. Thinking these thoughts, her expression turned sad.

Nicholas watched Meg as he spoke, saw the smile, and felt encouraged. Then he saw something in her eyes that looked like sadness and doubt, and quickly said, "I love you, Meg. Let's not think our time together is short. We'll enjoy the day, and whatever is meant to happen will."

Trying to maintain her happiness, Meg said, "I love you, too. It's a lovely day, and I'm having a wonderful time. I'm sure you're hungry. Let's race to the blanket." Meg, with her shapely legs, sprinted fast, but not too fast, as Nicholas, with his nearly six-foot frame and powerful stride, was quickly by her side and reaching for her hand. Their pace slowed, easing into a walk, until they reached the blanket, where they sat and ate their lunch.

As they nibbled at their food, they continued to admire the beauty of the Atlantic—the constant flow of the ocean and the rhythm of the waves. The sound created a peace and calmness; it was soothing to sit quietly and listen to nature's music. Meg and Nicholas, thinking of the other, turned slightly to let their eyes connect, and at the same time said, "I love you."

Meg quickly replied, "Pixie dixie, you owe me a Coke," and started giggling.

Nicholas started laughing and said, "Pixie dixie?"

"I haven't said that since I was a little girl. When we were children if we said the same words at the same time, we would say, "Pixie dixie, you owe me a Coke.""

"Did you get a lot of Cokes?" asked Nicholas laughing.

"No, we just said it for fun; I haven't even thought about the saying in a long time. I think being with you on Cape Cod makes me feel like I did when I was a child. I feel carefree, every day a joy, and so much happiness. I love you for making me feel this way."

"I love you, too," said Nicholas. He wanted to say *I want to make you feel this way forever* but didn't want to push Meg. He knew his proposal was rash, but he didn't care. He wanted a life with Meg and knew in his heart they were meant to be together.

When they finished their lunch, they noticed more people had arrived on the beach. It wasn't crowded, but there were people on blankets and beach chairs, couples walking along the water, people milling about on the shore, and a few brave swimmers enjoying the frigid Atlantic waters in the month of May. The atmosphere was pleasant and peaceful. They could have remained there all day and enjoyed the inspiring setting. But they had Jeanne's list; there was more to see.

They gathered their belongings and headed for the car. Meg drove through the parking lot and back onto Race Point Road. When she saw the sign for Herring Cove Beach, she turned right and merged with Providence Lands Road. Meg followed the road through a rugged mixture of dunes and shrubs and came to the parking lot for Herring Cove Beach. She turned right at the entrance and drove along the water to the farthest point in the lot, where she parked her car.

They saw people walking and biking toward the paved trail Jeanne wrote about in her note. In the distance, they saw the lighthouse at Race Point, sitting tall like the last outpost in the wilderness. It was a stunning postcard setting. They brought the blanket to the beach to sit for a while and enjoy the view. The ever-present seagulls were flying by, and some landed on the sand. An all-white seagull walked up to Meg. She smiled and asked, "Do you remember me?"

Nicholas smiled and said, "You really do love seagulls."

"I was always drawing and painting but never a seagull. I hope to someday capture the beauty of seagulls in my artwork."

"Were you planning to be an artist when you applied to Holy Trinity?"

"I was going to be a singer," said Meg, causing them both to laugh. Meg continued and said, "I hadn't decided. I love to read, and I love children; I thought about teaching. Art was something I always did for the joy of it. Now, if I ever have the chance, I'll make it my passion to paint the best seagulls I can."

"With the love you have in your heart, they will be beautiful seagulls."

"Thank you. I love this place so much. Everything we've seen, surrounded by all the beauty nature has to offer, has provided me with such peace. Wherever I am, this is the place where I will live in my thoughts and never leave," said Meg.

They sat quietly on the blanket holding hands, occasionally kissing, and mostly relaxing. They nearly drifted asleep when two young women who looked to be in their early twenties, approached them, and one said, "Excuse me, we saw your car when you arrived and noticed the Tennessee license plates. We were wondering; have you ever been to Nashville?"

Nicholas pointed to Meg and said, "I'm from Worcester."

Meg responded and said, "Oh yes, I grew up in Nashville. It's a wonderful place."

"We're planning to visit, and can't wait to go to Broadway and listen to the country music. You must love it there."

"I've driven on Broadway many times, but I never went to listen to the music."

"Really, wow. I would think living there you would love country music."

"I like it very much. I like all music. There's much more to do in Nashville, I just never really went down there, mostly because I was too young for most places."

"Oh wow, that's a bummer. When we go to visit, what else should we do?"

"If you love to be outside, my two favorite places are Radnor Lake Park and Cheekwood Botanical Garden. There are many other delightful parks, museums, and historical sites you should consider. If you really love country music, you must go to the Grand Ole Opry at the Ryman Auditorium. It's such a splendid old place to listen to music and just a short walk from Broadway on Fifth Avenue."

"Thanks, we will, and we'll try to remember some of those places when we go. Well, take care."

"Good-bye," said Meg.

"Take care," said Nicholas.

As the two young women walked away, they held hands. When they stopped near the water, they turned to embrace each other and kissed. Meg noticed and said, "Do you think the two women we spoke with really like each other?"

"I would think so; they're planning a trip together."

"What I meant to say is, do you think they like each other the same as we like each other?"

"I'm not sure. What makes you think so?"

"Well, I noticed they held hands, and then when they reached the water, they hugged each other and kissed. In the way that we would."

"I don't know if they love each other as much as I love you. No one has that much love. They must like each other very much. I'm sure they're very close if they're planning to take a long trip together."

"I don't know any women who like each other in a romantic way."

"I had a best friend since grade school who was gay. We were freshmen in high school when he told me. I wasn't sure what he meant. So, he told me what he meant by being gay. He said he felt he needed to tell me because we were getting older. We did what kids do, we wrestled with each other, played sports together, and slept over each other's house."

"What did you say?"

"I didn't say anything."

"What do you mean?"

"Well, he was my best friend. I didn't need to say anything."

"Do you still see him?"

"He went away to college, and the last time I saw him was last fall. We had an away game in Buffalo against his team. He played for the other team, and we saw each other during the game. Afterward, we had only thirty minutes to catch up before my bus was leaving. I was hoping to spend time with him over the summer, but he has a job near his campus and won't be coming home."

"I'm glad you're still friends. Everyone deserves friends, and everyone deserves to be loved."

"Some people are lucky like me. You're my friend, and I love you. I need a kiss from you right now to convince me you love me, too," said Nicholas, as he smiled and moved his face closer to Meg's.

Meg immediately responded and gave him a kiss with meaning. When they separated, she said, "Now I need a kiss from you, to convince me you love me, too." Nicholas wasn't sure Meg was convinced after he kissed her, so he kissed her again, just as passionately, and just to make sure.

With only a couple of hours remaining before meeting Toni, they decided to drive to Commercial Street. Meg drove her Beetle back onto Providence Lands Road. They were now driving on the bay side of Cape Cod with dunes and water on their right. Meg turned her car left onto the Bradford Street Extension, heading toward the center of town.

When Nicholas caught his first glimpse of the Pilgrim Monument, he recognized it immediately. He could see himself as a five-year-old boy, looking up at the 252-foot structure in awe.

"Meg, I remember the monument. Look how tall it is! I remember standing and looking up at it in wonder. I can't believe it. I know Jeanne said we came here in 1957, but to have a memory of this place means so much to me."

"Nicholas, I am happy for you. Maggie, Gall, and Jeanne said you had a wonderful time when your family visited. You have another memory for your scrapbook. It's exciting."

"Once we park, I'd like to walk over to the monument."

"We will. I'm so pleased for you."

Meg turned right when they came to Ryder Street Extension and followed the road to the parking lot near the entrance to the wharfs. Leaving the car, they made their way up Winslow Street to the rear of the Pilgrim Monument.

Standing behind the stone structure, Nicholas tilted his head back until it could go no farther and said, "All I recall is looking up and staring at the top. It looked like a giant castle. I suppose something like this would be hard to forget as a young boy."

"You remember it, Nicholas. That's what's important."

"It's like we've recreated 1957, the sunset at Rock Harbor, the fire on the beach, staying with Maggie and Gall, the marking on the wall, the pond in Wellfleet, visiting Jeanne, and now the monument."

"And you're visiting all these places with someone you love and who loves you very much. It's just like your mom and dad," said Meg, as she squeezed his hand.

They stood watching for a few more minutes and then started slowly walking away. Meg and Nicholas strolled back down Winslow to Brattle Street, and passed by a small park. Set on the grass was a large bronze plaque encased in stone, shadowed by a thick cluster of trees. Rising up from behind the greenery was the Pilgrim Monument, as if reaching the clouds.

Meg and Nicholas walked over to look at the engraving on the bronze plaque. They stood admiring the beautifully crafted portrayal of the signing of a document by the earliest pilgrims. They read that the artistry is a representation of the signing of the Mayflower Compact and was created as a tribute to the five pilgrims who died before the final settlement in Plymouth. They thought it was masterful and, once again, had Jeanne to thank for providing an itinerary for a terrific visit.

Leaving the Town Green, the couple walked toward Commercial Street. They were going to window-shop while waiting to meet Toni. The solitude Meg and Nicholas enjoyed most of the day was over. Commercial Street was a bustle of activity with people walking on both sides of the street, shops with their doors held open, people sitting wherever they could find a spot, and street vendors hustling to sell an assortment of goods.

As they strolled along enjoying the activity and feeling the energy of the crowded street, they heard someone call out and wave to them, saying, "Hey you, lovebirds." When they looked, they saw a four-inch round peace medallion hanging from the neck of a man standing behind a small table of jewelry. The vendor said, "Yeah, you," and motioned for them to come to him.

Meg and Nicholas walked over to the vendor, and he said, "I see it all the time. You two are in love."

Meg blushed and Nicholas smiled. They looked at each other and said, "Yes."

"I knew it, I knew it. You're not married, right?" said the vendor.

"No," said Meg.

"No," said Nicholas.

"I know, you'd love to marry someday, but you don't have the money? I'm right again, ain't I? Ain't I right?"

"Well, sort of," said Nicholas.

The vendor interrupted and said, "Well, you two are lucky, I'm here to help you. I have these beautiful, inexpensive friendship rings. They're just like wedding bands without the expensive gold or silver. Who needs that anyway? Now, if ya really love each other, you need these rings. I can sell ya two of these beauties for twenty dollars each."

Meg and Nicholas looked at the rings and didn't respond. The vendor, not wanting to miss a sale, said, "I know, you're short of cash. Let's see what I can do. I'll go half price, twenty dollars for the two, now that's a deal."

Meg and Nicholas continued to look at the rings. They weren't thinking of the cost or even listening to the vendor. They were imaging the possibility of being together, what the two cheap rings could mean. They still didn't know how they could be united, but it was very much on their minds.

"Woo, you're two tough customers. My bottom price, fifteen dollars for both. No, make it ten dollars. Only because you're young and in love. I can see it all over you."

Meg and Nicholas looked at each other for the first time and smiled.

The vendor saw the sign. He knew he had his sale, and he said, "Just because we're friends, eight dollars and the rings are yours. Now which one does the pretty lady want?"

Meg picked out her friendship ring with the most yellow around the band. Nicholas found one that fit him from the same box. After pooling their money, they paid the eight dollars for their friendship rings. They thanked the vendor and walked away holding hands. The matching rings felt like bonding, uniting them and strengthening the tie holding them together.

35

*I*t was getting close to the time Toni was expecting Meg and Nicholas to arrive. They had enjoyed their day exploring Provincetown and purchasing their friendship rings. As they walked along Commercial Street, there was a feeling of excitement. Nicholas told Meg that remembering the Pilgrim Monument was another step in really knowing the love his parents had for each other. Nicholas's joy became Meg's. She felt so much a part of his life; she could feel his happiness.

They started watching the numbers on the stores once they walked past Pearl Street. It wasn't long before they found Toni's shop. The name of the store was Arthur and Anthony's. Written under the name were the words, Nature's Art by Local Artists & More. When they walked through the door, they could see people in the rear of the shop who looked to be customers making a purchase.

Meg and Nicholas browsed through the aisles looking at the artwork. Meg shared her joy with Nicholas as they admired the paintings and photographs. There was stained glass with all the colors of the rainbow and clear glass designs and statues made from a variety of mediums. She especially loved the themes on display: wildlife and birds, ships and boats, and the natural scenes of Cape Cod.

As they ambled through the gallery, appreciating the many interesting pieces of art, Nicholas said, "One day you will have inspiring paintings on exhibit. You'll paint amazing seagulls, and everyone will want one."

"I hope to one day paint again and try to capture the seagull as majestically as I see them. I only wish my talent was a good as they are beautiful."

"Your love for them will make all the difference."

"Thank you. I do find them inspiring."

When the customers left, Meg and Nicholas seemed to be the only ones who remained in the shop. A slender man with curly, shoulder-length hair came out from behind the service counter and approached them. He said, "May I assist you with anything, or are you just browsing?"

"I'm Nicholas, and this is Meg. Jeanne called, and Toni's expecting us."

"You must be Peggy and Andrew's son. I'm Arthur. Toni's upstairs getting ready. He wanted to cook some local cuisine for you. He's very much looking forward to seeing you again. He loved your parents. I didn't know them well; we met only once, back in 1957. That was when your mom and dad came to visit with us and attend our friendship ceremony. Meeting her and listening to stories from Toni, she was really an incredible woman. I'm sure you miss her greatly."

"It's nice to meet you, Arthur. I do miss my mom. Over the last few days I've learned so much about her and my father. I'm starting to feel like I finally know something about them as a couple. Jeanne said Toni was a good friend of my parents. I'm sure I'll learn more about them from him."

"Your mother and father really helped Toni when he was in need. Jeanne's a special woman; she took very good care of him. It was my good fortune that she introduced us, and it wasn't long before we started dating. We've been together nearly nineteen years. Here we are now with a successful business and our own apartment in town. Why, shame on me for ignoring such a pretty young lady."

"That's all right, I'm here for Nicholas. We've had a most enjoyable time learning about his mom and dad and seeing all the beauty of Cape Cod." Meg paused then said, "The artwork in your gallery is beautiful."

"Why, thank you. Are you an artist? We're always looking for new talent."

"No, I'm just visiting."

"From the South?"

"Yes, Tennessee."

"I bet Nashville."

Meg smiled and asked, "How'd you know?"

"I spent some time there when I was younger. Your southern accent is only slight, but a very beautiful sound nonetheless."

"Thank you, Arthur," said Meg as she blushed.

Nicholas listened, waiting patiently to say, "Meg's a painter, and she loves seagulls. She wants to paint them and capture their beauty as she sees them. I'm sure they'll be terrific."

"Seagulls are the most majestic bird," said Meg.

"Well, sweetheart, when you start painting again, you make sure to bring them here. We're always looking for unique pieces." Arthur paused then said, "I don't recall seeing seagulls in Nashville."

As Meg hesitated, thinking about how to respond, Toni came walking from the back of the shop. He called out to Arthur and asked, "Have they arrived?"

"Toni, we're up front. I was just going to lock the door and close for the day," responded Arthur.

As Toni approached, they could see he was slightly taller than Arthur. He had the physical frame of a runner. His short brown hair was combed to the side. Seeing Nicholas, he stopped and said, "Oh my God, you look just like your father." He walked over and gave Nicholas a big hug. He then stepped slightly back, and with his tendency to speak quickly said, "The resemblance, the resemblance, it's just amazing. I'm sorry," he said as he extended his hand to Nicholas, "I'm Anthony, your mom and dad's friend. Everyone calls me Toni. I can't believe Peggy's boy is in our shop. I loved your mom. She was truly a wonderful woman. How's your dad? Sad, I'm sure. I knew he could never enjoy life without Peggy." Toni paused then said, "And who's this gorgeous young lady?"

Toni extended his hand after the hug, and Nicholas was still holding it as he said, "Nice to meet you, Toni. This is Meg."

"Why, you're beautiful," said Toni as he released Nicholas's hand and hugged her.

Meg blushed and said, "Thank you."

"Arthur, why are we still down here? You should have brought them upstairs right away. We've so much to talk about."

"Toni, we were just getting ready to go upstairs when you came down. I had a customer, and when they left, well, never mind. Let's go upstairs; I'm sure everyone's hungry. I know I am."

Arthur locked the front door as Toni led the way through the store toward the back room where they exited the shop. The four then walked up the wooden stairs to the second-floor landing. The entrance to the apartment was through a small foyer leading to the kitchen. The kitchen opened into a dining area, then a larger living room. The apartment was furnished with all the skills of an artist; a perfect balance between trendy and homey. The ambience was warm and serene.

"Welcome to our home. You're too young for wine, so will it be soda, iced tea, or water?" asked Toni.

"Iced tea," said Meg. Nicholas asked for the same.

"Let's sit in the front room and chat before we eat," said Toni.

As they walked to the front room, Arthur poured a glass of chardonnay for Toni and one for himself. Nicholas and Meg sat next to each other on the soft harvest colors of the love seat cushion while Arthur and Toni sat on the muted brown leather couch opposite them. Toni kept looking intently at Nicholas. He was trying to see Peggy in him. As he watched, Nicholas turned slightly and smiled at Meg, and she smiled back.

"Your smile, it's your mother's! It's exactly like your mom's. You may look like your dad, but you have Peggy's smile."

"No one ever said that to me. I've heard people say how much I look like my father, but no one ever told me I had my mom's smile."

"Well, you do. It's a beautiful smile. You must have used it to win Meg's heart. Now tell me how you two met. I want to know."

"Meg, why don't you tell Toni how we met," said Nicholas.

"Well, I love to be outside, the early mornings are my favorite time. That's when I find the most interesting things. On Monday, I was at Holy Trinity, visiting the campus. When I went back to my car, my tire was nearly flat. So, I found myself in some distress. Being a damsel, I did the only thing a damsel could do. I went looking for a handsome buccaneer to assist me. I merely asked quietly if there was a Nicholas about this fine institution. Well, this charming fellow, who enticed me with his smile, inspired me to believe he was a Good Samaritan. I was comforted when he also said he was a student. On seeing me, however, he declared he was now a thief who would become a sailor, and steal me away with him. This smiling buccaneer made me his treasure, and we sailed to this paradise you call Cape Cod."

Everyone laughed at Meg's story, and Nicholas kissed her on the cheek and said, "She's my treasure, I'll admit that. I love her, but she's the one with the car. I think I may be her treasure, too."

"A lovely story and a fine sense of humor. You're an attractive couple, and you seem very happy together," said Arthur.

"It's funny; Meg sort of resembles your mom. She's slim like her, the same height, dark brown eyes, and her hair length is similar, but there's something else that reminds me of her. Peggy had a presence about her that's hard to describe. She had a poise that was natural and welcoming. Well, I just miss her so much." Toni paused for a minute as he thought, then said, "Meg has that same presence as Peggy. I think it's a quality that makes them appealing. I don't mean just in looks. There is an attraction that is welcoming, and you sense the goodness of their hearts."

Meg was blushing. She knew she'd blushed several times since she'd left Jeanne's house. She also knew she'd tried to be funny. Meg hadn't been this happy in a long time. All of her lost joy had returned, and she had confidence in herself. She was loved by Nicholas, and she loved him. Meg felt she had friends, good friends who cared about her. There was Maggie and Gall, Jeanne and Francis, and now Toni and Arthur. She was happy, and she wanted to remain happy. She needed to be with Nicholas for all the days of her life.

"Nicholas is special, too. He's kind and loving. He makes me feel safe," said Meg.

"You sound just like Peggy talking about Andrew. You two gorgeous kids are meant for each other. Don't you dare tell me you only met on Monday. That's just not possible. You seem like you've been together forever," said Toni.

"We did; we met on Monday. If Meg hadn't called my name, I wouldn't be here, learning about my mom and dad. I owe her so much. She's been so generous and supportive of me. I can hardly believe we met when I think about it," said Nicholas.

"Well, you did, and I see the matching friendship rings on your fingers. That means you're committed to each other in love. I bet you bought them from Edward. They look like the ones he sells. How much did he charge you for those rings?" asked Toni.

"Eight dollars for both," responded Nicholas.

"Good for you, you gave Edward a run for his money. He usually holds the price at ten dollars for two rings, but only with really tough customers," said Toni.

"Standing there, we were looking at the rings, and we could hear him talking. We weren't really listening, and when he said eight dollars, he asked Meg which one she wanted. She picked out the one with the most yellow, and we bought them," said Nicholas.

"That's Edward. He never knows when to be quiet. He talks himself down on the price, and he's always complaining he can't make a profit. Now that you have your rings, you'll just need to seal your bond with a friendship ceremony."

Arthur interrupted and said, "Toni, I don't know about our guests, but I'm hungry, and I'm sure they're too polite to tell us. Not everyone is always on a diet like you are."

"I'm the same weight I was in high school, and I'm not going to say how long ago that was," replied Toni. He then said, "You can tell, I'm the one with the personality in this relationship. Arthur's the serious one, so deadpan, all business. I love him, though. He lets me do all the talking."

Arthur rolled his eyes at Meg and Nicholas as he smiled, making them laugh. Then with his eyebrows raised and speaking in a serious manner he said, "How about the three of us go eat, and we'll let Toni keep talking."

"All right, all right, I can keep talking at the table. See how serious he is?"

They moved to the dining table, and Arthur served the meal Toni had prepared for them. As they ate, Toni talked about their shop and asked Meg and Nicholas about the places they'd visited. Nicholas spoke about school and answered a few questions regarding his dad. He didn't mention football or how he no longer wanted to play.

Meg answered most questions with general answers. Arthur was mild mannered and agreeable. He listened politely. He was always attentive and would nod or smile when Toni told a story involving the two of them. Toni rarely gave Arthur an opportunity to respond to questions, and Arthur seemed happy to let Toni talk for both of them.

Toni thought Meg was a lovely person, but he was too astute to be fooled by her vague responses. He felt she genuinely loved Nicholas, but there was something she wasn't saying. He thought maybe it was his imagination because Meg looked so young and innocent. He asked himself, *What's this delightful young woman hiding?* He wasn't going to push, but he wasn't going to let it go, either.

36

$\mathcal{W}$hen the meal was finished, they returned to the front room. They sat in the same seats as before. In their short time together, the seeds of a friendship were already established. Arthur and Toni were very likable and friendly, and so were Meg and Nicholas. The relationship was sealed by the connection to Peggy and Andrew.

Nicholas thought anyone who had a loving friendship with his mom and dad would naturally be his friend. In Toni and Arthur's eyes, Nicholas and Meg were more than friends. They felt they were family and would do whatever they could to help family.

"Jeanne told me you were a good friend of my parents. She said my dad drove you to Truro. When I asked her about it, she said it wasn't her story to tell. I was hoping you would tell me about my mom and dad," said Nicholas.

Toni, reflecting on his memories of Peggy and Andrew, said, "I loved your mom very much and your dad, too. It's your mom who was my best friend; I have a debt to her and your dad they never let me repay.

"When your mom married your dad in 1943, they had a one-night honeymoon at the Parker House in Boston. The next day your father was on a train to the Finger Lakes region in New York. That's where some of the seamen trained in World War II. After your dad's train left the South Central Station in Boston, your mom was all alone.

"I was your mother's neighbor during the war when your father was away. We spent so much time together. She was alone, and I wasn't in a relationship at the time. We did things that didn't cost much money. We'd go to an occasional movie, usually a matinee, or to a local dance. Sometimes, on a Saturday we'd pack a nice lunch and picnic at a park." Toni gently rubbed away a tear and when he continued, he paused often to reflect on his love for Peggy.

"We'd pool or swap ration coupons, and your mom would cook one night and me the other. Most evenings we'd sit by an old mahogany Philco radio and listen to the war news, or the Bing Crosby or Glen Miller show. Oftentimes we'd just talk with the radio low and share our thoughts. Your mom was a very good listener. You felt you could open up and confide in her. She knew everything about me; it was very difficult back then and still is in many places." Again, Toni sat quietly as he fixed his eyes forward without seeing; he was lost in his own thoughts.

When he continued he said, "We'd read your dad's letters together; sometimes we'd laugh, and sometimes we'd cry. Your mom missed your father so much when he was away at sea. I remember one period when your mother hadn't received a letter for over a month. She was very concerned and unhappy. She always said Andrew would come back, and they'd have a wonderful life together. It makes me sad to recall how disheartened your mother was when she didn't hear from Andrew.

"But he did come back just like your mom said he would. He came back from the war happy and full of life. They had fun together. Most people didn't have a lot of money back then, but that didn't stop your parents from enjoying themselves. They loved the outdoors, going to Lake Quinsigamond, and being at the park. They especially enjoyed Holmes Field where they would walk and picnic in the warm weather, and ice skate in the winter.

"I remember in 1957 when Arthur and I had our friend-ship ceremony; your mom and dad were invited. I wasn't sure if they would make it with work, and well, at the time you were only five years old. They had expenses, so we weren't expecting them.

"Peggy called and said they decided to have a family vacation and were coming to Cape Cod. It was always something she'd talked about and wanted to do. When she said it was time, I thought she was using the invitation as a good reason to finally come to the Cape, visit with Jeanne, and tour the area. When Peggy told Jeanne and me she was very ill, then we understood what she meant by 'it's time.' I was heartbroken. She told me to buck-up. I said to her, 'Peggy, who says buck-up?' and she said, 'How do I know? It just came out.' I have a million stories of your mom.

"Once she found out about her illness, the end came fast. We never had the chance to say good-bye. I'd been planning to visit her in the fall when business usually slows down, but I was too late."

Toni was crying, and Arthur was rubbing his shoulder. Meg and Nicholas were holding each other's hand. Everything Nicholas was hearing was another painful reminder of how little he knew of his mom and how short the time was that they had together.

Toni continued speaking. "Your mom and dad had a terrific vacation despite Peggy's illness. Your dad had no idea your mom was sick. She didn't want him to know about her illness until after their vacation. Your mom was still active, and from appearance, you wouldn't have known she was dying. They soaked up everything Cape Cod had to offer that week and had so much fun. When I think about it now, it's as if Peggy had been trying to pack a lifetime of memories into the shortest possible time."

Toni stopped speaking, and silence hung in the air. Nicholas broke the stillness when he said "Meg and I have been reliving those memories since Monday. Gall found us sleeping on the beach and brought us home to Maggie. We came down to watch the sunset like I did with my mom. I had a memory of the two of us on the beach, watching the sunset. Then, one day I found an old photograph of Mom and me. It was just like I remembered. My father kept it in a book, but he never showed it to me.

"Then I remembered the fire we had on the beach, so I made a fire. Meg and I fell asleep. In the morning, that's when Gall found us and brought us to his home. Maggie remembered my parents. She showed us where my father carved our names on a wall in the cottage they'd rented. Then I swam in a pond in Wellfleet and remembered holding onto my dad's shoulders and waving to my mother.

"Maggie asked us to do her a favor and deliver cranberry muffins to Jeanne. When Jeanne saw me, she recognized me because I look like my dad. She told us about you, and on our way here we saw the Pilgrim monument. I remembered seeing it as a young boy. I love Meg for bringing me to Cape Cod. I would never have learned about my mom and dad, or experienced how my parents felt in 1957 without her help."

"I love you, too, Nicholas," said Meg as she squeezed his hand.

"Well, I'm glad we had the opportunity to meet you and Meg." Toni wasn't rushing his story. He was taking his time, reliving his friendship with Peggy, but he was overwhelmed by sorrow for the loss of his friend.

Continuing he said, "I want to tell you one more story about your mom and dad. It's the story of how indebted I always felt to them. You know what your mom said when I told her I was indebted to her for all the help she gave me? She said, 'Family doesn't owe family for love.' That's how she felt about me. It made me cry. It still makes me cry thinking about it.

"It's not a very pleasant story, and I don't need to tell it. I don't want to make Meg or you uncomfortable. But it really speaks to the love your mom and dad had in their hearts and souls."

"I don't want to upset Meg," said Nicholas.

"I know I'll cry. I know it will probably upset me, but you need to hear Toni's story. I need to hear it, too. Toni, please tells us."

Nicholas put his arm around Meg and pulled her closer to him. When she looked at his face, he gave her a kiss and then nodded to Toni, confirming what Meg had said.

"It was 1951 when I started dating a man that I thought was good and caring. We were together for about six months, and he wanted me to move in with him. It was hard for me. I treasured my small apartment and my two best friends. Your mom and dad were living next to me. I loved the man I was dating, and it broke my heart to leave, but I did.

"The person I thought I knew and moved in with was violent. He'd never shown it when we were dating, but when we were living together, everything changed. He was very mean and abusive. He started slapping me, and then the slaps became punches. He was very muscular and strong. When I tried to fight back, he'd say, 'I'll teach you to fight back.' He would just beat me more. He'd tell me to shut up if I cried. He would tell me to leave. He said he was sick of looking at me. When I told him I was leaving, he threatened to find me and kill me. I threatened to call the police, but he just laughed and said, 'What do you think they'll do for you?'

"One night he came home drunk and meaner than usual. He started hitting me, and I was tired of him hitting me; I slapped him good, right across the face. I knew he felt the sting when he looked at me with such hate. He suddenly exploded into a violent rage of punches. I was badly hurt, my face bloody, my eyes nearly closed from the swelling. He broke my jaw and several ribs. I could hardly breathe and was coughing up blood.

"When he went into the bedroom, I grabbed my jacket and an old hat. I ran from the house and waited in the shadows for a bus. I didn't want to take a taxi. I was afraid the cab driver would look at my injuries and drive away, or call his dispatcher. I had no choice. I had to take the bus. It took me two transfers and three bus rides to reach my old neighborhood.

"It was about nine o'clock when I arrived and saw the lights on in your parents' apartment. I felt like a little ship lost at sea in a storm, and when all hope is gone, there in the distance is a little speck of light. The flicker somehow makes its way through the darkness and shows the way.

"The light in your parents' apartment showed me the way. I had no place to go. I couldn't go to the hospital because there would have been too many questions, and the police would have shown up; your mom understood all this.

"I knocked on your parents' door, and your mom answered it. You'd think she saw people looking like me, all battered and beaten, every day. She just took charge. She gently washed the blood from my face and helped me remove my bloody clothes. Then she practically dressed me into some of Andrew's clothes.

"She called your dad at his second job and ordered him home. Then she was on the telephone with Jeanne. She didn't even say hello; she just said, 'Jeanne, it's Peggy, I need a favor.' I couldn't believe her. She was scolding Jeanne for crying and then for laughing. Your mom was making me laugh; it hurt so much.

"Your dad arrived in a panic. He didn't know what was going on. He saw me all packed and ready to go. He looked at Peggy and she said, 'No time to explain. You're bringing Toni to Truro; Jeanne's expecting you.' She handed Andrew a thermos of coffee and five dollars for gas, and said, 'Hurry back; you have to work in the morning.'

"Your dad nearly carried me to his car. We drove straight through to Truro. Andrew had only one thing to say. He kept repeating it for the entire ride, 'We'll take care of you, Anthony. Don't you worry.' I knew I looked bad because everyone always called me Toni. He meant what he said; he meant every word of it.

"We arrived at Jeanne's, and your dad nearly killed me, I laughed so hard. He said, 'Jeanne, honey, I need to use the head, I got to go.' I'll never forget those words. I thought he had to go to the bathroom really bad. No, he meant he had to go to the bathroom and go right back home. He hugged and kissed Jeanne and said to me, 'You're in the best hands possible,' and then he was gone.

"Peggy and Andrew were very special; they loved life and loved people. They were a happy couple. When I look at Meg and you, I see the same love they had for each other when they were together. The two of you remind me of your parents when your mom was still alive."

Jeanne had prepared Meg for what to expect when Toni told his story. When Toni started speaking, Meg went to her memory scrapbook and recalled the sunset at Rock Harbor. She concentrated on the image she had filed away. Meg blocked out the pain and agony Toni had experienced, and her own memories of the brutality she'd endured. She fixed on the sun slowly falling, vanishing into the bay. Meg now knew she had powerful memories to face Lewis if she couldn't find a way out of returning to him.

"Enough of this sad talk of the past. Tell us your plans. Where's your next adventure?" said Arthur after he had embraced and kissed Toni.

"We planned on driving back home tonight," said Nicholas.

"I'll have no such thing. It's much too late for you to drive all that way. You'll stay overnight and sleep here. Meg, you take the spare bedroom, and Nicholas will sleep on the couch," said Toni.

"That's all right, Toni, we sleep together on the floor. I wear my pajamas and my Holy Trinity sweatshirt, and Nicholas sleeps in his gym shorts and his football shirt. We watch the sunset every night like we did at Rock Harbor. Then we talk until we fall asleep. I mean, we don't actually watch the sunset. We sit on the blanket in the dark and imagine the fire in front of us. Nicholas pulls the window shade up, and in the darkness, we let our imaginations see the glow of the sun slowly slipping into the water."

"That sounds perfectly all right to me," said Arthur. He paused and said, "If that's not being too serious for you, Toni."

"I'm perfectly fine with the arrangement. I only suggested the other option to get my way. I'd planned to let them watch their imaginary sunset together from the very first time I saw these two innocent lovebirds," said Toni.

Arthur once more rolled his eyes, giving Meg and Nicholas another laugh. He then asked, "Now that you're staying over, what are your plans for tomorrow?"

"We'll leave in the morning, and if Meg wants, we can take our time. I won't make it back for spring practice, and the semester just ended. So, there's really no need to hurry." Nicholas paused for a moment then continued. "I just want to thank you for letting us stay the night—and for the delicious meal, and for all you told us about my parents."

"Your very welcome, Nicholas," said Toni.

As they all started to get up, Toni suddenly said, "I just thought of it. I have a tremendous idea! It'll be a special remembrance for you and Meg. You traveled the Cape together since Monday, recreating Nicholas's 1957 summer vacation. You said over the past four days, you've discovered wonderful memories of your parents when your mom was alive.

"Uncle Toni, yes, I'm adopting you, I owe it to your mom. I want you to feel the same happiness they felt on their honeymoon. You should experience all the luxury and excitement they did. The memories you create will be a comfort to you when you think of your mom. Uncle Toni is going to call a friend in Boston, and I'll take care of everything. You two lovebirds will recreate your mom and dad's honeymoon, without the hanky-panky, of course.

"I'll not take no for an answer. You'll be given a spectacular room and a fine dinner in their restaurant. After your meal, you can go up to your room and spread your blanket on the floor. You can sit in the darkness with the window curtains open and imagine the beautiful sunset.

"You'll be just like Peggy and Andrew in 1943. Only no one will have to ship out and leave the other all alone in the morning. How romantic! If Arthur's bones didn't need a soft mattress, I'd have him on the floor, and we would be watching the sunset together. Don't even think about the cost; it will all be arranged before you wake up in the morning."

Toni wouldn't take no for an answer. He said their only expense would be to promise to come back and visit him and Arthur. Meg and Nicholas thanked Toni for his generosity and promised to return. The two lovebirds, knowing they would now have two more nights together, looked into each other's eyes and smiled.

It was nearly eleven o'clock, and they were ready for bed. Toni showed Meg and Nicholas to the spare bedroom and told them to enjoy the sunset. As he was walking away, he remembered the fire and said, "Nicholas, there's a candle on the shelf you can use for your fire. It will create a very romantic atmosphere to watch your sunset. Please be sure to extinguish it before you fall asleep. Good night, and I'll give you the information about Boston in the morning."

Meg and Nicholas thanked Toni and told him good night. Meg went into the guest bathroom to shower. She dressed in her pajamas and the Holy Trinity sweatshirt. Nicholas was next and returned wearing his gym shorts and practice jersey. He retrieved the candle holder from the shelf while Meg spread the blanket on the floor.

The candle holder had a twelve-inch round base with a bowl of wax resting on top and a wick in the center. The bowl was multicolored with etchings of the seashore. Nicholas struck a match and lit the wick, and their makeshift campfire was glowing. He then opened the window shade and shut off the bedroom light.

Nicholas sat down next to Meg and wrapped the blanket around their shoulders. They pressed their bodies up against each other and were ready to visualize the fourth sunset of their improbable journey.

"Toni and Arthur are very nice," said Meg.

"They are. I can see why my mom and dad were very good friends with Toni."

"I think he's very funny, and he and Arthur have a wonderful relationship."

"They do, and I think if we spent more time with them, we'd learn that Arthur is the funny one. He doesn't need to say much to make you laugh."

"Were you surprised Toni was a man?" asked Meg.

"I didn't really think about it when Jeanne told us that Toni would be expecting us. The name could be a female or male. If you had asked me before we arrived, I would have guessed Toni was a woman. After hearing Jeanne speak about my mom, nothing would surprise me about her. All I know is that I washed a lot of convent floors for saying less than my mother did to the nuns."

Laughing, Meg said, "She was very daring when she was small."

"I would love to know how she thought. I'm not sure if that's the right way to describe it. She must have reasoned it out in her mind, why she felt she and the nun should be in charge of the class, and why she suddenly decided she should be called Peggy. Think about it, my mom thought it was perfectly acceptable to be best friends with a man in 1943, and she was married.

"My dad even thanked Toni for looking out for my mom during the war, and they were all friends. Not just friends. Toni said my mom called him 'family.'"

"I would have loved to meet your mom. She sounds amazing. I love the story when she called Jeanne. The world would be much better if everyone had a friend like Peggy."

"My mom must have made my dad feel like you make me feel. Since we've met, these last four days you've made me feel for the first time real joy and happiness. You gave me the strength to grieve all the sorrow I've carried over the loss of my mom and the courage to shed the tears I've been holding back.

"Since my mom died, I've kept all my sadness hidden, like my dad. I love my father, but I don't want to end up like him. I don't mean just losing my mom. He's been sad for fourteen years and has little desire for joy or happiness in his life. I don't want that kind of life. I want to have the life you've shown me, a life I now know really exists."

"I love you, Nicholas, so much. There's still time for us to find a way to stay together. I just need a little more time to think about how it can be done."

Nicholas turned to face Meg and kissed her eyes, then the tip of her nose, and slowly pressed his lips against hers. He then reached for her left hand and kissed the friendship ring on her finger and said, "I love you, Meg. If we're going to find a way to stay together, I propose we take the vows of friendship and seal our love."

Smiling, Meg said, "Nicholas, I accept. I love you, too."

Meg and Nicholas kneeled and faced each other, the candle's flame flickering on the floor between them. They extended their arms, held each other's hands, and together expressed their love by saying, "We promise to be true, to love, and honor all the days we are together."

Their eyes watering, the couple kissed. They felt the unity of their vows, and a hope that this was the beginning and not the end they were desperately resisting. Maybe Boston would no longer be their fifth and last night together. They allowed themselves to believe there would be many more nights to share in each other's arms.

Nicholas blew out the candle and returned it to its original place on the shelf. He sat back down next to Meg, the blanket pulled tightly across their backs. They relaxed their bodies and quietly watched the setting sun. As they imagined the glowing sphere peacefully descending into the bay, they once again quietly drifted off to sleep. It was the fourth night Meg and Nicholas lay fully clothed and slept serenely under an imaginary Cape Cod sky.

37

*M*eg woke early and gently kissed Nicholas while he slept. She slipped from under the blanket and went to the bathroom to change out of her pajamas. When she left the bedroom, the apartment was still quiet. She opened the door leading to a small outdoor deck and headed down the wooden stairs in the rear of the shop. She walked toward the front and onto Commercial Street.

Meg was shivering and glad she was still wearing her Holy Trinity sweatshirt. The morning air was cold, and the sun was still sleeping soundly. The streetlights were on as she walked in the direction of the wharfs. She could smell the salt air and feel the breeze off the bay.

Meg was the happiest she'd felt since she had received her acceptance letter from the College of Holy Trinity. She had the same feeling of hopefulness she'd felt reading the admissions letter. She imagined the freedom, the opportunity she would have had if she could have lived the life she dreamed about since childhood.

She loved the Green Hills section of Nashville where the houses were shrouded in old oak, pine, and walnut trees. It was her anchor, and she had thought it would always be her home. Even though she had always wanted to travel to experience new things, meet new people, and expand her knowledge academically and spiritually, to her the Volunteer State would always be a part of her.

But Meg knew all those dreams were in the past. She had new dreams since meeting Nicholas. She wanted to explore, to learn, to see, to feel. She still wanted to be the independent and confident person she created in her mind, the woman she was with Nicholas. She and Nicholas were exploring Cape Cod together. They'd shared their thoughts, their hopes, and the joy and sadness they had experienced. Meg felt she could make this paradise her new home.

Nicholas loved her and supported her. He was proud of her and had confidence in her. He loved that she painted and encouraged her to pursue her dreams. She knew Nicholas's hope was to be free of football. He dreamed of becoming a doctor. He wanted to join the Navy and be a corpsman so they could be together. Meg wanted to be with Nicholas, to be his partner, his wife, his lover. She could be like Peggy waiting for Andrew. She would live on Cape Cod surrounded by her new friends, the same friends that Nicholas's parents had, the people who loved them and loved Nicholas. They would love her, too.

Meg felt the excitement, the adrenaline rushing through her. She thought of the friendship vows they'd exchanged. She decided she was going to take real vows with Nicholas. They would be married, husband and wife, wife and husband, united as one.

She would tell him everything she had been holding back, all that was too terrifying to say. Meg felt the courage;

she would be brave. She would walk through that darkness with Nicholas at her side, and she would not fear Lewis's evil.

When Meg arrived at the wharf, her heart was racing. She walked down to the small strip of sand that ran along the water. She strolled the tiny area looking for a treasure. Meg noticed a small patch of greenery behind some of the houses lining the beach. She walked over to look at the small shrubs and the scattering of colorful flowers.

The sandy soil was harsh on the delicate plants; some were thriving and others wilting. Meg noticed a single yellow rose among the pink and the red. She could see the yellow rose was struggling to survive. She wanted to pick her favorite flower as a gift for Nicholas. Meg didn't have the heart to remove it from its roots, its life source. She plucked one of the healthy wildflowers and started back to sing to Nicholas. She couldn't wait to see him. This would be the start of their new beginning.

When Meg opened the door to the apartment, Toni was dressed and sitting at the kitchen counter. He was reading the *Cape Cod Times* and drinking coffee. Seeing Meg, he said, "Good morning, sweetheart. You're an early riser, aren't you? Arthur is down in the shop, and sleepyhead is dreaming of you, I'm sure. How was your walk this morning?"

"Good morning. It was wonderful. I walked to the wharf and to the little strip of beach by the water. I picked a flower for Nicholas."

"What a lucky boy. I'm going to have to remind Arthur there are still people who get flowers these days."

"I'm sorry, Toni. I should have picked one for you, too."

"That's sweet of you. Thank you."

"You're welcome."

"Meg, I would like to say something, and you don't need to say anything. I don't want to pry. I just know it's important that I do."

Meg tensed. She wasn't sure what Toni would say. She didn't think she'd revealed anything about her past. Maybe it was just advice from Uncle Toni about sleeping in the same room with Nicholas. Meg knew she was happy and determined. She was not going to let anything bother her, so she said, "Uncle Toni, you can tell me what you want to say. It's okay."

"You know I'm a friend of Jeanne's and you know the work she does. I am also a friend of Maggie and Gall, and well, I know when she sends her cranberry muffins to Jeanne, there's a reason. I know they said it's a long ride, and they don't get up this way too often. I'm sure she said that Gall is a bad driver. They say those things to send someone to Jeanne who needs help. They'll send someone directly or through a friend. It's always on an errand to deliver her delicious muffins. No one suspects anything, and Jeanne does her best to help those in need.

"I told you my story of how Jeanne helped me after Andrew dropped me off that night. I was the first abused man she'd helped, and she now helps other men victimized in relationships like me. The work she does is primarily with women who are abused, and she does good work.

"All I'm trying to say is if you know someone who needs her help, you should let them know."

"Thank you, Toni. I know how caring Jeanne is, and I want you to know, I will visit her again when I return from Boston. I want to speak with Nicholas tonight and let him know everything about me. I know he loves me, and he will help me."

"You're a good girl, Meg. You deserve happiness and love. We all deserve to be happy and loved."

Meg walked over and hugged Toni and held him tight and whispered, "Thank you, Toni. I love you."

Toni, with tears in his eyes, said, "That's Uncle Toni and don't ever forget that. You come see me when you get back like you promised."

"I will, Uncle Toni. I will."

"Now go wake up that handsome boyfriend of yours."

Meg knew she was ready to tell Nicholas. Speaking with Toni had been a test she'd passed without any difficulty. She wanted to tell Nicholas everything about the abuse she'd suffered, and she wanted Jeanne's help. Meg knew leaving Lewis would not be easy, but she felt she had all the support she needed on Cape Cod. She thought with Nicholas's love, anything was possible.

When Meg went into the bedroom, Nicholas was still asleep. She wondered if he would sleep all day if she let him. Smiling, she admitted to herself she was selfish. She wanted to hug him and kiss him, and get him up so they could just do, do anything, as long as they were doing it together.

Meg knelt on the floor next to Nicholas and held the flower to his nose. She let him inhale the fragrance. When he continued to sleep, she gently rubbed the flower on the tip of his nose. Nicholas was surely dreaming of Meg because he hadn't stirred; he was still sound asleep.

Meg had only one more thing she could do to wake him up. It was something she loved to do most and that was to sing. She took a deep breath and let her vocal cords do the rest. "You got to wake up every day . . . With a happy face on . . . And tell me how much you love me . . ." Meg continued to hold the "me" sound until Nicholas opened his eyes, smiled, and hugged and kissed her.

"You not only get a song today, and of course the hug and kiss, but you get this pretty flower that I picked for you."

"Wow, you do love me. You look very happy. Your walk this morning must have been invigorating."

"It was splendid! I walked down to the beach near the wharfs. There was a little patch of plants where someone was trying to grow small shrubs and flowers. I noticed a pretty yellow rose that I wanted for you, but it looked so weak. I knew if it remained attached to its roots, the flower had a chance to survive. If I picked the yellow rose, it would surely have wilted away. Instead, I picked you a healthy wildflower. I hope you like the color pink."

"I do like the color, and I love you for sharing your treasure with me. I love you for the vow of friendship we took last night. Most of all, I love you," said Nicholas as he hugged and kissed her.

When Nicholas released Meg from his embrace, she said, "I spoke with Toni when I came back from my walk, and he said Arthur was already in the shop. I thought it would be nice if we left Provincetown early. We could take our time driving to Boston. It would be good if we could stop and say good-bye to Jeanne and Francis and also Maggie and Gall. They were generous and kind; I thought it would be nice to see them one more time."

"That's why I love you. You're always thinking of other people."

"Well, I have to. You're always sleeping," said Meg as they laughed.

"If you want to get ready first, I'll go say good morning to Toni."

"Thank you, I won't take long."

As Meg showered and changed, Nicholas went to see Toni. They shared good mornings, and Toni gave Nicholas directions to the Parker House. He said to ask for Gerard at the front desk, and he would take very good care of them. He told Nicholas that Gerard managed the hotel and was a dear friend. When he visited Provincetown, he always stayed with Toni and Arthur.

Meg came out of the bedroom and was all packed. Nicholas went to take a shower and collect his belongings. When Meg left Nashville, she'd brought enough clothes for her trip. She had packed the few tops with three-quarter length sleeves she had at her parents' house. Before her marriage to Lewis, Meg didn't normally wear sleeves that long.

Meg had plenty of clothes in her old bedroom because Lewis insisted on having his mother purchase her a new wardrobe. She brought slacks and two sundresses with hems slightly below the knee. She also had a couple of lightweight sweaters, sandals, and a pair of low-wedged heel slip-ons.

Nicholas left Holy Trinity with the clothes he was wearing and the clothes he had worn to football practice. He also had his athletic shorts and practice jersey tucked into his gym bag. He was thankful when Maggie gave him a set of the summer ballplayer's clothes. She'd washed the ones he had worn the night he and Meg fell asleep on the beach. Nicholas knew he needed to find a laundromat soon; he was running out of things to wear.

Meg had emptied her keepsake box of all the money she had kept in her room at her parents' house. She had bought gas for her Volkswagen Beetle. Because it got such great gas mileage, they had to stop only once to fill the tank after leaving Holy Trinity.

When Nicholas was at school, he had a twenty-dollar bill in his wallet. The face of Andrew Jackson had been hibernating comfortably between the leather for over two months. Nicholas didn't have much money, and what little he had, he wasn't apt to spend.

He ate all his meals in the cafeteria with the exception of Sundays, when he would visit his dad. With football and all his courses, he didn't have the time or desire to just hang out or spend money. Nicholas used two dollars at Howard Johnson's when he went Dutch treat with Meg for lunch. The friendship rings cost him four dollars. He wanted to pay for both rings, but Meg had said it would mean more to her if they purchased each other's ring.

As Nicholas was packing the last of his belongings into his gym bag, he reflected on how fortunate they were on this trip. It was their fifth day on Cape Cod, and except for that first cold night on the beach, they'd enjoyed the comfort and hospitality of good people who had been friends of his parents and filled in the blank pages of his memory with vivid stories and examples of his mother and father's love for each other, and for the love they had for their friends. He was grateful for Meg. She had made their fantastic voyage possible. Nicholas knew Meg made him better than he could ever be without her, and he felt blessed.

Nicholas had such a good feeling as he was about to depart Provincetown. He had exchanged friendship vows with Meg and could feel the union of their two hearts strengthening. Nicholas believed experiencing his parents' honeymoon would change the trajectory of his life. He would not live a life of sadness like his father. All that mattered to him was loving Meg and honoring her. He told himself, *I will take a real vow to be true to Meg for all the days of my life.*

When Meg and Nicholas were ready and packed, they thanked Toni. The three then went down to the shop to say good-bye to Arthur. They all embraced, and Arthur and Toni each kissed Meg. Toni wished them good luck and winked at Meg. Arthur told Meg he wanted first dibs on all her paintings.

As they drove away they could see their two newest friends waving good-bye. What they couldn't see was Meg's Holy Trinity sweatshirt, her shield from all that was cold, hanging on a hook behind the bathroom door. Anthony would later find it and pray that one day the sweatshirt and Meg would be united.

38

$\mathcal{M}$eg was happy to be back behind the wheel of her VW driving to Truro. Toni told them to take Shore Road that ran along the bay. They had plenty of time and wanted to enjoy their last day on Cape Cod.

They arrived at Jeanne's house mid-morning, and Jeanne smiled when she saw them. Francis was home from work. His first class on Friday was at two o'clock, and he usually left by noon. Jeanne asked Nicholas if he wouldn't mind going to the market with Francis. She wanted them to pick up a few items for lunch. Since they surprised her with their visit, she decided to make them something to eat before they continued on their journey.

Jeanne said she was hoping Meg would take a short walk with her since she'd enjoyed her company. Nicholas, agreeable by nature, was happy to take a ride with Francis.

Once the two men drove away, Jeanne and Meg walked to the peaceful reserve and sat on the garden bench. Jeanne took note of how vibrant Meg looked. She saw there was a glow of excitement about her, and she looked happy.

Jeanne wanted to speak with Meg once more, now that she'd stopped to visit.

"You look terrific. Did you have a pleasant time in Provincetown?" asked Jeanne.

"I did, yes, it was wonderful. Toni and Arthur were delightful and very funny. Toni was brave to tell us everything about the time Nicholas's mother and father helped him. Arthur was so caring when Toni became emotional. I could see he was suffering telling his story. It broke my heart."

Jeanne looked directly into Meg's eyes and asked, "How are you doing?"

Jeanne only wanted to help. Meg needed to want her help, to be ready for it. Jeanne could not make the decision for her; it was Meg's alone. There was nothing else Jeanne could do. Meg was the one at risk. She was the one who needed to decide her future.

Excitedly, Meg responded and said, "Oh, Jeanne, I'm so happy. I love Nicholas. I'm going to tell him everything about my life tonight. If you still want to help me, I will come back, and you can help me figure everything out."

"Can you stay now?" was Jeanne's quick response.

Meg didn't want to disappoint Jeanne, but she wanted to go to Boston for Nicholas. She wanted to help him feel his mother's presence one more time. Meg tried to explain why she couldn't stay and said, "Toni is sending us to the Parker House to experience Nicholas's mom and dad's honeymoon. It's important that we go to Boston tonight. That's where I want to tell Nicholas everything about my past." Meg paused for a few seconds as Jeanne watched her intently. Meg, suddenly feeling the pangs of guilt, looked down at her interlocked hands resting on her lap and solemnly said, "It will be painful for me to recall all that I need to tell Nicholas. But he deserves to know everything about me. I have to be honest with him. I love him so much." Looking up at Jeanne, Meg had tears in her eyes, and after pausing said, "Nicholas will accept me with all my scars, and with all my heart. I know how much he loves me, and I love him."

Jeanne heard the pain in Meg's words. She could also see how good Nicholas and Meg were together. Jeanne knew how much Andrew loved Peggy, and she could see that Nicholas and Meg shared that same love for each other. She just wasn't convinced going to Boston was the right thing for them to do. Meg was here now. She didn't want to risk her leaving. Jeanne delicately asked, "Would you consider not going to Boston and staying? You could tell Nicholas about everything here."

Meg looked back down and hesitated before speaking. She wasn't sure how to say no without seeming ungrateful or offending Jeanne. After sitting in silence for a few minutes, Meg looked back up, held her gaze on Jeanne, and slowly shook her head. Her eyes began to water, and sensing her distress, Jeanne reached out and embraced her.

Jeanne with regret said, "You can come back tomorrow. I'll be here to help you. You don't have to worry. I'll always be here for you."

With sadness Meg said, "Thank you. I want to come back. I don't ever want to go home. I want to come back with Nicholas and be safe and happy. I will come back."

"I'll be waiting for you to return, I promise." Jeanne again embraced Meg, and when she released her said, "Why don't you go wash your face before Francis and Nicholas return."

"Thank you," whispered Meg. They stood up and walked back to the house.

Jeanne would always keep her promise and wait for Meg to return. She just didn't believe she would ever come back.

When Francis and Nicholas returned, Jeanne prepared an early lunch for them to eat. After the meal was finished, Francis left the table to get ready for work, and Meg and Nicholas helped Jeanne wash the dishes. They said their good-byes when Francis returned to the kitchen. The four friends walked to the driveway, and Jeanne waved as the two cars drove away. Francis was on his way to work, and Meg and Nicholas were headed to Rock Harbor.

Meg was determined not to let anything interfere with her plan for Boston. Heading down the highway, she and Nicholas had the windows down and the radio playing. Meg would show her joy once again. She was singing and humming to her favorite songs.

As the car traveled down Route 6, they were quickly out of Truro. They continued through the towns of Wellfleet and Eastham before entering Orleans. The twenty-mile drive was over in forty-five minutes. Before they knew it, they were back on Rock Harbor Road.

Arriving at the familiar house, Meg drove her Beetle onto the shelled driveway. When Maggie and Gall heard the car arrive and saw it was yellow, they quickly went outside to greet them. Nicholas exchanged a handshake with Gall, then hugged Maggie. Meg embraced both of her new friends, who now felt like family.

Maggie was disappointed she couldn't feed them because they'd eaten with Jeanne. That didn't stop her from packing a lunch for their ride to Boston. Nicholas and Meg spoke about the fantastic time they had on the Outer Cape. Nicholas shared the story of Jeanne's friendship with his parents and how they'd gone to Provincetown to meet Toni. He told Maggie and Gall that Toni was another friend of his mom and dad who shared all of his beautiful stories about them. Nicholas also said he now felt like he was really beginning to know his parents' happiness when his mom was alive.

The visit was short but packed with all the details of their travels. As they prepared to leave, Meg said, "Thank you, Maggie, for asking us to bring your cranberry muffins to Jeanne. She's an incredible and helpful person. We really have you and Gall to thank for sending us on a fantastic journey."

"You're very welcome, honey. I hope you come back and spend some time with us, but don't wait too long. We're going to miss you until you return and visit again."

"I will, Maggie. I very much want to come back and see you again."

The two women understood the real meaning of their exchange and were both hopeful their paths would cross again.

Back on Route 6, it wasn't long before the Lower Cape was behind them, and they were traveling through the Mid-Cape, and into the Upper Cape. As they crossed the Sagamore Bridge Meg shouted out, "Good-bye, Cape Cod! See you soon!"

Nicholas laughed and said, "Wow, you not only talk to seagulls, you speak to islands. I just hope they don't talk back."

"I believe Cape Cod is a peninsula, but anyway, they do speak back to me, just not in words. I try to feel them. When I see my seagulls, I feel free. With Cape Cod, I feel all the happiness and joy we experienced together. When we're not speaking, I feel like we are and can sense your love and hear your voice. Like now, you're not talking, but I can hear you saying, I love you."

"You have a wonderful heart and a beautiful soul, Meg Elizabeth Gabriel."

"You do, too, Nicholas Andrew Avellino."

They were cruising up Route 3 heading to Boston. Meg and Nicholas were leaving the peace and natural wonder of Cape Cod. The farther north they drove, the yellow Beetle began to merge with the congestion of urban traffic, crowded and noisy streets, and the bleak shadows of concrete buildings. The transition infected their joy and happiness; hopefully, it would not metastasize and alter their trajectory.

39

*M*eg preferred the wide-open roads of Tennessee to the narrow ones of Boston. She wasn't used to one-way streets, bumper-to-bumper traffic, or honking horns. Nicholas didn't drive, so Meg piloted their way through the urban terrain, finally reaching School Street and the Parker House.

When they arrived at the hotel, Nicholas could see the stress leave Meg's face. She quickly transformed back into the optimistic young woman who had left Provincetown six hours earlier.

Toni had told them about the valet service and to not worry about parking the car. Their bags were light and they carried them into the lobby. When Nicholas asked for Gerard, he suddenly appeared out of nowhere. He was very gracious and asked about Toni and Arthur. He said he visited them regularly, but that Toni was reluctant to leave the Cape. Gerard said when he received the call about a room for Toni's nephew he was thrilled to help. He told them he owed Toni and Arthur for their hospitality and friendship and was glad to reciprocate.

Gerard escorted Meg and Nicholas to their room on the fifth floor. Before leaving, he said, "The maître d' will be expecting you this evening. Just tell him you're under Gerard's reservation. You'll love our restaurant, but if you prefer, just order room service and charge the cost to the room. Now, don't worry about the prices, I've taken care of everything."

Meg and Nicholas thanked Gerard for his generosity, and when he was gone, they started laughing. They couldn't believe the size and beauty of the hotel, the wood-paneled lobby with the elegant lighting, the rich carpeting, and the spaciousness. Meg had never traveled with Lewis, but she'd traveled with her parents. They'd stayed in hotels, but nothing like she was experiencing now. Nicholas would be spending his first night in a hotel and felt intimidated by his surroundings.

Their room was grand with rich cream-colored walls, a king-size bed, and gold-colored hardware in the bathroom. It had everything Nicholas had never dreamed about because he didn't know it existed. When he looked at Meg, he was smiling. He was excited that they would have another memorable experience together.

"I wonder if my mom and dad felt like I do right now. I'm overwhelmed by everything about this place. It makes me want to jump into your car and head back to Cape Cod. I felt like we were living a dream down there. In this beautiful hotel, it's more like a fantasy," said Nicholas.

Meg walked over to Nicholas and stood in front of him. She reached out and held his two hands and said, "It's overwhelming for me, too. I'm sure your mom and dad felt the same way we do. They probably laughed just like we had, and with your dad going to war, your mom and dad deserved one night together living a fantasy."

"I can't imagine how my mother felt when my dad boarded the train the next day and was gone, not knowing when or if he'd come back to her. The loneliness, the sadness she must have felt. It was good she had a friend as considerate and caring as Toni."

"He was a very good friend, and your father thanked him for being there for your mom when he couldn't."

"Still, to think of her all alone."

"Your mom was very strong. Jeanne told us how brave she was when she became ill. Your mother was determined for you and your father to have wonderful memories. That's why she wanted the summer vacation on Cape Cod."

"I'm not sure how she would feel about my father never sharing the experience with me. He must feel such sadness when he looks at the picture of me and Mom."

"Nicholas, your mom loved you, and she loved your dad. She would forgive his sadness just as I know you do."

"I don't hold it against him. I'm a lot like him in many ways. He didn't want a sad life. He would have died for Mom if he could."

Meg gave Nicholas a light kiss on the lips and seductively said, "I bet when your mom and dad were in this big room, they were thinking exactly what I'm thinking."

Meg got Nicholas to smile with her enticing words. He asked, "And what are you thinking?"

Meg looked into his eyes and then let her warm brown eyes wander toward the king-size bed. "Well, I'm thinking . . ." she said, as her eyes slowly drifted back to Nicholas, "that we go for a walk." They started laughing, kissed, and headed for the door.

The young couple feeling like newlyweds walked out of the hotel, holding hands, and felt the heat of the city. The cool breezes of Cape Cod were in the past. They proceeded down Tremont Street strolling by the Granary Burial Ground, and shortly, the golden dome of the Massachusetts State House, as they wandered through the Boston Common.

Meg and Nicholas were back where they felt the most comfortable. They were outdoors, surrounded by grass and trees, and plenty of birds and squirrels. People were walking or sitting on blankets or benches. The green grass, trees, and sloping terrain all combined to create the illusion of being in a town square and not in the center of the state's capital city.

They crossed Charles Street and entered the public garden. Meg and Nicholas walked along the center path toward the small lagoon. From the pedestrian bridge, they watched ducks with their ducklings, and beautiful white swans floating on top of the water. They noticed several comfortable looking places to sit and chose one with soft grass next to a colorful bed of flowers to talk and pass the time. As they spoke quietly of their short time together, they watched the light of the day dim and turn into an evening gray.

As darkness set in, they followed the streetlights back to the hotel. Meg needed to call home to tell her mother that she wasn't returning. Her father was sure to have noticed her car missing from the garage. She'd left her wedding ring on her bureau and clothes scattered about the bedroom when she rushed out of the house. Lewis would still be away, and she didn't think her parents could contact him. Meg knew her mother and father would be worried about her. She was very concerned about her dad's health but couldn't help it; this was a trip she'd needed to make.

Meg wanted to have fond memories to block out Lewis's brutality. But she decided she was never going back. Once Meg made the telephone call to her parents, she would tell Nicholas everything about her past.

Meg didn't know how she would call home with Nicholas present. She couldn't think of a way to leave him long enough to make the call. When they arrived back at the Parker House, Nicholas helped by saying he wanted to use the restroom in the lobby. Meg then asked if he would go into the hotel shop and buy something cold to drink. She told him she was going to use one of the nearby telephones to call home and let her mother know she was in Boston.

Meg closed the sliding glass door to the booth so she could have privacy. She dialed the operator and asked to make a collect call to Nashville, Tennessee. When Mrs. Gabriel answered the telephone, the operator spoke and said, "I have a collect call from your daughter Margaret. Will you please accept the charges?"

"Yes, yes, we, I will," said Mrs. Gabriel.

"Thank you, ma'am. You may speak now," said the operator.

When Mrs. Gabriel spoke, she was not kind to Margaret. She used guilt as a knife and her wedding vows as a club. It was part of the trap the Barrens had set for Meg in 1970. Mrs. Gabriel used her last verbal weapon, and it left Margaret shaken.

Meg hung up the telephone. She needed to compose herself before she saw Nicholas. She rushed from the booth and ran into the ladies' room. Her face was red and her cheeks moist. Meg splashed water over her tears to wash away her sadness and waited until she felt calm. As she gazed at her reflection in the mirror over the sink, she stared hard at the face looking back, trying to visualize

Jenny. Instead of conjuring up the fictional character, Meg recalled the photograph Jeanne had shown her, and imagined Peggy's reflection. Meg then looked up to the heavens and quietly whispered, *I need your strength and courage to be brave—I need your strength and courage to be brave—I need your strength and courage to be brave.*

When Meg walked out of the restroom, she was composed. She forced a smile on her face. She was yearning for Nicholas. Meg wanted his arms wrapped around her, so she could feel his strength and love. She needed all he had to block out her mother's words. They were words that ran through her heart and penetrated her soul. Meg was determined to conceal her anguish; she didn't want to appear upset. She wanted everything to be perfect for Nicholas.

Meg could see how handsome Nicholas was as he walked out of the shop and approached her through the lobby. His hair was a little lighter than it had been on Monday when they'd first met. His face was tanned, and he showed the full width of his natural smile when he saw Meg. The five days in the sun had lightened his hair and brought out the natural color of his skin. The dark complexion framed his white teeth perfectly. Meg thought if Nicholas was the image of the man Peggy had fallen in love with, she could certainly understand why.

It would be their fifth night together. Meg wanted the imaginary sunset to be special. The room would be dark; she would make it so very dark. Nicholas would not see what she was hiding. When he felt the ridges of the scars on her body, she would say, "Shh, tomorrow." She would be with Nicholas; she needed to be with him. He would make love to her. He would always make love to her. They would make love all the days of her life.

Part Four

*Even when I walk through
a dark valley, I fear no harm
for you are at my side;
your rod and your staff give me courage.*

40

argaret let go of her beautiful thoughts of the time she'd spent with Nicholas. She had to return to the task she needed so desperately to complete. The letter was still not finished, and she knew her time was running out. Margaret continued to feel nauseous, weak, and now a pounding in her head and dizziness were her new burdens. She had been fighting against her body's will to die.

Discharging the contents of her stomach gave her a little relief. The water from the faucet helped her shaking ease to a cold shiver. Margaret sensed a temporary truce with her physical being. But now her mind was attacking her. She was fighting with a voice inside her head telling her to surrender, repeating over and over the deafening sound of defeat, *You can stop the pain. You don't need to finish the letter. End your suffering. Do it now!*

Margaret picked up the bottle of sleeping pills she'd brought from the medicine cabinet. She opened the plastic lid and poured the contents into her hand. She looked at the glass sitting on her desk. She dropped the little white pills into the warm water and watched them break down into tiny, colorless specks as they slowly dissipated.

Margaret would not succumb to defeat just yet. With her hand quivering, she picked up the pen and spoke the words so she could hear the sound of her voice. *I am with you, Nicholas. I will walk through this pain with you at my side. I will not fear Lewis's evil.*

Tears trickling, her reservoir nearly empty, it was all the water that remained in her eyes.

With the little strength she had, she let her mind return to September 1970, her wedding day. She would now write about her marriage to Lewis.

Before Margaret met Nicholas, she could recall every detail of her wedding. She would try to determine what caused her life to crumble. She had been told so many times that it was all her fault, the abuse, what Lewis did to her, her inability to get pregnant and give him a child. She had wanted to find answers to make things right, and then maybe the pain and loneliness would evaporate. After being with Nicholas, his goodness and love, she no longer remembered or searched for answers from that horrible day.

Nicholas had restored in Margaret her love, happiness, and joy. She no longer blamed herself or accepted the blame that rightly belonged to Lewis. He alone owned his anger and violence. Margaret would feel all of Nicholas's love through the memories of their time together and the thoughts she had stored in her heart. He had given her the strength and courage to want to leave Lewis and never return to him. She had wanted desperately to stay with Nicholas, but her mother's words, penetrating, biting, pulled her back home.

Margaret had felt Nicholas's love was enough to save her from her husband's sins. She was so agonizingly wrong. There was a deeper love for her father that five days could never erase—a decision that had broken her heart, but one she'd made because she had greater love for her father than she had for herself.

Margaret knew she would have Nicholas's love forever. She would always carry him in her heart, and it would have to be enough. She believed the goodness of their love was a gift from God and the only faith she needed. Margaret would never believe the love they had for each other was wrong. To her, their love was not a sin. She would never ask forgiveness for a love so beautiful.

Margaret remembered the verse in Ecclesiastes in the Old Testament, "You had better not make a vow than make it and not fulfill it." But she'd learned from Jeanne to let your conscience guide you, that in your final judgment it would be known you broke a vow, but you loved and were loved. Margaret no longer believed in the sanctity of a vow when there was no love and only evil. She would be judged because she loved.

The brutality and trauma Lewis had inflicted on Margaret when she returned to him caused her to repress his violence. She endured the pain of Lewis's assaults by concentrating on the joyful, loving memories she had with Nicholas. It helped her block out the horror.

Margaret thought of the only moment from her wedding ceremony she could now recall. It came back to her as the nausea passed through her and she vomited. She had her arms wrapped around the porcelain bowl when her vision of that moment became clear. Margaret had been standing on the altar and looking directly at Lewis. She had just finished saying, "All the days of my life," and for a flash, she caught a glimpse of the malicious grin on Lewis's face. His eyes were dark and cold. His look was so frightening. Margaret blinked, and the evil expression vanished. Margaret's gaze was still fixed on Lewis. She could see his lips moving as he said his vows, but she couldn't hear the words he spoke. When his mouth stopped moving, he kissed her lips. Margaret felt nothing. She was lightheaded, dizzy, and blamed the horrid vision of Lewis on her anxiety over the wedding.

Margaret could not recall the reception or how she'd arrived home, but she would never forget her wedding night.

41

*T*he two most memorable events of Margaret's wedding night were the punch to the face and the throbbing, awful pain between her legs.

When Margaret opened her eyes, the room was dark. She couldn't see through the blackness. She sensed Lewis was in the bed beside her. His breathing was slow, steady, and even; he appeared to be in a deep sleep.

Margaret's body was incapable of moving. It was as if she was encased in a solid block of ice. She wanted to get out of bed and go to the bathroom, but her body wouldn't move. When she recalled Lewis hitting her and forcing himself into her with such savageness, she was thankful for her paralysis. She did not want to disturb the monster sleeping next to her. Margaret desperately tried to remember why it happened. The fatigue from concentrating on the horror overwhelmed her, and she fell back to sleep.

When Margaret awoke for the second time, the room was no longer dark. She had a sudden recollection of waking in total darkness, unable to move, and feeling such agonizing pain. She wasn't sure if it had been a nightmare. It only took a moment for her to recall just how real it was; her pain was so intense she squeezed her eyes shut. The sudden blankness frightened her. Before she could open her eyes, her body flinched. She remembered Lewis's powerful fist striking her cheek, knocking her to the bed. He had the horrid look on his face. His weight was crushing her tiny body, and suddenly there was terrible pain between her legs and violent thrusting. Seeing Lewis's evil stare had shocked her. She could hear his snorts and his grunts, and then everything went blank.

The vividness of this recollection engulfed Margaret. Everything came at her at once: the throbbing of her face, the aching pain between her legs, the need to relieve herself, her fear of Lewis. The thought of his name brought her back to the present. She struggled to suppress her suffering. She needed to know if Lewis was in the room. Cautiously looking around, she let her eyes and ears search for his presence. The bathroom door was closed. She listened intently for water running, the flushing of the toilet, or any movement at all. She could hear no sound; there was only silence.

Margaret felt a sudden solace, but it was short lived. Her physical pain was increasing, intensifying, throbbing. She raised a hand to her face and when her fingers lightly touched her battered cheek, she cried out. She reached between her legs to stop the pain and felt dampness. She removed her hand and saw the smear of pasty dark red: her blood. Her bladder bursting, she ran to the bathroom, sat on the toilet, and relieved herself.

Margaret couldn't determine how long she remained on the plastic seat before she found the will to stand. When see looked at her face in the mirror, her one brown eye didn't recognize her own reflection. She could see the blackish-blue color. Her left eye was swollen and closed. Her tears were falling for the first time since the terrifying assault. As she continued to stare at her face in the mirror, her despair was jolted by a sudden sense of smell. Her perspiration, the dried blood, and the smell of Lewis's sweat on her body was nauseating. She needed to cleanse herself of his filth.

Margaret stood under the shower, she wanted to feel clean. She let the water spray hot until it burnt her cream-colored skin. She was scrubbing and washing, washing and scrubbing. She lost track of time until she felt the goosebumps on her body and her hands begin to shake. She realized the hot water had run out. Her delicate lips were blue, and she was shivering.

Margaret turned off the water, stepped from the shower, and gently dried herself. Her movements were driven by memory. She was nauseous, weak, and cold, and she couldn't stop shaking. Her confusion was driven by a single thought, *Why did this happen?*

Margaret had left some of her clothes in the bathroom the night before. Through her pain and tears she slowly dressed herself. When she was ready to leave the bathroom, Margaret placed an ear against the door. She was trying to listen for Lewis. The room was quiet, and she was afraid. She couldn't decide what to do. She cried out, *Daddy!*

Margaret cautiously entered the bedroom. She was bracing herself for the sight of Lewis standing naked by the bed, as he had been the night before. When she'd been in the bathroom preparing herself for their first night as husband and wife, Margaret had stalled for time. She'd been nervous and a bit fearful. During her courtship with Lewis, her physical contact with him had been limited. Margaret and Lewis held each other's hands and kissed, but never passionately.

Margaret thought Lewis had grown impatient waiting for her, but as she entered the bedroom he immediately opened his arms as if to reassure her. Margaret thought the gesture was an expression of understanding, that Lewis was being sensitive. She had momentarily felt reassured and comforted. She had never been so wrong.

When Margaret exited the bathroom this time, the room was empty. She knew she would never let herself relax in the bedroom again. Her pain had not diminished, and she felt its burden as she stood motionless trying to decide what to do. Her first thought had been to call her father, but she was afraid Lewis would return while they were speaking. She didn't know what to expect when he came back. She asked herself, *What could Lewis possibly do or say to explain his behavior last night? How can I live in this house with him?*

Margaret wanted to speak with her father. She shivered when she realized what her call would do to his weak heart. She would need to rely on her mother. She knew her mother loved her and would tell her what to do. Calling her mother, she reasoned, was worth the risk. Margaret thought if she was on the telephone with her mother, she would be safe. She believed Lewis wouldn't hurt her, at least until she hung up. She then said to herself, *What could he do to me then? I would have told mother everything.*

Margaret recalled there was a telephone in the hall just outside of the bedroom. Again, she proceeded cautiously. She waited at the door to listen for movement. When Margaret was satisfied Lewis wasn't in the hallway, she opened the door. She picked up the telephone and dialed the number to her parents' house. She waited nervously through five rings. On the sixth, her mother winded said, "Hello."

Margaret, hearing the familiar voice of her mother, began to cry. She couldn't speak. She kept trying to say, "Mother," but through her sobs the words came out garbled.

Her mother spoke into the telephone with concern and asked, "Margaret, is that you? Is that you, Margaret? You're crying. What's wrong?"

Hearing her mother's soft southern accent helped Margaret regain some control. Her crying slowed enough to speak and she said, "Oh, Mother, last night was so frightening. Lewis hurt me badly."

Margaret's mother did not fully comprehend the meaning behind her daughter's words and abruptly said, "Margaret, please stop what you're saying. Pull yourself together. You're a married woman now."

Pleading, Margaret said, "But, Mother, it was so awful."

With firmness her mother said, "My dear, you need to pull yourself together. Of course, it was awful the first time. What did you think would happen when you fell in love and were married? Love isn't always so pleasant."

"Mother, you don't understand, Lewis—"

Her mother cut her off when she mentioned Lewis for the second time. She remained firm, saying, "Margaret, you need to hear me. Now please listen. What goes on in your bedroom is up to your husband. You have a duty to him. I will not discuss this topic with you."

"Mother," cried Margaret.

Softening, her mother said, "Darling, I love you very much and want you to be happy. You need to try harder to satisfy your husband. It will get easier. Now, is that clear?"

Margaret was unable to respond. She couldn't believe what her mother was saying. She struggled for words as she said, "I want to come home."

"This is not your home anymore, Margaret. You have your own home and a husband to satisfy, a man who will take care of you once you learn to take care of him. You need to give yourself time to learn his needs. Do you understand what I am telling you?"

"Mother, Lewis."

"Margaret, you can talk to me about the weather, you can ask me how your father is doing, but you cannot ever speak with me about your husband or your bedroom. Is that clear?"

"Mother, I'm not sure I can stay here."

Raising her voice, her mother said, "Margaret, you can and you will."

"I want to talk with Daddy."

With anger in her voice her mother said, "Listen to me. You will not discuss Lewis, your marriage, or anything else with your father. He had a very severe heart attack and nearly died. He may never fully recover. You'll not upset him. Is that clear? Do you understand me?"

In a tone of utter despair, she mumbled, "Yes, Mother."

"Now, Margaret, you're a smart girl, and you'll figure it out. We all had to learn how to satisfy our husbands. Believe me, I will cherish your telephone calls and your visits, as long as you respect my wishes. You will not discuss what goes on between you and Lewis with me. Now I need to say good-bye. Please give my love to your new husband."

As the telephone line went dead, Margaret gasped for air. She felt dizzy and nauseous, and couldn't comprehend the conversation she'd just had with her mother. Her body was aching; the bedroom door stood ominous. Fear gripped her, and the only sound was the echo, *How can I live here?*

Margaret made her way down to the living room. She wrapped herself in a cotton throw blanket and sat on the sofa with her legs tucked under her. She quietly recited her prayers for the first time since the wedding ceremony.

She wanted to remain awake until Lewis came home. She was too afraid to sleep, but she was so very tired.

42

*M*rs. Barren entered the house through the back door. She walked through the foyer that led to the kitchen. She didn't know where she would find Margaret. She did know she was still in the house. When Lewis had left that morning, Margaret had been asleep. He'd set the security alarm, and it was still activated when Mrs. Barren arrived. Margaret didn't know about the alarm. It was one more thing she would have to explain to her.

As Mrs. Barren was making her way through the house, she caught a glimpse of Margaret wrapped in a blanket and asleep on the sofa. She quietly entered the room and sat in a chair that allowed her to watch Margaret without disturbing her rest. She did not want to startle her. She had her instructions from her husband, and there was a lot she needed to discuss with the new Mrs. Lewis Isaak Barren.

While Margaret continued to sleep, Mrs. Barren reflected on the conversation she'd had with her husband earlier that morning. When Lewis had left the house the first full day as a married man, he'd gone directly to see his father at the office. Lewis had known his father had not planned to travel on business the day after the wedding. He had chosen the office because he wanted to avoid his mother until first speaking with his father.

Lewis had been in trouble before, and he'd presumed that his father would be annoyed with him but would neither judge nor scold him. His father had dealt with previous incidents by simply opening up his wallet to solve the problem. When Lewis entered his father's office, Isaak looked at his son and knew Lewis had already been violent with his wife. He became concerned when his son told him about the punch to Margaret's face. Lewis provided his father with a good description of the injury. Isaak knew from experience that in a matter of an hour, the severity of the bruising and swelling would magnify and look significantly worse.

Isaak had always protected his son and had never told his wife about Lewis's latent tendencies for violence. He knew it was inevitable; Doris would one day need to be told. Like him, she would do anything to help her son. Isaak was well aware that whoever Lewis married would eventually feel his wrath. He just hadn't expected it to be on Lewis's wedding night. Isaak wouldn't dwell on this detail. He knew protecting Lewis was about protecting the family name.

After some reflection, he told himself, *Since it was going to happen, it's probably best it happened quickly.*

There would be no honeymoon. Isaak sent Lewis out of state on business for a few days. He then telephoned Doris. He explained to her that their son had inherited certain behaviors from Vernon Exuvial Barren. He told her she would need to attend to Margaret. Doris was already prepared to assist Margaret in her role as a Barren wife. This new matter was simply another piece of family business to handle.

Doris Barren wasn't very sentimental or emotional. She either liked or disliked people. Doris loved very few people. She was manipulative but not hateful—that was an emotional response. She tried never to let herself become emotional. She was prepared to comfort Margaret to gain her trust, but then it would be down to business.

As Margaret began to stir, she felt a presence, a silhouette. In the fog of her fatigue, she wasn't sure. As her eyes adjusted to the haze, her body tensed. She could see the outline of a figure sitting in a chair in the far corner of the room. Before Margaret's vision was clear, Mrs. Barren said, "My darling girl, I didn't want to disturb you."

Margaret felt such relief hearing the voice of Lewis's mother, her eyes quickly began to tear. Her voice whimpered when she said, "Mrs. Barren." As she tried to move, she winced and let out a grunt. The pain immediately consumed her. The pounding in her head as she sat up to face Mrs. Barren made her dizzy and nauseous. She moved her hand to her battered cheek and flinched, as the pain reminded her of last time she touched Lewis's hate.

Mrs. Barren in a tone of concern said, "Oh dear, Margaret, that looks terrible. We need to put some ice on that bruise immediately. You shouldn't have waited so long. Now it'll take much longer to heal. Let me get you some ice."

The little attention Margaret received from Mrs. Barren was a relief to her. She couldn't understand her mother's reaction to her distress. Mrs. Barren seemed concerned, and her helpfulness in caring for Margaret's swollen and bruised face was a comfort to her. Margaret ached for someone who would help her and tell her what to do.

When Mrs. Barren came back to the room, she sat next to Margaret. She then handed her ice wrapped in a cloth. Mrs. Barren held the hand with the ice, and assisted Margaret to carefully place it against her face. She continued to help her hold the cold pack while it gently rested on her swollen, purple-bluish eye.

Margaret thanked Mrs. Barren, her voice filled with despair. Mrs. Barren didn't respond immediately. She needed to know if Margaret had called and spoken to anyone prior to her arrival. She didn't think she had because she was alone; however, she wanted to be sure. When she did respond, she said, "You're very welcome." She paused for a couple of seconds then asked, "How long did you sleep on the couch?"

"I'm not sure. I don't even know what time it is."

"How did you walk to the couch? You must have used the stairs. You seem unsteady. My goodness, you could have fallen."

"I don't clearly remember. I went into the hallway to call Mother, and I must have walked down the stairs to the sofa."

Mrs. Barren wanted to give Margaret time to think about the call before she questioned her further. She needed Margaret to talk as much as she wanted before asking her questions. Mrs. Barren wanted Margaret to feel she was her ally, someone she could trust.

Gently prodding, Mrs. Barren said, "Did you reach your mother."

To her surprise, Margaret burst out crying and said, "She told me to try harder and do better. It's my duty to satisfy my husband. I don't even know what I did wrong."

Mrs. Barren suddenly knew she would have no problem with this young girl. She hugged Margaret and said, "Dear, dear, if you want to cry, just let the tears flow. You can count on me for help. We'll figure it all out. You'll become a good wife to your husband. Now don't you worry."

Margaret let go of her tears and through her sobs said, "Thank you, thank you. I love you. I'm so sorry. I just don't know what I did wrong."

"Don't you worry, my dear. Everything will work out just fine. I'm sure your mother knows best when she told you to try harder. We all want to satisfy our husbands. After all, they do work hard to take care of us."

"I do want to be a good wife. I love Lewis. I just don't know what I did wrong."

"I think the best thing is for you to tell Lewis you're sorry for what you did, and ask him how you can do better. I'm sure he'll appreciate your words and your desire to be a good wife. We all had to find our way when we were first married. I'm sure your mother was talking to you from experience."

"I do want to be a good wife. I'm not sure I know how."

"Lewis had to leave for a few days on business, and when he gets back tell him you're sorry. I'm sure he will tell you what he wants from you. You'll see, it will all get better."

"I do hope so. I don't have anyone to talk with. Mother told me she loves me and looks forward to seeing me, as long as I don't talk about Lewis. I only wish I had someone to talk with, someone to help me."

"Margaret, you sweet dear. If I had a daughter, I would give her the same advice your mother gave you. Mothers know their sons best. I certainly want to help, but only if you truly want me to."

"Thank you, Mrs. Barren. I do want your help."

"Margaret, darling, I only want what's good for you. You can always count on me to be your very best friend. Now don't you worry, everything will get better," said Mrs. Barren.

43

*W*hile Lewis was away on business, Mrs. Barren would spend several hours every day with Margaret. She tended to her injured face, making sure it healed properly. Margaret was lonely and always grateful for the company. Since the beating, she hadn't left the house. Mrs. Barren had advised her not to go anywhere until the bruising disappeared completely.

Mrs. Barren was satisfied she had prepared Margaret for her son's return, and Margaret was pleased she had someone who cared about her, helping her to be a good wife to her husband.

On the morning of Lewis's return, Mrs. Barren called Margaret on the telephone to let her know Lewis would be home at six o'clock. She told her it would be a nice gesture if she were waiting by the door when he arrived. She then said, "Good luck," and asked Margaret to call the next day.

Margaret was a bundle of fear and anxiety as she waited by the front door as Mrs. Barren suggested. She was trembling and suddenly hit with a nauseous feeling. In order to calm herself, Margaret rehearsed in her mind what she was going to say to Lewis. She felt that somehow, she had done something wrong and wanted to make things right with him. Margaret convinced herself that Mrs. Barren and her mother had given her good advice and that they knew best.

As Margaret stood waiting by the front door, it had dawned on her to recite her prayers and ask God for guidance. She was surprised she hadn't thought of it before. She then realized how little she'd looked to the Lord since moving into her new house. It bothered her to think that when she'd needed God's grace the most, she had neglected to ask for his help.

At ten past six the door opened and Lewis entered the house. He looked directly at Margaret, saw her bruised and swollen face, and handed her a bouquet of red roses. Looking uncomfortable, he spoke hesitantly and asked, "Did you receive my mother's telephone call?"

Margaret stood motionless. She was anxious and scared. Lewis towered over her as she cautiously said, "Yes," and as an afterthought added, "Lewis."

"Well, she must have told you how sorry I am about what happened on our wedding night," said Lewis defensively.

"Oh Lewis, yes, she did, and I'm so very sorry for what I did. I want you to know, whatever I did to make you angry, please know it was not done deliberately. Please tell me what I did wrong, so I can be a good wife to you. I love you and want you to be happy," responded Margaret with her voice cracking and tears escaping from her eyes.

Lewis approached Margaret and embraced her. She could smell the alcohol on his breath. Margaret pulled back impulsively, but Lewis held her tight. She buried her face in his chest and let herself cry. When the tears slowed, he was still holding her loosely, and he said, "Margaret I'm sorry. I didn't want to hurt you. But you have to know, you just can't make me angry. I know you're sorry and how much you love me. Well, I love you, too, and I've missed you these last few days. And, I really want to show you the love I have for you. Now go up to the bedroom and get yourself ready for me. I'll give you ten minutes then I'll come up. I want to give you a chance to show me how much you love me and want to make me happy. Margaret, but please, I don't want to be kept waiting for you. After we make love, we can talk, and I'll tell you how you can be a good wife to me."

Margaret stood still while listening to Lewis speak. She felt relieved talking with him, but the thought of returning to the bedroom frightened her. She wasn't sure she was ready for sex. She still had a lingering ache and soreness between her legs. The thought of Lewis entering her made her tremble. It would hurt too much, and she was scared.

Her thoughts were interrupted when she heard Lewis say, "Now give me a kiss before you go upstairs."

Margaret was too frightened to try to explain she was still in pain. As Lewis drove his tongue into Margaret's mouth, the taste of alcohol made her feel ill. Margaret's anxiety intensified, and she felt nauseous and dizzy. When their faces separated she managed to say, "I won't keep you waiting this time, Lewis." Margaret then turned around and hurried up the stairs, fighting the urge to vomit. She needed to prepare herself for her husband.

When Lewis walked into the bedroom, Margaret lay waiting for him on the bed with the covers pulled over her body. Lewis casually undressed and then moved toward Margaret. He pulled the covers down quickly, exposing her naked body. He climbed into bed and said, "I've missed you so much, Margaret. I know you're sorry about our wedding night. I'll let you make it up to me now."

Lewis kissed Margaret hard on the mouth, forcing his tongue deep into her throat. The smell and taste of alcohol was gagging her. He was breathing hard as he squeezed her small breasts. Margaret winced from the pain. Lewis then spread her legs and forced himself into her. She let out a scream and with every stroke her pain increased. Margaret closed her eyes and tried to hold back her tears. The pain was intense. Lewis was through with her in a matter of minutes. For Margaret, every uncaring stroke was hell.

Lewis rolled off Margaret. He was breathing hard and said, "That was awesome." He then turned to face her, saw the tears, and continued talking. "There's no need to cry, sweetheart. It only hurts in the beginning." He then gave her a quick kiss on the lips and said, "Why don't you clean yourself up, and we'll have something to eat in about an hour. I'm going to work out for a while, then I'll meet you in the kitchen." Naked, Lewis picked up his clothes and left the room.

Margaret felt she had been brutalized. It was the second time she had intercourse with Lewis, and the pain between her legs was more pronounced than the first. Lewis hadn't punched her this time; it had been his head banging against her cheek that caused a throbbing so painful she cried. Margaret could hardly move. She wasn't sure she wanted to. This was not what she had expected when her mother and Mrs. Barren had told her to try harder, insisting it was her duty to satisfy her husband. She wasn't ready for Lewis so soon. She needed time to recover and feel better. Margaret thought, *What just happened to me couldn't be love. It was so cold and forceful and the pain so agonizing.*

Margaret left the bed and went into the bathroom where she threw up. She washed her face then stood under a cold shower, trying to numb her feelings. She was shivering as she dried herself and then hurried to get dressed so she could meet Lewis in the kitchen. Margaret knew she wouldn't be able to eat, but at least they would talk, and she would learn what Lewis expected from her. She hoped to tell him she needed more time to heal, and that intercourse was too painful.

Her mother had told her she was smart and to figure out how to satisfy Lewis. She couldn't do it alone, she needed someone willing to help her. She thought of Mrs. Barren and couldn't wait to call her in the morning. Margaret would tell her how painful it was and ask her what to do. She didn't want to keep Lewis waiting. She had already learned violently he didn't like that, so she hurried downstairs.

Only moments after Margret arrived in the kitchen, Lewis walked in carrying a bottle of Jack Daniel's. He opened a cabinet door to retrieve a glass and filled it with ice from the freezer. He poured the honey-colored liquid over the cubes, then dropped his one-hundred-and-ninety-five-pound body on the chair across from his new wife.

Margaret felt tentative as she looked at her husband. She wasn't sure what to expect from him. Their only time together in their short marriage had been extremely painful for her. She could see he was happy because he displayed his white teeth through his broad smile. She couldn't rationalize his joy with the mournful feeling that consumed her.

Margaret had been very lonely when Lewis was away for several days. She couldn't leave the house with her swollen and bruised face. She'd been concerned with what people would think, and besides, Mrs. Barren advised her to stay in the house until her bruises disappeared completely.

Margaret didn't want to call her mother so soon after her previous call. She was afraid she would only anger her by mentioning Lewis and what he did to her.

Margaret's two best friends from high school were away at college. She hadn't seen them much on Saturdays after she started dating Lewis. Then when her friends were preparing to travel abroad, her father had his heart attack. She'd really lost contact with them over the summer months when Terese was in Haiti and Mary was in France. She had no one close by she could call and talk with.

Margaret thought, *If there were someone to talk with, what would I say to them anyway?* She considered her savings at her parents' home and her car, then asked herself, *Where would I go? What would my parents think if I ran away?* Mrs. Barren was her only contact. Margaret felt Mrs. Barren was her friend and wished she were sitting at the table with her and Lewis, speaking on her behalf.

Lewis interrupted her thoughts when he said, "Margaret, I want you to know how happy you just made me. The sex was fantastic. I love your body, the feel of your skin in my hands, feeling your breasts. It was great, and it won't be long before you'll be looking for it every day. Admit it, you liked it even though it hurt."

Margaret turned red and looked down. She was embarrassed and shocked by what he said. Margaret asked herself, *How could he enjoy what was hurtful and unloving? How could he think it was enjoyable?* She didn't want his upbeat mood to change. She knew what her response had to be, so she said, "Lewis, I'm glad you were pleased. I know it will get easier for me to enjoy."

"You bet you'll enjoy it, Margaret. You can be such a good girl. Now let's be serious for a minute. I don't want to punish you because you're my wife and, well, you know how much I love you. We're partners now, and like my mom and dad, I'll sometimes need your help with the family business. You'll have an important part to play, but you need to be prepared. My mother will teach you everything you need to know. She told me how close you and she have become. You do enjoy spending time with her, don't you?"

Margaret felt her ever-present anxiety rise, and she tried to control her breathing. She didn't understand this person she thought she knew and loved. He enjoyed violating her body and thought it would be pleasurable to her. He called her his partner and said he needed her. She was thankful he wanted his mother to help her and she said, "Yes, Lewis, I love your mother. She's already been a big help to me."

"Well, that's fantastic. Of course, she'll be a big help to you. She can be your best friend."

"I'm planning to call her in the morning if that's okay with you."

"It sure is. Call her anytime. But listen, we're both sorry about the wedding night. It's just that certain things make me angry, and it's not my fault. It will be your fault if that happens. You know, it was very inconsiderate of you to keep me waiting. Do you know what I mean?"

Margaret could feel herself tremble when Lewis's tone became serious. She didn't want to make him angry, so with remorse she said, "Yes, Lewis, I do, and I'm sorry for keeping you waiting."

"Good, that's good. One more thing, and I know this will be hard for you, but you can't be crying all the time. It's really embarrassing. How do you think it makes me look if my wife's all teary-eyed and crying? You need to control your emotions and not always cry. You understand what I'm saying? You do want us to be happy, right?"

Trying to restrain her tears, Margaret responded. "I do want to be a good wife, and I don't want to embarrass you. I love you, Lewis. It's just so hard. I do get emotional."

"I know you do. I'll give you time to learn to control your crying, but you need to learn not to always cry."

"Yes, Lewis."

"Great. I just want you to know that I will work very hard to give you a good life and provide for you. You'll be the mother of our children, and the sooner we have kids the better. We need little Barrens running around our big house."

"Thank you. I know you'll work hard for our family, and I do appreciate it. I want to be a good wife and mother for our children," responded Margaret.

"I know you do. Now let's go to bed. I have to be at work early and will be gone before you're awake. If you hear me in the morning, there's no need to get out of bed until I'm gone," said Lewis. He paused, winked at Margaret, and continued. "You'll need all the rest you can get for when I come home. You know what I mean?"

Margaret forced a smile and said, "Yes, Lewis. I'll always look forward to you coming home."

44

*O*ver the next three months, Margaret received her indoctrination into the Barren world. Mrs. Barren was indeed Margaret's only friend. She escorted her to various types of functions, and introduced her as Mrs. Lewis Barren. Margaret had impeccable manners and was always courteous and polite. She didn't need instructions on how to behave.

One suggestion in particular concerned her. Mrs. Barren said, "Margaret, sometimes it's important to appear to worship in the same faith as someone we do business with."

Margaret said, "Mrs. Barren, I wouldn't want to deny my faith and deceive another person."

Mrs. Barren's lips tightened, and she said, "It's just a little white lie, Margaret. Sometimes people feel better about you when they think you believe the same things they do. Besides, it's only religion. It doesn't really matter. After all, it helps Isaak and Lewis. I'm sure you would want to do it for Lewis."

The stern look, and the mention of Lewis's name, frightened her. Margaret knew what Mrs. Barren was saying, and she didn't want to be punished. Since that horrible first week of her marriage, Margaret had learned to navigate the unpredictable world of Lewis Barren. She had occasionally felt his wrath through his words, a push, or a stinging slap, and once from a vicious punch to her arm that turned her right bicep the color of an eggplant. Lewis wasn't one to get drunk. He would limit himself to one or two drinks, even though most of these incidents would occur when he'd been drinking or stressed over something at work. He would blame Margaret for his anger and intimidate her into saying she was sorry. Only then would he apologize. To show her his love, he would give her flowers or a small gift, and then penetrate her in his usual unloving manner. Lewis would then make Margaret tell him how much she enjoyed his love making.

Margaret didn't want to discuss anything with Lewis, so with little enthusiasm she said, "I'll always do my best to help the family and Lewis."

"Thank you, my dear. You're a good girl," responded Mrs. Barren.

On a rare Sunday when the Barrens were in town and attending a Catholic service, Margaret was asked to invite her parents. The Barrens were always looking to enhance their image and project themselves with an extended family, united and committed to their Catholic faith. Margaret felt guilty about frequently missing Sunday Mass, and she was thankful when there was an opportunity to attend a Catholic service. She wasn't going to mention her guilt to Mrs. Barren, not after their last conversation.

Margaret started accepting all of Mrs. Barren's directions and explanations, more as an act of surrender than agreement. She felt the mention of Lewis was intended to scare her. Margaret had subtly tried to speak with her mother and was always rebuffed. Her father had an unhealthy ashen look with a shrinking physical frame, and Margaret was afraid for his health. She was very lonely and felt isolated. Living in Franklin, Margaret had even lost contact with casual friends from high school. Most of her time was spent in the company of Mrs. Barren, her acquaintances, or wives of business associates.

After Margaret's damaged face healed, she started to visit her mother on Saturday. Her only enjoyment was to drive her yellow Volkswagen Beetle to the botanical gardens or Radnor Lake. She would cherish the freedom to sit alone, gazing through the trees and looking out over the water lost in her own thoughts. At the botanical gardens, she would walk along the foot paths, but rarely smelled or noticed the flowers. She would usually choose a random spot to spread her blanket and eat her lunch. Margaret rarely read anymore. She found it difficult to concentrate and felt little joy. She stopped going to confession on Saturday afternoons because she had to meet Lewis at the club at five thirty. She wouldn't have time for confession if she was going to be punctual, and she couldn't risk being late.

Margaret's contact with her mother was limited to a telephone call in the middle of the week and the Saturday morning visit before her mother headed out for the day. When Margaret would talk on the telephone with her dad, she could hear her mother standing next to him just in case she told him something that made him upset. On her Saturday visit, her mother would always remain at home until after her husband departed.

When her mother left the house, Margaret would go up to her old bedroom to sit on her bed. She'd spend time opening the drawers and holding her personal belongings. Margaret desperately wished she could go back to be a little girl living in her lovely old room. She'd imagined listening to her father's soft, mellow voice as he read her stories from her favorite books.

Margaret was trying to learn not to get emotional or cry. She would spend time in her room waiting to become sentimental, and when her eyes welled, she would force herself to hold back the tears as long as she could. When she felt she would cry, she quickly left the room. She was a Barren now, and according to Lewis, Barrens shouldn't cry.

Margaret found it hard not to cry. She was never embarrassed when she cried. Her tears came when she was happy or sad; it was simply a way to let people know her feelings. Her time to learn not to cry would soon end. She could see the look Lewis gave her when she couldn't control her feelings and cried in public.

Margaret's life with Lewis was just an existence; she felt no real love. Margaret would hear Lewis say the word *love*, and she would say it back, but there was no feeling. When Lewis wasn't angry, she sometimes felt his companionship and even his laughter. Every couple of days, she would be reminded of how little affection he had for her. With liquor on his breath, he would mount her and penetrate her with the same unloving, robotic motion. Lewis would then tell Margaret how great the sex was, and as always, she would have to tell him how much she enjoyed it.

Margaret was spending more and more time alone in the house. She was lonely and even began to welcome Lewis's physical presence. She was managing her life with her husband and watchful of his moods. He could be considerate and show affection but never in the bedroom. She had finally settled into her lonely life with an unpredictable and violent man.

It was now December 1970, their first Christmas married. Margaret and Lewis went to a party at the club attended by members and their children and grandchildren. Margaret became emotional, watching all the young girls and boys playing with their happy faces and smiles. She felt so much joy, she let herself become emotional and cry. At first, she seemed able to control her tears, but once they started flowing, she ran to the ladies' room. The restroom was occupied by several women at the time Margaret entered. When they noticed her crying uncontrollably, one of the women went to find Mrs. Barren.

On the way home with Lewis that evening, Margaret knew he was angry. She couldn't help herself from thinking about the children with their innocence and how much her life had changed since she was a child. Margaret knew when they were at the club, everyone had seen her crying. Driving home she couldn't look at Lewis; she didn't want to see his face. She was afraid he would have that horrid evil look he sometimes showed. When they arrived home, Margaret quickly jumped out of the car and ran to her room. She sat on her bed and cried. She hoped Lewis would not come up and find her still crying.

Margaret was in her room for nearly twenty minutes before the tears stopped. She went into the bathroom to wash her face. She returned to the bedroom and stood trying to decide what to do when suddenly Lewis pushed opened the door and entered. Margaret froze, she could see the veins on his neck swell as his angry voice spewed out, "Margaret, what did I tell you about crying? What am I going to do with you?" He paused, his face red, and said, "Just know, what I'm about to do is your fault. You're making me punish you. I can't believe it. You know I don't want to. You must know how disappointed I am with you." Once again, Lewis paused. He was breathing hard. There were beads of perspiration on his face. "We've been getting along so well and enjoying each other's company." His tone began to rise. "I told you not to embarrass me with your crying. Everyone was watching you. How the *fuck* do you think that looked? How do you think it made me look? Did I *fucken* tell you to control your crying? *Did I not*?"

Trembling, Margaret responded in a barely audible voice. "Yes, Lewis." Her tears were blinding her.

Lewis moved toward Margaret until his nose pressed up against her cheek and with a slow haunting tone said, "You'll remember this day, and you will learn from it!"

Margaret squeezed her eyes shut. She could feel his breath and hear the gnashing of his teeth. Lewis's evil glare so frightening. With fear in her voice she cried out, "Lewis."

Lewis ripped off his leather belt. His heavy breathing menacing. He folded the leather in half and gripped the buckle. Margaret was shaking. She wrapped her arms around her upper body and held herself tightly. This was a nightmare too gruesome to believe, and it was happening to her.

The first of many blows was quick and slashed across her back. The stinging pain was intense. Margaret shrieked and collapsed onto the bed. She heard Lewis shout her name. She tried to concentrate on his words. Screaming, he yelled, "I told you not to embarrass me!"

She couldn't think. Her voice was paralyzed. The words *Lewis, I'm sorry* never left her mouth.

Margaret was curled up in a fetal position, her dress pulled high, her flesh exposed. Several more blows from the harsh leather landed across her backside. Lewis let her pain linger before he yelled, "Whose fault is this?"

Margaret tried to speak. Her mouth was dry, her lungs felt empty, and she was gasping for air. She wanted to say, *My fault, Lewis, it's all my fault,* but all that came out was a guttural wail.

With sweat staining his white shirt, Lewis's vice-like grip clutched the fabric of Margaret's fraying dress and tore the thin silk covering from her body. Lewis then raised his muscular left arm as high as he could. His bicep bulging out of his short-sleeve shirt, and with lightning force whipped his belt downward, letting the leather once again slice through her soft, delicate skin.

Lewis barked his final words as he walked out of the room. "This was all your fault, Margaret. You made me do it!"

45

*T*he next morning Mrs. Barren entered the bedroom. Margaret was wearing only her panties and lay corpselike on the bed. Her body was stiff and motionless, her head slightly tilted toward the door. Her eyes were opened and bloodshot. Her look was blank and unresponsive. Dried blood tarnished the crisp, white sheet. The two women stared at each other, neither one speaking. Margaret felt the inferno raging through her lacerated flesh.

What made her current pain even more intense was that it had disrupted her equilibrium. She felt her life was a tightrope stretched over an abyss, and she was walking that delicate walk from one end to the other, when suddenly her balance was shuddered. It wasn't her fault; something made her stumble. Someone wanted her to stumble. Someone enjoyed her fall.

Margaret's ghostlike stare fixed on Mrs. Barren. She wasn't going to talk. She wasn't going to move. She wasn't going to pray. She was going to lay in pain and waste away at the bottom of the abyss until she died.

Mrs. Barren wasn't prepared for what she saw lying on the bed. She was stunned by the evil she had nurtured in her womb. Margaret looked fragile, broken; it was as if she were willing herself to die. Mrs. Barren was frightened. She suddenly felt dizzy and nearly fainted. Her mind told her to sit. She could feel a force pulling her to the bed. She rested her weakening body on the mattress. Sitting next to Margaret, she clasped her hand and flinched at the heat of it.

Mrs. Barren felt a strange sensation from the comfort of human contact. A shock bolted through her extremities. Reflexively, she tightened her grip on Margaret's hand and tried to speak, but her words were absent. Margaret was not moving. Her breathing was shallow, and her body was still. She remained motionless, seemingly comatose. Mrs. Barren felt tightness in her chest and a sudden harsh stabbing sensation through her shoulder blades. She let go of Margaret's hand and reached for her heart. The pain intense, and her arm felt numb. She hit the floor. Mrs. Barren was dead.

Margaret did not move when she saw Mrs. Barren grip her chest and fall from the bed. She saw the expression on her face and the fear in her eyes. She knew something was very wrong. When she heard the thud of the body hitting the hardwood, she didn't have the strength to move. Margaret's despair was gripping her, holding her firmly against the mattress with a force so powerful her shoulders ached.

It took persistent effort for Margaret to roll to her side and move her legs off the mattress. Agonizingly she pushed herself to sit up and let gravity pull her legs toward the floor and dangle over the side of the bed. Margaret's exertion exhausted her, and she needed to rest. She felt welded in place while looking at the stillness of Mrs. Barren. It wasn't her pain from the sting of Lewis's leather belt, it was the oppressive hopelessness that made her feel helpless to move.

Sitting and watching, it struck Margaret as she kept her eyes fixed on Mrs. Barren's face that only yesterday she would have been crying at what she was seeing. She felt no emotion, so there were no tears to shed, and still her body never moved.

Margaret continued to sit staring, mostly with her mind blank. Time passed slowly, and still her body never moved.

The blankness of Margaret's gaze was interrupted by the words that entered her thoughts, *The Margaret of yesterday would be praying for what you're seeing*. She had no words for prayers, and still her body never moved.

Margaret had no experience with death, but staring at the lifeless cadaver, she was seeing death for the first time in her young life. She didn't recognize death; it was too difficult for her to see through the murkiness of her depression. Margaret saw only how she felt, a lifeless body not moving, numb in its stillness.

It was Margaret looking at herself in the mirror. Gradually she noticed something peculiar on the face looking back. She moved her hand to touch her own face and felt the searing heat of her skin.

Margaret wanted to touch the face in the mirror, but she couldn't reach it. She needed to move in order to feel her reflection. She groaned as she strained to stand up. She could feel her pain in the distance. Margaret was plodding, moving slowly. When she reached the mirror, she dropped to her knees. She slowly extended her right hand, gently placing her fingers against the face looking back. She felt chilled by the emptiness. It was not a coldness she recognized; it was odious and unfamiliar.

Margaret touched her own face and felt the burning. She then reached out and touched the face in the mirror. Again, the unpleasant bite of emptiness, of cold. As she stared hard at the reflection, she kept her hand still against the image of herself, the vile coldness penetrating, merging with the fire burning inside her. Suddenly, flushed, she was jolted from her trance.

Mrs. Barren, thought Margaret. *Why is she in my mirror? No, it's not a mirror, it's Mrs. Barren lying on my bedroom floor.* Her face was frozen and impiously fixed.

Margaret now recognized the unfamiliar; it was death. She had little doubt that Mrs. Barren was dead on the floor. Her death stirred no emotion in Margaret; she felt empty of all feelings. It was a drought that began on her wedding night and climaxed with the last sting of Lewis's belt. She was now a Barren wife, with the last glint of her emotion buried so very deep down in her soul.

Without much thought, Margaret stood up and walked to the telephone in the hallway. She dialed the number Lewis told her to call in the event of an emergency. A woman answered on the second ring, saying, "Good afternoon, you have reached Barren. May I help you?"

Margaret said, "This is Mrs. Barren. May I please speak with Mr. Barren?"

The receptionist was startled. Mrs. Barren had never called her husband at the office. She said, "Certainly, Mrs. Barren. One moment please."

"Thank you," replied Margaret as she waited patiently for Lewis.

"Why are you calling me on this line?" asked Isaak.

Margaret was jolted by the sound of the voice and the tone. It snapped her out of her malaise and she spoke quickly. "I'm sorry, Mr. Barren. This is the telephone number Lewis gave me to call in the event of an emergency."

"Margaret, my dear, no need to worry. Lewis is out of town. If there is truly an emergency, I'm sure I can straighten it out. Now what's this emergency?"

Without emotion Margaret said, "Mr. Barren, it's Mrs. Barren. I believe she's dead."

Isaak had sent his wife to visit Margaret after his son told him of the whipping with his belt. He knew Doris was to arrive at Lewis's house by nine that morning. It was now two in the afternoon. He'd seen how emotional Margaret could get, so when she said Mrs. Barren was dead, he found it difficult to believe Margaret was correct in her assessment.

Isaak responded and asked, "Margaret would you please explain to me what you mean when you say Mrs. Barren is dead?"

"Mr. Barren, when Mrs. Barren came into my bedroom, she sat on my bed and held my hand. She suddenly grabbed for her chest and fell to the floor. When I felt her face, she was very cold, and I could see she was not breathing," responded Margaret in a neutral informative tone.

Isaak was struck by the way Margaret was calmly responding to his questions. He thought for a moment then asked, "How long has Doris been on the floor, Margaret?"

"I'm not sure, Mr. Barren."

"Did she just arrive?"

"I'm not sure, Mr. Barren."

"Margaret, do you know what time it is now?"

"Mr. Barren, I do not."

"Margaret, did you do anything else since you got out of bed?"

"No, Mr. Barren."

"Margaret, I need you to get dressed, then wait downstairs by the front door. I'll send someone to look after Mrs. Barren. I will be over to see you shortly," said Isaak.

Margaret did as she was told. She went to her bedroom and walked past the grayish waxy body of Mrs. Barren. As she showered, the burning from the water running down her body was an unwelcome reminder of the slashes imprinted into her soft, delicate skin. Margaret found a loose-fitting dress to reduce the pain caused by fabric rubbing against her raw flesh. She put a black dress on and covered Lewis's hate. She then waited by the front door as Isaak instructed. It wasn't long before two men arrived. They entered the house with a gurney and left shortly, hauling a big black vinyl bag containing the remains of Mrs. Barren.

Isaak arrived as the two men were placing the gurney in the back of a wagon. He spoke to them for several minutes and then walked into the house, where he met Margaret. Seeing her, he misread her pale, withdrawn look for grief. He stood looking at her; she was silent. He then approached her and gently put his arms around her. He tightened his embrace and said, "Oh, Margaret, Mrs. Barren is gone."

46

*I*saak had not been prepared for the death of his wife. He would mourn her passing, but it wouldn't take long. After all, he had a company to run. He still needed to prepare Margaret to help Lewis for when he assumed the stewardship of the family business. He would also need to find someone to keep Margaret and Lewis together. Isaak wanted a grandson; it was time for boy named Exuvial Lewis Barren. He felt his son would stop abusing Margaret once she delivered a baby. That was what his father had done when Isaak was born, and he would have Lewis do the same.

Isaak was concerned about the publicity should Margaret divorce Lewis. He knew once court documents were filed in probate court, they would be quickly leaked to the press. The Barrens were a prominent family who made news, and reporters would readily expose Lewis's deviance. His son had abused other women, and he didn't want any media attention that may motivate victims of his previous violence to come forward and publicly accuse Lewis of his crimes. He knew how important it was for Margaret and Lewis to stay married. He wanted them to produce a son who would eventually succeed Lewis as the head of the Barren business.

With all these thoughts going through Isaak's mind, he knew he had to act quickly. Isaak wasn't concerned; he knew how to solve problems. After some reflection, he knew what needed to be done.

He decided to first speak with Lewis and make explicit there would be no more violence against Margaret. When Isaak had spoken with Lewis, he'd told him to control his anger with his wife, treat her with kindness, and be a loving companion. Isaak had made it clear that Margaret needed to know Lewis's brutality was in the past. Lewis had been told to convince her that he was sorry for his behavior and to ask for her forgiveness. Isaak knew Margaret was a good Catholic girl, and she would forgive his sins. Isaak had also told Lewis that Margaret needed to conceive, and that would guarantee they stayed together.

Isaak would then rely on Mrs. Gabriel to manage Margaret. He would appeal to her as the heartbroken husband, devastated by the loss of his beloved wife. Isaak would let her know how shattered he and Lewis were over the sudden death of Doris. He would tell Mrs. Gabriel that Lewis needed Margaret, now more than ever, to console him and make him a better person.

Isaak told himself, *It's so much easier to exploit good people; simply appeal to their most personal and cherished beliefs.* He felt sure that getting Mrs. Gabriel to speak with Margaret would take little effort. He also knew she loved her daughter but was scared about her own future. Mrs. Gabriel worried that if her husband's heart failed him, she would be left alone. Isaak knew he needed to reassure her that she would never have to worry about money or living alone. He would let her know that Lewis would open up his home to her if there were ever a need; and with all the room they have in their big house, she would have all the privacy she needed.

Isaak believed Mrs. Gabriel had convinced herself that what she told Margaret was in Margaret's best interest. When Mrs. Gabriel did speak to her daughter, Isaak surmised that she used her husband's bad heart to manipulate Margaret when she needed to.

Isaak would confide in Mrs. Gabriel and let her know that there had been unpleasant times in the young couple's marriage, but it was all in the past. He would tell Mrs. Gabriel that Lewis was sorry for hurting Margaret, and he begged for her forgiveness. Isaak would convince her that his son wanted to be a better and more loving husband to his wife. He would tell Mrs. Gabriel how a child would make all the difference in the marriage and would brighten up all of their lives.

Isaak was confident that Mrs. Gabriel would remind Margaret of her belief in the love for family, the sanctity of marriage, and her commitment to love and honor until death. He knew she would prompt Margaret to remember her obligation to forgive as a Catholic.

Margaret knew true and deep faith was about love and forgiveness. She read what was written in the Bible: "The Lord has forgiven you, so you must also do." Mrs. Gabriel was all too willing to drive Margaret deeper into the Barren fold with her words of faith and love.

It wasn't long ago that Margaret, with all her goodness and grace, would have readily listened to the religious doctrine her mother was preaching. But she was now a Barren, empty of faith and religion. Because of Margaret's anguish and pain, the depression, and her loss of feeling, her mother's words held no meaning.

Margaret would obey her mother but not because of religion; she would do as she was told because she had no hope. She was hopeless. She was barren.

47

*I*saak was determined not to waste time dealing with the formalities of his wife's death. The funeral and a reception would occur the day after Mrs. Barren died.

The service for Doris Barren was private and held in a crematorium. Isaak, Lewis, and the mortuary staff were the only people in attendance. They watched as Mrs. Barren's body was loaded into the combustion chamber and the temperature increased to the maximum 2,000 degrees Fahrenheit. Isaak and Lewis could feel the surge of heat as Mrs. Barren dissipated. Once her body was reduced to ashes and bone fragments, the father and son quietly departed.

Isaak had arranged for a reception at his club in order for members and, more importantly, the people he did business with to pay their respects for the loss of his wife. Isaak was not going to miss the opportunity to use Mrs. Barren's death to enhance his business relations. Nothing, in Isaak's view, worked better with the churchgoers than the death of a wife. He thought of the comments he would hear, *I'm here for you, Isaak. You can count on me. Call me any time at all, day or night."* Isaak would indeed call if he needed to, and it would be strictly about business.

In his own unsentimental way, Isaak had paid tribute to Doris and moved on. He now had to focus his attention on protecting his son from himself. To do that, Isaak needed to follow his plan and speak with Mrs. Gabriel.

As Isaak and Lewis were driving to the reception, Mr. and Mrs. Gabriel were on their way to pick up Margaret at her house. They had planned to drive her to the memorial service at the club. Margaret was standing by her front door when her parents arrived. She had on the same long-sleeve, black sheath dress she wore the day Mrs. Barren died. The color made her look frail and fatigued. Margaret had the appearance of someone overburdened with grief.

As the Gabriel's car approached the front of the house, her mother saw Margaret and said, "Oh, Joseph, Margaret looks heartbroken."

Mr. Gabriel didn't respond. He looked at his daughter, and his eyes quickly filled with tears. He couldn't wait to embrace and comfort her.

Mrs. Gabriel loved her daughter very much, and she too wanted to console her. She had convinced herself that Isaak had been sincere in his expression of sorrow. She believed Lewis needed Margaret's support as he grieved the loss of his mother. Mrs. Gabriel also felt reassured by Isaak's generosity when he told her she would be cared for as long as she needed.

When the car stopped, Mr. and Mrs. Gabriel got out to extend their condolences to Margaret. Mrs. Gabriel lightly hugged her daughter. When her father embraced her, she began to cry. Margaret was crying for the first time since the holiday party at the club. She couldn't stop her tears. Her father held her tight, as her mind raced through the eighteen years he had always comforted her when she needed him to. Margaret thought of all that her father meant to her and what she wanted to say to him. She knew he would protect her if she told him about all of her pain, but she wasn't sure his heart was strong enough to hear her misery.

Mrs. Gabriel interrupted the embrace when she said, "Margaret, we're so very sorry for the loss of Mrs. Barren. I know how close you and she had become."

Margaret stepped back from her father. Standing in front of him, she could see his diminished size, the droopiness of his clothes, and the grayness of his face. He looked so weak. She turned to her mother, her face moist with tears, and said, "Yes, Mother, thank you."

On the drive to the reception, Mrs. Gabriel said, "Margaret, dear, this is such a terrible loss for Mr. Barren and Lewis. They will need a lot of support from you to overcome the sudden and tragic death of Mrs. Barren."

Margaret could hear her mother speaking but felt no emotional connection to Mrs. Barren or her death. She responded, "Yes, Mother."

"Darling, I'm sure you're still in shock at witnessing Mrs. Barren's heart attack. It must have been so frightening for you."

"I don't really remember it, Mother."

"Oh dear, Margaret, it was frightening. I'm so sorry."

"Yes, Mother."

"Well, my darling girl, you need to be strong for Lewis. His beloved mother has passed so suddenly, and his grief needs to be consoled. Lewis needs your love now more than ever. You need to comfort him, and let him know how much you care for and love him. Help him to be strong as he deals with his loss."

Margaret could not fully rationalize her mother's words. She could certainly comprehend the meaning of console, love, comfort, and care, but these words were the antithesis of Lewis. Lewis didn't console, love, comfort, or care; Lewis hated, brutalized, tormented, and punished.

Margaret knew her mother was adamant she not discuss her relationship with Lewis with either her or her father. She had been very harsh when she told Margaret she would not be allowed to call or visit if she tried to talk to them about Lewis. Margaret couldn't tell her what she was saying to herself, *No Mother, you're wrong. Lewis doesn't need any of those things. Lewis needs to punish, to punch, to whip, to enter me without love or affection, and then force me to say I'm sorry.*

The only possible response Margaret felt she could say to her mother was, "Yes, Mother."

"Margaret, you know we love you, and we know how much you love us. When you were born, well, it was the happiest day of our lives. I know there are difficulties when two young people first start out but, darling, having a baby will change all that. The baby helps you become closer as husband and wife. You will have a common purpose— you'll both want the best for your baby. I do believe a baby will bring joy to your family, particularly now with Mrs. Barren's death. Mr. Barren expressed to me the same sentiment. It would bring Mr. Barren and Lewis so much happiness if you became pregnant."

Margaret listened to her mother but didn't want to respond. She wanted to sit in silence and not think about Mr. Barren or Lewis. The mention of Mr. Barren speaking with her mother about her marriage and a baby horrified her. Margaret's mind was telling her, *If Mrs. Barren knew Lewis abused and beat you, then Mr. Barren must surely have known. How could he let Lewis hurt you? And if he hurt you, what would they do to your little baby.* After listening to her own thoughts, Margaret silently expressed one certainty, *I will never become pregnant.*

"Thank you, Mother," was all Margaret could say.

Mr. Gabriel had remained silent during the ride. He was very worried about his daughter. He knew she was troubled. He wanted her to open up to him like she always had. He was just so tired all the time. He knew his life was fading away, and it broke his heart to see his daughter unhappy. She had always been full of life, and now, he only saw sorrow.

As the car pulled into the parking lot of the club and approached the front of the building, Mrs. Gabriel said, "Look, Margaret, Lewis is out front waiting for you. He's so very considerate."

Margaret didn't respond to her mother. She hadn't seen Lewis since his leather belt ripped through her pale, soft skin, but she'd felt the pain every second between then and now.

Lewis fidgeted as he stood outside near the entrance to the club anticipating the arrival of the Gabriel's car. He'd been told by his father to treat Margaret with respect and control his anger. Lewis had given assurance he would obey his father.

Lewis hated himself when he hurt Margaret, but he hated her more for making him angry. He never wanted to be angry; he just couldn't understand why the woman he was with always made him mad. When he did get angry, he knew it wasn't his fault; it was hers. With Margaret, he felt that if he punished her, she would behave just as he wanted her to, and then he wouldn't have to punish her anymore.

After Mr. Gabriel parked the car, Lewis approached and embraced Margaret. Her parents moved slightly away to give them a little privacy. Margaret could feel his physical strength gripping her body. Emotionally, she felt nothing. As he held her, she whispered, "Lewis, I'm sorry." To Margaret her words were a courtesy; his mother had died. Even saying them, she had no feeling.

Lewis wasn't considering his mother's death when Margaret said she was sorry. He quietly responded, "I know you are, Margaret. I'm sorry, too. I love you. You know that, don't you? I promise you everything will be better, sweetheart. I need you so much." As he released his embrace, his eyes welled. Margaret looked at his face and recognized sadness. She could only nod.

Mr. and Mrs. Gabriel then paid their respects to Lewis, and the four entered the club. The Gabriel family extended their condolences to Mr. Barren.

Isaak welcomed Joseph and Elizabeth Gabriel and thanked them for their support and comfort. The Gabriels moved on as other people were waiting to pay tribute to Mrs. Barren and convey their sorrow to Isaak, Lewis, and Margaret.

Later that afternoon, Mr. Barren found a way to speak confidentially with Mrs. Gabriel. He was using all his skills as the heartbroken widower, a father, and a hopeful grandfather. He sought out Mrs. Gabriel and when he'd cornered her said, "Mrs. Gabriel . . . Elizabeth . . . our children look so heartbroken."

"Mr. Barren, Margaret is just so distraught over the passing of Mrs. Barren. She loved her so much."

"Please, you know I prefer you call me Isaak. We're family, after all. Lewis is grief-stricken. He needs Margaret's love now more than ever; I'm sure she knows that."

"There's no need to worry, I had a long talk with Margaret, and she loves Lewis very much. She's looking forward to starting a family. She told me she can hardly wait to be a mother and bring happiness into her home."

"Thank you, Elizabeth. You do know what's best for our children."

"Isaak, you can always count on me to keep our little family together."

"I'm grateful to you. You know you'll never have to worry about anything. We'll always be there for you, and Lewis loves you. If the unfortunate time comes, you'll have all the support you need from the Barren family."

With tears in her eyes, Elizabeth said, "Thank you, Isaak. Thank you very much."

As the reception concluded, good-byes were exchanged, and Lewis and Margaret left together. On the drive home, Lewis said, "I'm very sorry for what I did. Sometimes I just can't help myself. I feel like it's not me doing what I'm doing. I need you to forgive me, Margaret. Will you please forgive me?"

Margaret looked at Lewis. He looked humble and sincere. She heard his words and saw his face; she wanted desperately to believe him. With ambivalence she said, "Yes, Lewis, I forgive you." She paused and without emotion said, "I'm sorry you hurt me."

"Thank you, Margaret. You're always so considerate. I love you. I feel lonely now that my mother is gone. I need you, sweetheart. I need to be with you tonight. Will you please do that for me?"

Margaret had no strength to resist either the kind Lewis or the violent Lewis. In a voice that held no emotion she said, "Yes, Lewis, I will do that for you."

That night his penetration was cold and unfeeling. Margaret lay awake through the night silently staring into the darkness. She didn't have the will to leave her bed the next morning until Lewis was well on his way to work. After Mrs. Barren's death, every day became a blur. Lewis's sexual appetite increased to four or five nights a week. It was always the same unloving penetration and mechanical thrusting that left her feeling cold. Lewis in his own distorted way felt he was compassionate, kind, and loving. He told himself Margaret wanted him, and he gave it to her as often as he could.

Initially Lewis refrained from hitting Margaret, but her failure to conceive a child was driving him toward releasing his barely containable rage. He wanted a son, his father wanted a grandson, and Margaret hadn't gotten pregnant. He rationalized it was Margaret's fault, and because it was her fault, she needed to be punished.

When Lewis penetrated Margaret, he believed it was the way you treated women. To him, it wasn't violence at all. Lewis was physically strong, but he didn't consider himself violent. When he was violent, it was always someone else's fault. With Margaret, he felt she was his possession, and it was his responsibility to punish her when she was bad. After months of intercourse produced no pregnancy, Lewis concluded it was time to punish Margaret.

Lewis's violence had been in a short hibernation. By the end of February 1971, it had restarted with intimidation. He would take off his belt as Margaret lay motionless on the bed watching him. He would fold the belt in half and hold an end in each hand. Then he would extend his arms away from his body and bring his hands together to slacken the leather. He would very quickly open his arms, bringing the two sides of the leather together, creating a snapping sound. Margaret had no doubt what the sound meant.

When the punches came, he avoided Margaret's face. He would punch her arms, her back, and her legs. Lewis didn't want to have to tell his father he had disobeyed him. He would not hit her in the face a second time. After Lewis had abused Margaret, he would follow the same pattern. He'd coax her until she said she was sorry for making him hit her. He would then apologize, ask for forgiveness, and bring her all the usual gifts. The cold sexual intercourse would never change, and Lewis would act as if they were just a loving couple, enjoying the intimacy of each other's company.

Over these months, Margaret suffered in silence. She did as she was told and continued to visit her mother on Saturday mornings. Their time together was short and their conversations perfunctory. Her father was either resting or trying to spend some time at work catching up when the office was quiet. Her mother's question was the same every week. She would ask, "Margaret, darling, when are you going to get pregnant?"

"I'm trying, Mother," was all she said.

Margaret would leave her parents' house and drive her Volkswagen without enthusiasm to the botanical gardens or the lake. She'd lost all interest in the things she enjoyed. Margaret no longer prayed or read books. She hardly ate, and she looked anemic. At home, she never slept and never cried.

It was now the beginning of May 1971, three weeks before Margaret's nineteenth birthday, when Lewis informed her that he and his father were traveling on business. They would be away for ten days. That same night Lewis gave Margaret a going-away present. He entered the bedroom, ripped off her nightgown, and gave her what he

314

said she wanted, his unloving penetration. When he was through, all that was heard was a single slap of his belt on her bare flesh and his throaty voice saying, "You make sure you're a good girl while I'm gone. You wouldn't want anything to happen to your parents."

As Lewis walked out of the room, Margaret lay motionless. Her pain held no meaning; it had become too much a part of her. She never thought what ten days without Lewis could mean.

48

$\mathcal{L}$ewis and his father had been gone three days when Margaret woke on the second Saturday in May feeling different. Old joys were on her mind. She thought of prayer but didn't pray. She thought of smiling but didn't smile. Margaret didn't feel unhappy, but she wasn't happy either. She realized she'd slept the night and thought, *Maybe even insomnia needs to rest.*

Margaret showered longer than usual and was particular in the clothes she chose to wear. As she drove away from her house, everything she viewed while driving was much clearer. She noticed the flowers, the colors, and the trees— all the ordinary things she used to enjoy. She felt she was somehow able to see again.

When she arrived at her parents' house, Margaret felt the anticipation of seeing her mother. As she entered the kitchen and saw her, she had an urge to hug her. Margaret hadn't felt this way in a very long time. Her mother was happy to see her, and they had a pleasant talk. Surprisingly, she didn't ask Margaret when she was going to become pregnant.

Margaret was hoping to see her father, but her mother said he'd felt refreshingly well and joined some friends for golf.

After Mrs. Gabriel left, Margaret didn't go to her old bedroom. She went to the garage feeling excited. When she saw her yellow Volkswagen Beetle, she suddenly felt impatient, wanting to get behind the steering wheel and just go. Margaret hurried into the driver's seat and drove to Radnor Lake. She had an expectation she couldn't describe.

As Margaret drove, Lewis suddenly emerged in her thoughts, as if trying to assert control. The sudden blast of frost that normally accompanied such thinking was absent. She had no fear of him just then, and in a way, she felt empowered. As if the time he was away from her, and the distance between them, was lifting his veil of vile and evil that had been smothering her. An ember of emotion, kindled, trying to ignite, was fueled by her unexpected awakening. Margaret felt an urge to break free of Lewis.

By the time she reached the lake, she had a hope that renewed her energy. She sensed her dormant happiness surfacing. She found her favorite spot. She spread her checkered blanket and sat on the grass with a view of the lake. Margaret perused her surroundings and saw only beauty. She was no longer seeing darkening shades of gray. Margaret was seeing the vividness of colors: red, yellow, blue, green, orange, and purple. By seeing, her sense of sound was awoken. She could hear the chirping of birds, and the ruffling of leaves as the warm breeze passed through the tress. By hearing, her sense of smell was aroused. She could smell the freshness of the morning air, the trees, and the aroma of flowers.

Margaret could feel the internal struggle to suppress her happiness. The joy traversing through her was now racing.

She could feel her body resisting, pushing back. Her joy began to sputter, and she felt weary. The unexpected bolt of hope that had arrived so quickly drained her. She was overwhelmed with fatigue. Slowly, resisting, failing, Margaret drifted off to sleep.

When she awoke—the sun's rays on her face—the vision of a dove—the all-white seagull—flying to her parents' house—praying they weren't at home—her migration north—soaring over roads one thousand miles long—floating through the campus of Holy Trinity—drifting across Cape Cod—landing in Boston—all that had happened during that wonderful week in May with Nicholas was like a dream to Margaret. All of the events, the circumstances, the people who could have and should have changed her life, saved her, protected her, and nested her.

Margaret's fate had been determined when she'd called home to tell her mother she would not return to a marriage without love. She said there was no love in Lewis. Margaret told her mother she needed to love and be loved, that she'd found someone she loved and who loved her. Margaret said, "God loves and commands us to love each other."

Margaret will always remember her mother's response to her pleas.

"Margaret, you don't know what you are saying . . .

"Margaret, Gabriels do not leave their husbands . . .

"Margaret, the sanctity of your marriage . . .

"Margaret, you took a vow before God to love and honor your husband until death . . .

"Margaret, you'll be a divorcee, consider how hurtful that is to your parents . . .

"Margaret, your father is very sick, it's his heart. He had another heart attack. He's in intensive care. You did this to him when you ran away from home. He could die! We need you home, your father needs you. I need you, I can't be alone. Lewis will care for me if your father dies . . .

"Margaret, we are your parents, and we love you. Have you lost your love for us? Have you lost your love for your father? Don't you want to see your father?"

All these words coming at her, breaking her resistance, and suddenly her wings were clipped. Her flight home would be painful.

What had freed Margaret was also what pulled her back. All her love and goodness returned to her when the Barren grip was weakened by the time she'd been away from them and distance created by her flight. All the things the Barrens had deadened in her, she felt again. It was because Margaret was good, compassionate, and loving that they could pull her back home. The Barrens would make sure Margaret never flew away again.

It had been Lewis's threat to harm her parents, and Margaret's compassion for her mother's mental health, and her unselfish love for her father that had deprived her of love and a life with Nicholas. She needed to be home for her father. He couldn't die without her seeing him once more. She needed to tell him how much she loved him. Margaret, with a crushed heart, would return to the horrid life that had chosen her. She would fulfill her vow to love and honor until death. She would do as the Bible said, "Love your enemies, do good to those who hate you."

Nature is not kind to a bird without wings. Life ends quickly and violently. The predators who prey on the fragile and broken are not the strong or courageous. They are the weak and cowardly with an appetite to devour the isolated and defenseless.

Margaret returned home with a broken heart. It was not the flight of joy that had brought her to Holy Trinity. She returned out of love for her mother and father. It was part of the cunning scheme Isaak had designed for Margaret when Mrs. Barren first told him about her. He knew all along it was Margaret's love for her parents that would contain her in a marriage until death, and not her wedding vows to Lewis. Without her wings, Margaret was defenseless. She was returning to the worst predator of all, the abusive, violent husband insulated by a marital contract.

The drive home would be vacant of the music that had filled her heart with joy as she migrated to Holy Trinity. Margaret would not hear the songs that reached her soul and inspired her. She had felt reborn as she headed north seeking memories that would reopen her heart and make it strong and unbeatable.

During Margaret's drive south, there was no music, only the old gloom returned, smothering her, and forcing all the joy, happiness, and love from her heart. The closer she drove toward home, the darker the cloud of despair inflicted her. She could feel Lewis's evil sitting beside her, his demonic smile and leather belt. Margaret wanted to cry, needed to cry, but there were no tears. Her tears had refused to come; they knew Margaret's fate if they did. Her tears would not betray her.

Margaret was closing the book that contained her happy ending. She thought how the books you read determine your story, your outcome. Jonathan Livingston Seagull had to return to those who were evil and hated him. Jenny, so young and beautiful, had to die. Margaret knew the ending of her book. She was returning to evil and hatred, and she would die so very young.

She continued thinking of the most important book in her life, the Holy Bible. *So many words, so many words to guide you, and to live by. The Book in all its majestic authority could be reduced to a single word. Love. Love, as God commands, "Love one another as I love you."*

So many songs have been written about love, and so many people listen to the words, recite them, sing them; but how many really hear the words, their meaning, or have lived their life with love?

Margaret had learned so much about love on her quest to Holy Trinity. She discovered the beauty and uniqueness of love, the goodness that cements and forms an unbreakable bond between two people. She'd found it with Nicholas, and she had seen it in those who had shared their stories, Gall and Maggie, Jeanne Marie and Francis, and Anthony and Arthur. It had often been confusing and conflicting for her, but she'd been certain of its goodness and its beauty. She'd seen for the first time a love between two people that was eternal.

These had been Margaret's last thoughts as the bleakness of her previous life inundated her and the last embers of hope went out. Her future would be barren; she would spend it with Lewis.

49

When Margaret pulled into the driveway of her parents' house, Lewis stepped outside and looked directly into her eyes. He was staring with a vision. He imagined an inferno engulfing Margaret and destroying her yellow Beetle. Margaret could feel the heat of his hatred in the scars of his whippings and the bruises of his punches. At that moment, she knew all the memories she'd collected and placed neatly in her scrapbook would not help her endure life as a Barren.

Margaret's father was indeed hospitalized, but it was Margaret's mother who was critical. She'd suffered a stroke and was in intensive care. Her death came two days later when her heart hemorrhaged. It was as if the Barren evil had infected her parents with a vile curse. Her father, with his failing heart and weaning strength, was unable to recover from the loss of his wife and succumbed to death within the month. Margaret was heartened in her grief only when she heard someone mention the age-old superstition that death came in threes, and she thought, *my time is near.*

Lewis took full advantage of Margaret's isolation and loneliness. She would suffer for four months as Lewis tried with renewed energy to impregnate her. He would penetrate her five or six nights a week. Isaak could no longer control Lewis's violence; he had lost his will to try.

Margaret had been feeling sick; the same nausea and vomiting she had experienced a couple of months ago was back. She had developed a little belly on her slim body and became frantic. She knew she was depressed. She had no appetite, lost weight, felt exhausted, suffered from insomnia, and a deep sense of hopelessness consumed her. She had witnessed all the same signs in her mother. Pregnancy frightened her. If Lewis thought she was pregnant, he would stop penetrating her and hurting her. He would force her to get well. He would protect the unborn child. Isaak and Lewis would turn the baby into a monster like them, an image too horrible to imagine.

Margaret didn't want to know if she was pregnant; she couldn't face the consequences of knowing. She decided she would never get pregnant. She would guarantee it. Margaret knew there was only one way to prevent it, and that was death. Lewis would kill her, or she would kill herself. She would not be a conduit for evil.

Margaret wanted to end her life that night. Lewis had not had intercourse with her the day before; she surmised he would penetrate her that evening. Margaret loved Nicholas so much that she never wanted to hurt him. She couldn't explain the compelling need she felt to write to him and say a final good-bye. She knew it would torment him as he read her letter, but she had no choice; she felt as if she were writing against her will.

As Margaret sat at her writing table, she thought she wouldn't have the strength or courage to finish the letter.

She had started writing in the morning and continued all day, but it didn't seem to be enough time. She struggled for words and knew she was rambling. And there were the interruptions — the nausea and vomiting, the sudden lack of courage, and her need to get lost in her thoughts of Nicholas and all the love they had for each other. When Margaret needed to write about the darkness of Lewis's evil, she could only do it with Nicholas at her side. His courage and strength were her courage and strength. She would not surrender to defeat.

Her letter finally finished, Margaret ran out of the house dressed in a white slip and sandals. She raced to the post office near her parents' old home. Margaret was frightened. In her despair, she believed Lewis would learn of the letter and find a way to prevent Nicholas from reading it. Margaret didn't care if she made Lewis wait for her. She wanted him to wait. She wanted his rage to rise and his violence to finally end her life.

Margaret felt nauseous, dizzy, and weak as she ran up the steps of the post office. Her heart was racing and her breathing was shallow. The shortness of breath made her feel faint as she stood in front of the blue mailbox. Her hand was shaking as she grasped the metal handle and pulled open the lid. Margaret released the white envelope and watched it vanish from her fingers. When she heard the clang of the rectangular door closing, she had a moment of clarity. She now knew for certain why she had desperately needed to write the letter to Nicholas. Through the dense fog engulfing her mind, she could hear the words she never spoke, *I have the courage to deprive Lewis of a child. Only you, Nicholas, have the strength to destroy his evil.*

Part Five

You set the table before me
As my enemies watch;
You anoint my head in oil;
my cup overflows.
Only goodness and love will pursue me
all the days of my life;
I will dwell in the house of the lord
for years to come.

50

My Dear Nicholas,

You truly have a sensitive soul. You are beautiful and kind and gentle. You were oh so gentle.

But I know you have strength. You are strong. I needed to be strong; your love gave me strength.

I will always love you, Nicholas, I will always love you. But now I'm weakening,

I want to say so much to you.

I know you were confused by the note I left behind.

I watched you walk out of the hotel, I saw the tears you wiped away; your heart was broken. My heart was broken long ago. But you restored it; you gave me my heart back when I needed it most.

You are the life and love I'd always wanted.

I know it will be hard for you to understand, but I needed the memory of you in order to survive.

I thought it would be enough.

I know it's unfair for me to write this letter, but I needed to say goodbye.

To thank you for all the happiness you gave me.

My time is short, but my love for you is strong.

I tried to take courage in your courage.

But the pain, the physical and emotional pain, is overwhelming.

I am all alone—so lonely.

I know your kindness, I don't have to say I'm sorry for hurting you.

But leaving you was my destiny.

I took a lifetime vow to love and honor.

I no longer love nor honor.

I am weakening, I no longer have the strength to sustain me.

I know I am rambling, trying to say so much. My heart weeps; I am weeping, Nicholas. I am weeping.

This will be hard for you. But I need you to know.

I thought of you when he humiliated me, threatened me, slapped me, punched me, and whipped me. I focused on your love. It gave me the strength to remain stoic to his abuse.

I am now weak and can't go on. I need your strength and courage one more time, not to survive but to die.

I am mailing you this letter to say goodbye.

I am telling him tonight that I found love in another man. He will kill me or I will kill myself.

I have sinned, Nicholas, I will sin. I am a sinner. This has been my hell.

Tomorrow it will be over.

I love you, I love you, I love you.

51

*W*hen Nicholas arrived home on leave from the Navy, Meg's letter was waiting for him. It was postmarked September 16, 1971, from Nashville, Tennessee.

Just holding the envelope, seeing Meg's handwriting brought back the ache in his heart he'd struggled to suppress. He had tears in his eyes. He was trembling as he recalled all the memories of their time together.

To read about the abuse Meg had endured, and how her love for him had sustained her, brought him to his knees. He couldn't breathe. The violence, the torture her husband had inflicted upon her was incomprehensible to him. He was sick to his stomach, burning with anger and hatred.

Nicholas had read Meg's note when she'd left him in Boston so many times, he knew every word by heart. He spoke them out loud and said, *You will protect me, and that means, you must never find me.* As he recalled the lines on her back that his fingers had felt, the seeds of guilt began to sprout.

He heard his words of guilt in his thoughts, *I never even looked for you, so how could I find you. Now you're dead.* In his grief, his despair, Nicholas convinced himself that if he had looked for Meg, he would have found her. He could have protected her and loved her. She would still be alive. He blamed himself. He heard the words, *It's your fault.*

Nicholas thought of his father and his sadness. He knew he blamed himself for his wife's death, but there had been nothing he could have done. His dad could not die for her or kill the cancer with all its evil. Nicholas believed it was different for him. Meg had died, and it had been his fault. But unlike his dad, he could kill the cancerous evil man who took her life.

While Nicholas's anger and hatred would be used to avenge Meg's killer, the guilt he felt would be his demise. He'd read Matthew's words in the Bible, "An eye for an eye and a tooth for a tooth." He knew what he should do, "turn the other cheek." Nicholas wouldn't do that; it was the sadness he saw in his father, the loss of joy, the happiness, and the sharing of emotions. He could not live his life that way, not after the love he had found with Meg.

Nicholas loved her so much and had always prayed she would walk back into his life. That was his dream, his hope; it had gotten him through the day. Now Meg was gone, the victim of the vilest abuse.

In his naïveté, Nicholas thought, *This is 1971. How could this happen? How could a man beat a woman, his wife, the person he had chosen to spend his life with? The person who had accepted him? The vow he'd taken, the promise he'd made to love and honor?*

How could he get away with it?

As he thought about it, he considered some of the families in his neighborhood. *There was Mrs. Giovani, Mrs. Murphy, Mrs. Kowalski, Mrs. LaFontaine, mothers of his friends. There had been many subtle signs and whispers of physical and emotional abuse. People had known, and shamefully everyone had ignored it. They'd said it was a family matter and no one else's business. People had kept quiet for the good of the family. The family had to stay together; that's what had mattered.*

Nicholas's mom had passed when he was still young, but he had learned so much about her because of Meg. He now knew she'd been the center of their family life. She had been respected and loved. His father had walked in his mother's shadow. His dad's love of life had died when the love of his life died.

Nicholas didn't want his father's sad life. He couldn't tell him about Meg or what he planned to do. If he talked about it, he might change his mind. Nicholas wasn't going to allow that to happen. Nothing was going to change his mind. He would suffer the eternal consequences of his sins.

His dad had been a combat veteran of World War II. When Nicholas told his father, he was shipping out early and couldn't stay, his father told him to be careful. He asked for no explanation. Nicholas hugged his dad and held the embrace a little longer than the one he'd given him just a few short months ago. He kissed him for the second time since he was a child.

"I love you, Nicholas," said his father before Nicholas could say the words.

"I love you too, Dad."

In less than fourteen days Nicholas would be shipped overseas. He didn't have much time.

52

Franklin, TN—October 1971

*T*he encounter that had brought Nicholas face-to-face with Meg's killer had not been chance. The truth is, once he found him, he had stalked him for six days. He knew his name, who he was, and the routine he followed.

To Nicholas, this person would remain nameless. He was Meg's killer.

The killer worked out every morning, lifting weights one day, then running the next two. His runs took him into some isolated areas adjacent to the property surrounding his business.

Nicholas could clearly see the killer was bigger and stronger than him. His one advantage was that he would pick the time and place of their confrontation. Nicholas had spent his afternoons studying the terrain where the killer would take his morning run. He found the spot where they would ultimately meet. He made his plan.

Killing would not come easy for Nicholas. It was not just another neighborhood fistfight that oftentimes ended in a handshake. The act of taking another life transcended faith; it had always been unimaginable to him. His military training had now prepared him to take the life of another when he was shipped to a war zone. Before Nicholas boarded the plane that would take him overseas, he would fight his own battle against the evil man who had destroyed goodness.

As a youth, Nicholas had been educated by the nuns and imbibed with the dogma that his guardian angel stood strongly on his right side. He believed this and took comfort in the angel's presence. He often prayed to him for guidance and grace. He also knew the forces of evil, always present on the opposite side. The ongoing battle between good and evil for every soul was never ending.

Nicholas felt he was no longer in control. He knew he'd already succumbed to the forces that were moving him to take another life.

His first encounter with the killer was when he saw him exit the gym after his morning workout. Nicholas made eye contact with him and held the stare. His adversary returned the glare, seeking recognition but then turned and walked away. Nicholas had no doubt; Meg's killer would remember his face.

The next day, the killer was running at a good pace. He was heading north on a narrow trail, and approaching a rocky gully, with a steep sixty-foot drop. Nicholas was running south on the same narrow path. He'd timed the killer's run and had selected this site for the confrontation to take place.

As they approached, Nicholas slowed his pace. He moved to the edge of the gully to let his adversary pass. He stared hard into the killer's eyes, and saw confusion. The killer reduced his speed and began to move by Nicholas. As their paths crossed, Nicholas slightly lowered his left shoulder, bracing for a jolting impact, and drove his shoulder into the killer, causing him to stumble.

As his adversary lost his balance, Nicholas grabbed his left arm to help stabilize him and whispered, "You killed her." Nicholas then released his grip on the killer's arm and continued to run, moving away from him. The killer was slow to react, but within seconds the confusion was gone, and he remembered the face. He heard what Nicholas said. The killer was shaken.

In a questioning voice that morphed into screams, the killer said, "What did you say? Hey, you, I know you . . . what did you fucking say? Asshole, what the fuck did you say? Fuck you! Fuck you!"

His echoing rant faded as Nicholas moved farther away from him. The killer had been warned, and Nicholas's conscience was clear. This was not a coward's errand.

The final encounter would be a meeting with no surprises. It was much more than Meg's killer deserved.

The fatal morning was clear and cool, a good day for a run. The killer followed the same route as the day before, and true to his routine, he was moving toward Nicholas from the opposite direction. They could see each other from a distance. Neither was going to turn around.

As they approached the same narrow pathway that ran along the gully, the killer rapidly increased his speed. Nicholas could see the killer's right arm rising slowly, and suddenly a hammer was plainly visible above his head.

Nicholas also increased his pace, running hard, and quickly approached their collision. Slightly slowing his pace, Nicholas began to lower his upper body. He was relying on his football skills to reduce his center of gravity. He'd been taught that this technique was a great equalizer when confronting a bigger and stronger opponent.

Nicholas braced for the impact, then within two feet of the killer and moving from his right, he drove his shoulders across the killer's lower legs, sending him airborne. Within seconds Nicholas heard the sickening thud of the killer ricocheting off a large, flat boulder. He landed hard, rolling, and descending into the cavernous chasm.

Nicholas picked himself up and walked to the edge of the path. Looking downward, he fixed his gaze on the motionless body. He felt no triumph, no satisfaction. He spoke the words he'd been thinking, *Meg is dead. Her killer is dead. I'm now a murderer, no better than the lifeless corpse.*

Nicholas continued to glare at the body and realized his world had changed forever. He knew there was no happy ending and only one hero in this tale, and she had died at the hands of a savage. As he walked away he whispered, *"I am now a savage."*

Nicholas cried as he thought he would never say good-bye to Meg or tell her how sorry he was for not protecting her. He wanted to hold her in his arms and let her know how much he loved her. He had seen the picture in the *Tennessean* of the yellow VW Beetle Meg had cherished so much that had been found in a pile of ashes and debris. He read in the article that Meg's body was never identified. All Nicholas had of Meg was her favorite book, the note she'd left in Boston, and the letter he'd received much too late to save her from her fate. He now knew his father's turmoil and his pain.

Meg had not received a final blessing or a Mass to pray for her soul. There was no grave to mark her death.

Nicholas could not place the flowers she'd loved so much over her final resting place. There was no headstone where he could stand and talk with her or pray for her. He would not live with his sadness and his guilt.

53

*N*icholas's plane had landed on November 2th in a mountainous lush green coastal country in Southeast Asia, a country consumed by the violence of war.

To pass the time between assignments, he sought the quiet and isolation of the outpost's makeshift chapel. There in solitude he would spend his days and nights waiting for the end.

On December 24, 1971, Nicholas boarded a Boeing CH-46 "Phrog" on an early morning assignment. As was his custom, every time he entered the helicopter he would say a prayer for the safe return of his comrades and beg that this would be his final mission. He did not want to see Christmas.

The assault came quickly, the gunfire fierce, the explosion deafening, the fire an inferno.

Nicholas could see Meg calling for him; he knew the end was near. He would not receive the last rites of his Catholic faith. There would be no absolution for his sins.

Maybe the saints and angels, invisible in the Chapel, had heard his story after all and would grant him relief from his suffering by allowing him to die.

His world had suddenly flashed dark, or was it light?

54

Worcester, MA — May 1994

"Andrew Nicholas Avellino."

That's my cue to walk across the stage and receive my degree from the College of the Holy Trinity, Class of 1994.

My parents, Margaret and Nicholas, are so proud, watching me graduate. They are both crying. My mom and dad carry so much love in their hearts for each other. I've always felt the love they share and the love they have for me.

My father, Nicholas Andrew Avellino, nearly died in Vietnam the day I was born. He was hospitalized for five months before he returned home. We were waiting for him when he walked into his father's house in May 1972.

Even with all the sadness my mom endured, she's the happiest person. My parents raised me to be happy, joyous, and loving like my mom and to be good, kind, and loving like my dad. They said, "These are the true qualities that give you the strength and courage to deal with life's challenges."

My parents shared their past with me; they have no secrets. I know the evil and hate that nearly took Mom's life.

I know Mom collapsed at the post office the day she mailed her letter to Dad. I know the nuns from Saint Thomas Hospital, who saw her battered body, concealed her from her abuser. I know about the depression that hospitalized her through her pregnancy and my premature birth. I know how many times I nearly died and received the Catholic sacraments for the dying.

I know the man Mom first married didn't die on a running trail. I know he and his father were killed in a fiery crash the day after my birth. I know their company no longer exists. I know my dad prays daily for the forgiveness of his sins. I know Mom carries the physical scars of abuse. I know Mom has forgiveness in her heart.

I know my grandfather cries, hugs, and kisses me and says, "My boy," when he sees me. I know I cry when I see my dad's reflection in my face. I know how very much I love my mother, my hero.

Dad's a doctor and Mom's an artist, and they live on Cape Cod. Mom is a painter and paints seagulls. She says they're majestic and loving. Mom walks the beaches most days looking for bits of happiness in things most often overlooked. She searches for small keepsakes for my dad. I know his eyes still tear when Mom brings him a seashell, a pinecone, or a flower.

I cry every time I think of it. I cry because I love.

CPSIA information can be obtained
at www.ICGtesting.com
Printed in the USA
LVHW02s2008160718
583906LV00001B/49/P

9 781545 631034